SOME DIAMONDS ARE
BLUE

ELIZA GREY

Copyright © Eliza Grey, 2020

Paperback ISBN: 978-1-8380406-8-0
.mobi (Kindle) Ebook ISBN: 978-1-8380406-0-4

Published by Grey Publishing

The right of Eliza Grey to be identified as
the author of this work has been asserted in
accordance with the Copyright, Designs and
Patents Act, 1988.

All rights reserved. No part of this publication
may be reproduced, stored in a retrieval system,
or transmitted, in any form or by any means
(electronic, mechanical, photocopying, recording
or otherwise), without the prior written permission
of the publisher.

This book is a work of fiction.
Names, characters, places and incidents are either
a product of the author's imagination or are used
fictitiously. Any resemblance to actual people living
or dead, events or locales is entirely coincidental.

Acknowledgements

I have to start by thanking my mum. You always believed in me and never doubted this moment would come. It breaks my heart that you are not here. I know you would enjoy the personal significances I've weaved into the story. They are there to remember you, always.

I must also give very special thanks to my dad. I will forever treasure the memories that never fail to inspire and motivate. Thank you for fuelling my imagination and teaching me that anything is possible. I know you are always with me.

I'll always be grateful to my husband, David, for encouraging me to devote all my time and energy to writing. The journey began in the Maldives, August 2019, where my favourite part of the book was written. I'm not sure I did justice to the song 'Witchcraft' by Frank Sinatra after several cocktails, but what beautiful memories. Thank you for always being on my heels to cross the finish line.

Very special thanks go to my daughter, Lauren. You never fail to show your love and support. Thank you for reading the manuscript, dedicating your time to drawing a unique piece of artwork, and for being such an important part of my journey.

To my youngest daughter, Molly. With all my love and thanks for your creative, thoughtful, and inspiring ideas. Thank you for all the little things you do that mean so much.

Thanks to Jake for all the hard work researching, designing the website, and looking at things from a different angle.

And thanks also to Beth. Your passion for your degree inspired me to realise we are happiest doing what we love.

To my sister, Amanda. Thank you for being my rock. You have given me so much love and support writing this book, and always. Thank you for supercharging me with confidence and for your unwavering faith. I cherish our extraordinary bond.

My love and thanks go to Beverley. You have given me more strength than I can put into words. Your feedback after reading the raw manuscript will forever make me smile.

To Claire - otherwise known as 'Little Miss Sunshine'! Thank you for believing in this book and always being there to chase the clouds away.

And to Sarah. Thank you for all the love, laughter and support on this journey, and over many years.

I want to give heartfelt thanks to my editor, Judith. You transformed the manuscript from a rough diamond into something that truly sparkled.

This book was made possible by the love and support of so many amazing, inspiring and special people. I can't list everyone here, but I dedicate this book to you all, with all my love.

SOME DIAMONDS ARE BLUE

Midnight blue
Sparkling bright
On her finger
Perfectly right
In this moment
Made to belong
Yet the journey
Surreal and long
Back in time
Nature created
Something magical
Then simply waited
In his hands
The story began
He had a dream
Fate had a plan
Left African skies
Crossed stormy seas
Like a feather
Tossed in a breeze
Yet guided by
A divine power
Exquisite luck
Or luck turned sour
Towards the end
You can decide
Did fate and magic
Conspire or collide?
A conclusion
You may now treasure
Is to love truly
With no value or measure.

© Eliza Grey 2020

PART ONE

CHAPTER 1

LONDON, 1968

The solid steel doors closed like jaws snapping, sealing Prisoner AA157 off from the outside world. Anticipation throbbed in his veins; his muscles tense. But this cocky new prisoner with polished shoes and perfectly combed hair was of no obvious concern to the armed police officers flanking him.

In the criminal world of the late 1960s, everyone in London knew everyone. The excitement of a fresh arrival on the block was akin to throwing pellets into an overcrowded fishpond. But as the officers accompanied this particular prisoner to his cell, they were greeted with absolute silence. They had over seventy years' prison service experience between them, but this had never happened before. One of the officers deliberately dragged his baton along the cell bars like a xylophone, allowing the noise to reverberate around the corridor.

The prisoner walked calmly past each cell, his chin deliberately lifted and his eyes fixed straight ahead. He did, however, glance sideways long enough to spot one of the officers wipe his brow several times while his colleague appeared to be hanging back slightly. Unbeknown to the prisoner, the cell they were about to approach was the ultimate litmus test; this feral inmate, Jimmy, knew everyone who operated in the depths and shadows of the criminal underworld. He had black onyx eyes and a soul to match.

The staccato rhythm of the officers' heeled shoes clacking on concrete came to an abrupt halt as Jimmy reached forward and clasped the bars with his tattooed fingers. Prisoner AA157, Charlie White, turned his head. Their eyes locked and Jimmy looked visibly pained as he tried to recollect why the face in front of him was familiar. Seconds passed and Jimmy's eyes rounded, as he registered who Charlie was.

Charlie raised his left eyebrow, asking unspoken questions. In response, Jimmy gave a short nod and dropped his hands, taking a step back: an undisputable sign of hierarchical respect. Charlie stood still, waiting for the officers to stop gawking, shut their gaping mouths, and continue. Their reaction silently amused him; Charlie knew who Jimmy was and it was likely every officer inside these walls danced like a ballerina on eggshells to keep on the right side of him.

As the officers opened his cell door, Charlie noticed their treatment of him shifted. They were courteous and quick to leave. Charlie knew the system was rife with silent corruption. It would only take the wrong word or deed, and strange things would begin to happen: a mugger waiting in the shadows on the way home; slashed tyres; a break-in. These were all gentle warnings. Some officers attempted to play both sides of the system, but crossing the line was like flipping a coin and keeping it air bound. At some point, inevitably, it would drop.

And there was always a price to pay when it did.

Charlie looked around his cell. It was small, threadbare, and damp, but thankfully there was only one bed which at least meant he wasn't sharing. He tipped out the contents of the small bag he'd been carrying on his shoulder. Only basic clothing was permitted and his allowance had already been scrutinised. Charlie tipped the contents of the bag onto the bed and shook his head in disgust. The toothbrush and shaving kit, courtesy of the prison, would probably snap in his hands the first time he used them. Sighing, he unfolded then refolded his clothes before carefully storing them in the child-sized wardrobe. He cursed under his breath. Whatever had been stuck to the inside of the wardrobe had been ripped off, leaving streaks of paper hanging. It irritated him. Everything felt cold, musty and sordid. He forced himself to smile; it was prison not the Ritz.

He placed his shoes carefully side-by-side, knowing he would be able to tell if anyone touched them. He slowly took in his surroundings, mentally photographing everything in the room. If anyone took the liberty of entering his cell or moving his things, they would be lucky if he only broke their fingers. He turned his attention to the small sink and toilet in the corner of the room. They needed a good clean, especially the toilet. Charlie scrubbed and polished them until he was satisfied. Afterwards, he washed and changed and only then did he lie on the bed, after re-making it, and for the first time thought back to what had happened in the courtroom earlier that day. But all his mind could focus on was the image of the girl he loved with flowing dark hair and startling blue eyes.

He pulled a photograph of her out of his shirt pocket and stuck it neatly to the wall beside his pillow. That morning she had sat in court looking angelic and frightened, a kid-white gloved hand resting on her heavily pregnant stomach. Her performance had been worthy of an Oscar, and even the judge had wiped a tear away.

Charlie squeezed his eyes shut, as though somehow he could see her more clearly. He recalled the sensation of her eyelashes tickling his cheek when she snuggled close, and the hint of fragrance left from her lips on his. In the dull silence of his cell, he laughed. She had once slapped him hard across the face with a force that had sent him reeling; he would never forget the rage in her eyes or unbridled strength as her elflike frame knocked him off balance and almost straight over. Maggie Jones was no ordinary girl.

Earlier that day, Charlie had watched her dab her eyes with a lace handkerchief and smile with relief as the judge read out Charlie's sentence. Both Charlie and Maggie were fully aware that the judge had been softened somehow. Charlie's boss, Bobby Blower, was important; moreover, he had a particular soft spot for his young protégé. In turn, Charlie was fiercely loyal and trustworthy. It was, however, these very attributes that had now landed Charlie in a prison cell.

Bobby had misjudged one of his men in their elite circle. He'd ignored Charlie's gut feeling that something didn't feel 'right'. Everyone knew Charlie fussed if a hair was out of place or a molecule of dust fell on his shoes, but his meticulous nature usually resulted in him being bullseye right when it came to instincts. Charlie had followed Bobby's order and let the net fall around him, to prove his point. Not in an arrogant way, however. He knew Bobby would pull strings, and it was more important for him to see Charlie had been right without actually saying the words 'I told you so.' Bobby would get that message loud and clear. Criminals like Bobby could murder a dozen men in a single night and sleep like a baby a few hours later but still needed old-fashioned manners and respect.

Charlie planned to keep his head down in prison, then slither back to the underworld. His foot had been snared in a trap, but by the time he walked free, the man responsible would no longer be in intensive care; he would be in a morgue.

In the end Charlie had only been given a light knuckle-wrap for grievous bodily harm and would be out in just under two months, if he behaved, which he would. He had the patience of a saint, which he wasn't.

CHAPTER 2

The monotony was the hardest thing about being behind bars. Charlie knew this from previous experience. It could be soul destroying, especially if you had a conscience vying for retribution. Charlie was forced to listen to the other inmates' mental states come undone late at night as he stared out of the window, stealing a glimpse of the moon. He especially enjoyed the rain; it felt cleansing somehow. He focused on anything but the nightly drama detonating somewhere within the prison. The need for distraction gave him ample time to dissect what happened the night he held out his wrists and let Sergeant Hounslow snap the cuffs tightly around them.

Charlie remembered every part of that night with photographic clarity. He had raised the alarm earlier with Bobby. Something just hadn't felt right.

"You must be getting suspicious in your old age, son," Bobby had replied, patting Charlie on the back and laughing.

Charlie noticed Bobby had a particular laugh whenever he felt tense, but either way, he let it drop. Bobby was in charge. He was the lifeblood that dominated London during the 50s,

60s and early 70s. He owned nightclubs, pubs, restaurants, hotels, and taxi firms. His businesses were not just successful; they also provided camouflage for certain underhand activities to take place. The police had tried to catch Bobby for decades, the ones who had law-abiding morals still intact anyway. They only got so far up the ladder with their evidence before it would be carefully dismissed. That was the deal those in power had struck with Charlie's boss: shredded paperwork, manufactured alibis and fabricated evidence. In return, their pockets were amply lined and their families kept safe. Ironically this fear gave the streets of London protection and control. Petty criminals didn't amount to much and soon got quashed. Everyone had heard of Bobby Blower, just as schoolchildren knew the Big Bad Wolf.

The plan had been simple enough. Go in hard, return with the cash owed. The interest on top would be a large quantity of cocaine. An informant had provided the location of the money but had been unable to describe the type of safe, which wasn't very helpful when you needed to get into it. Charlie hated any job that involved a safe; they usually took up valuable time and excessive bloodshed getting the combination. His ace card had been a sixteen-year-old boy who was a genius at picking any safe. The safe, however, wasn't the problem.

What irked Charlie that night was one of Bobby's men called Joe, or Big Joe as everyone called him. It was an unimaginative nickname due to his sheer height and brawn. Charlie's whiskers had been twitching; Big Joe was behaving differently. He was usually loud and cantankerous, but that night he appeared restless, telling crude jokes and laughing before he reached the punchline. He was also sweating profusely and couldn't sit still; it was like watching a bull cooped up before a fight.

Big Joe had cut several silky lines of almost pure cocaine before they went out that night, and sharply inhaled it up each nostril. As first in, perhaps he needed the shot of confidence. Charlie declined any and simply followed his usual routine, feeling Bobby's steely eyes upon them all. Unperturbed, Charlie polished his black shoes, round and round with the cloth until the leather gleamed. His white shirt was immaculately pressed and carefully tucked into black trousers, also brushed and pressed. His beloved black leather jacket was lifted and dropped onto his shoulders last of all, and his inner pockets inspected. The thin comb was always the last item to go inside, after a final sweep through his thick jet-black hair. Charlie always insisted physical preparation and mental warm-up made the crucial difference between success and failure on any job. Men like Charlie needed to be agile, prepared and focused. Men like Big Joe, however, were necessary for initial impact and destruction. If Big Joe was left to do the thinking, the risks to the job would be incalculable.

Checking his hair in the mirror again, Charlie had been re-arranging theories to pinpoint what was bothering him about Big Joe that night. Maybe he had been thinking about this job too much and the clues were obvious. Had there been one too many small coincidences to ignore? Charlie had seen someone turn Queen's evidence before. The signs were extremely subtle but retrospectively blatant.

Charlie knew Bobby would not want to listen to his

concerns. It was, after all, only a gut feeling. Someone owed Bobby a lot of money, and he wanted it back with interest.

As he watched his men leave, Bobby caught Charlie's arm. "Something still bothering you?" he asked.

Dark questions lurked in Bobby's eyes, and Charlie met his stare. He was one of the few people brave enough to tell Bobby the brutal truth.

"Yes, sir."

Charlie knew Bobby well enough to assume this question arose because his boss also had a gut feeling. Bobby hadn't got to his position without trusting his instinct too.

"Give me three reasons why," Bobby said.

Charlie instantly heard the well-rehearsed patience in Bobby's tone. Bobby had prospered in the murky criminal underworld for years and this had taught him the value of listening occasionally. However, this time, it was too late.

Charlie looked into Bobby's slate-grey eyes and quickly considered three solid reasons. Bobby always thought of everything in threes. Except if you crossed him, then there was only one thing on his mind, and you were in trouble.

"First, Big Joe is too jumpy. I think he knows how this might play out already. Second, the safe is apparently on the left, but there is a window there, so that doesn't sound right. Third, if there is already enough cash and coke to clear the debt, why not just clear the debt? It doesn't add up… unless someone has set it up."

Charlie looked deliberately at Big Joe. Bobby followed his gaze and nodded. But the dice were already rolling.

◈ ◈ ◈

The boy Charlie hired to pick the safe was waiting for them at the address. Charlie had seen him open a safe in minutes, admittedly with a gun held to his head. It had also been Charlie's gun. The boy looked up to Charlie as though he were some sort of superhero. Flattering as it was, Charlie needed him focused.

"Ready?" Charlie asked.

It wasn't a question, more of a statement. The boy nodded, trying not to show he was shaking.

Big Joe gave the boy a derogatory poke in the shoulder. "Who the fuck is this?" he asked.

Charlie glared at him. "If you need to know, I'll tell you. Meanwhile assume you don't need to know."

Big Joe clenched his fist until his knuckles turned white, then relaxed it.

Every nerve in Charlie's body prickled. Charlie knew then he was right. Big Joe had arranged a net to fall down and catch him.

Charlie observed Big Joe again. He was clearly jittery, flicking a cigarette before finishing it and then re-lighting another. Having the jitters was not necessarily unusual; Big Joe would be first through the door and facing an ugly, bloody massacre. But he couldn't seem to sit still or stop talking. Charlie considered the copious amounts of cocaine he had watched Big Joe inhale and shook his head. No, Big Joe always inhaled and his behaviour was never like this.

Condemned yet focused, Charlie was ready. He reached

inside his jacket pockets to check again. In his left pocket: a flick knife, knuckle duster, pistol, and his comb. In his right, a rounders bat. Prepared, he turned to the boy.

"When we go in, dive low and get to the safe. It will be on the right, not the left. Got that?" The boy nodded. "Don't look back for me. Open the safe, take everything out, don't wait for anyone. Go straight back to Bobby. Tell him I got caught in a net."

The boy bit his bottom lip. Charlie shook his head; this kid would need to find his bollocks and quickly. He spun the boy around, squeezing his shoulder.

"If you don't do as I've told you, you will be dead within the next half hour."

The boy's head shot up.

"Got it."

Charlie knew he still had the option to bolt to save his skin. Cowardice, however, was worse than consequences. What mattered now was moving the chess pieces to his advantage, knowing his queen was going to be taken from him, but he was going to take her back. It was a tactical game, and sometimes you had to take a fall. Charlie still didn't know who he could trust among Bobby's men as they walked silently up to the target building, the tension feverishly high. There were five of them in total, six including the boy, which complicated things. Charlie always preferred to work alone for this reason, but the job tonight needed heavies to tackle other heavies and Charlie's skill to take out the nucleus. Except, if Charlie was right, the nucleus was a high-ranking police officer about to put cuffs around his wrists. It made sense now. This set-up didn't have the hallmark of a rival gang. They wouldn't need everything so neatly pre-arranged. If he was right and Big Joe had been picked up by the police and turned Queen's evidence, Charlie would be their prize. He was closest to Bobby and a formidable assailant in the sinister underworld.

Charlie would take the money owed, out of principle. He hoped there'd be at least one other person in their group loyal to Bobby, but there was bound to be more in cahoots with Big Joe. It would be a quick process of elimination. Each man had a role, even the boy who was walking behind Charlie and praying the mechanism on the safe was one he knew well.

The building they were about to storm was just ahead. The tension between them crackled like sparks of electricity. Charlie hooked the car keys out of the driver's jacket pocket and tucked them into the boy's hand. The boy would use the car to drive back to Bobby, hopefully bringing with him a highly valuable quantity of cocaine and cash, if the situation panned out as Charlie expected.

They moved stealthily up the stairs towards the sound of voices. Big Joe was upfront, as expected. The man behind him Charlie had marked; how he reacted to Charlie's first move would confirm his alliance and therefore, fate. The boy kept pace behind Charlie.

Charlie quickly ran a comb through his hair and replaced it in his pocket. His throat tightened. Big Joe glanced back then crashed through the door. That was Charlie's cue. He pulled out the knife from his leather jacket and stuck it straight into Big Joe's lung, bringing him quickly down, gulping for air. The man behind immediately swung a punch, but Charlie was ready and headbutted him square in the face, knocking him out cold. Bobby's second rat. As the door swung fully open, Charlie pushed the boy down low and fired several shots from a pistol as the boy scurried like a ferret to the safe. The two other men, clearly loyal to Bobby, looked shocked but had cottoned on fast. They followed Charlie into the room, taking his lead. Two men were already dead on the floor. Three other giant, angry men circled Charlie, who raised his fists, showing them the razor-sharp edges of his knuckle dusters. Seconds before they launched a trio attack, Charlie pulled out a second pistol and shot their kneecaps in rapid succession. He watched as they tumbled in agony. Bobby's other men quickly tied them up. Most likely policemen, Charlie guessed. Out of the corner of his eye, Charlie saw Big Joe slithering towards a man in a dark-grey tailored suit. With clothes like that, he was likely to be the nucleus in this set-up.

The safe was now open and empty. There was no sign of the boy. He would be on his way back to Bobby. If he got greedy and took off with the cocaine and cash, they would find him, and he would be dead by morning. But Charlie couldn't think about that right now. So far, the plan had played out exactly as he thought it would, and now he just had to finish it.

"It's over Charlie." Big Joe grimaced as he forced out the words.

Big Joe clung to his chest, struggling to breathe but trying desperately not to let it show. Charlie appraised the man next to him carefully, knowing he was probably a high-ranking officer. Most likely uncorrupted but certainly corruptible. In the end, they all were, once you found the right pressure points and slowly squeezed.

The other men loyal to Bobby stood beside Charlie and waited for his next move. Charlie was conscious that they were relying on him now. He would be responsible for whatever fate lay ahead.

Charlie took a cigarette out of his jacket and lit it slowly, unnerving Big Joe. When Charlie White was this calm, there would be consequences – measured and shocking. The police officer watched, waiting. Charlie pointed to the only chair in the room behind a large desk.

"Take a seat."

He looked at the police officer.

Big Joe laughed condescendingly. "You aren't calling the shots here, Charlie."

Charlie pulled out his knife and hurled it at Big Joe, skillfully catching his shoulder and pinning his shirt neatly to the wall behind him. He had spent long hours throwing knives at trees as a kid, much to his mother's horror, but it paid off in moments like this. Big Joe yelped loudly in pain. The police officer quickly sat down. On the desk in front of him were two heavyset briefcases.

"What's your name?" Charlie asked the officer.

"Peter Hounslow."

Charlie nodded. "Sergeant?"

Reluctantly Sergeant Peter Hounslow nodded. Charlie knew that the opportunity to net the elusive Charlie White would have been tempting to the officer. But the policeman's slumped shoulders and nervous eyebrow twitch indicated that the sergeant wished he was elsewhere.

Charlie pointed to the briefcases. "Can you open those, please?"

The sergeant fumbled with the brass numbers until they were correctly aligned and the latches popped open. The neat stacks of notes in the briefcase would be genuine; the stage props needed to be legitimate.

"Thank you, Sergeant Hounslow," said Charlie. "These your men?" He pointed to the men on the floor, blood from their kneecaps seeping into the floorboards.

"Yes."

Charlie nodded and lit another cigarette, taking his time.

"Here's what's going to happen. You can take me in, no fuss."

Sergeant Hounslow laughed.

"What's the catch?"

"No catch." Charlie paused. "A few conditions."

"Same thing."

"Depends on your interpretation. All you have to do is watch and learn."

Charlie took off his leather jacket, placed it carefully on the desk and rolled up his shirt sleeves. He turned to Bobby's men and nodded in Big Joe's direction. They smiled. It took them ten minutes of rough kicking and punching to subdue him enough to get him onto his knees and drag him across the room to face Charlie.

Sergeant Hounslow watched uncomfortably. "Is this necessary?"

Charlie shook his head. "Not necessary, no. It is essential. You need to see what happens to scum like this, and the consequences when you fuck with the wrong people."

"Are you threatening me?"

"No. Threats are idle. What you are about to see is more of a guarantee. You are going to take me in. I'll do my time, and you will get a nice pat on the back. Your involvement stops there. After we leave, everything here will get cleaned up, including these briefcases."

He gestured with a curt nod of the head at the rest of the men in the room. "You never saw these men here."

"What makes you think you can dictate the terms?"

Charlie raised his eyebrows.

"You are Sergeant Peter Hounslow. You live in a four-bed detached house on Pettifield Lane with your wife Lorraine and two daughters. One is prettier than the other, the blonde. She works on Oxford Street, hosiery department, third floor. Your younger girl works in Suzie's Bakery. She has a really nice smile." Charlie paused, allowing Sergeant Hounslow to get the full measure of his words. "You just can't get iced buns anywhere else in London quite like Suzie's Bakery, now can you?"

The sergeant's face turned ashen. As often as she could, his daughter left work with a packet of the buns for her father. The sergeant felt physically sick.

Charlie continued. "Lorraine walks your dog, a Yorkie, every morning and evening like clockwork. Surely in your position, you wouldn't encourage such a predictable routine?" He shook his head, mocking the helpless policeman. "Your house has an alarm system, but honestly, why bother? You haven't bought your wife any jewellery worth nicking. Your dog might yap but not for long. I *know* you, Sergeant Peter Hounslow."

The room fell silent.

"What do you want?"

It was all Peter Hounslow could say.

"I've told you already, and it's nice and simple. You have to cover your tracks, so you have to take me in. Your boys got caught up in the fuss, but the others ran. However, your informant, Big Joe here, well now that was a sad ending."

Sergeant Hounslow looked into Charlie's dark menacing eyes. The policeman knew those eyes would haunt him for the rest of his life. It was as though the Devil himself had driven his gaze right into his soul.

Charlie turned to Big Joe.

"Thought you'd been clever, didn't you?"

Before Big Joe could muster enough breath to respond, Charlie punched his face several times. Under the teeth of the knuckle duster, bones cracked, and blood squirted from Big Joe's nose and mouth. Strange animal-like sounds gurgled from his throat. Threading Big Joe's blood-soaked hair through his fingers, Charlie dragged the limp seventeen stone body across the floor and dumped him at Sergeant Hounslow's feet. Reaching into his right pocket, he pulled out his rounders bat and belted it hard across Big Joe's back. Bobby's other men pulled Big Joe up onto his feet. Charlie put all his physical force into the bat as he hit both kneecaps.

Big Joe slipped into unconsciousness but not before he had wet himself and thrown up. Charlie could have finished him off, but Big Joe's final fate was ultimately Bobby's decision.

Charlie watched unfazed as Sergeant Hounslow retched into a nearby wastepaper bin. He had understood the rules loud and clear.

Charlie focused on the fat fingers of sunlight pushing through the bars of his prison cell and onto his off-white bed sheet. He was bored. There were five weeks left of his sentence, and they were the hardest. By then, he knew the boy had returned to Bobby that night, with every ounce of cocaine and every pound note. Bobby's men had walked away from the crime scene as agreed. They owed Charlie their freedom and lives, as did Bobby.

Word had gotten around like little birds flittering between treetops. Inside, no one bothered Charlie. Once, a few cocky lads had pressed their luck. Charlie had asked them to clear off when he wanted to take a shower. The ringleader had stepped forward confidently.

"Fuck off you tosser. Who the fuck do you think you are? *You* fucking leave." The lads had stood there boldly, jeering with their towels wrapped around their waists. Each one left less than five minutes later with a piece of ripped shirt stuffed into their mouths and blood pouring from their groin. After that, no one bothered Charlie in the shower.

It was a harsh world of sink or swim, and even if you had the strength and stamina, there was no lifeboat on standby. Charlie preferred it that way. It kept everything simple when he worked alone and relied on only himself. Except, he remembered, he wasn't entirely alone. There was Maggie and now their unborn baby. For the first time, Charlie was also vulnerable. It created a dilemma he didn't yet know how to fix.

"White, you have a visitor," came a gruff voice from outside his cell.

This particular officer was a bastard. Even his colleagues

shook their heads, pretending not to see, or preferring not to hear. He used his power like weaponry, usually on the weaker prisoners. He tended to let the well-known prisoners get away with murder, exacerbating the pun. Not for any financial gain, just purely for amusement. Charlie had heard the officer took some sort of sick satisfaction from watching grown men cry like babies in the urinals when cornered by hormone-fuelled inmates desperate for relief. So far, he'd steered clear of Charlie though, having probably received the standard warning from Bobby Blower. Bobby wouldn't want his protégé to come out of prison seeking revenge against a psychotic officer and ending up back behind bars.

"Who is it?" Charlie asked.

"I ain't your private secretary. Get off your arse and find out."

Charlie shot him a look. It was, however, a fair point. He went through the humiliating security checks, another reason for not enjoying visitors, and waited in a side room until he heard his name. He was the first one called. A heavy barred door was opened deliberately slowly by an officer, finally permitting him to enter the communal area where the visitors would be waiting. Charlie happened to know this particular officer took a regular supply of cocaine from one of the other inmates. For a few days at least, his supply channel might also be frustratingly slow.

Appeasing himself with this small act of satisfying revenge, Charlie's eyes swept the room. He saw her instantly. Her pregnancy bump had swollen considerably in the past few weeks since that day in court. She wore a pretty pale pink dress with a white cardigan and delicate heeled sandals. Even heavily pregnant, she was stunning. Her long dark hair had been woven into an immaculate bun high on her head, framing her exquisite face. He reached for her hand, breathing in the sweet magic of the perfume she always wore. The muscles in his arms twitched with the desire to pull her into an embrace, but it was against the rules. Their eyes met and locked. Charlie smiled, breaking the reverie. The clock was already ticking.

"How's the baby?"

She looked down matter-of-factly.

"Good, I think."

"I've missed you so much."

His heart raced. For a man who could maintain a perfectly average heart rate firing a round of bullets or be calm when outnumbered five to one, this girl had a profound effect on him.

"Charlie, we need to talk."

She released her breath. He knew she meant business. There was no messing with those startling blue eyes.

"Maggie? What's wrong?"

"You mean aside from the fact I'm about to have your baby and you are in here? And…" She paused. This was indelicate even for her.

"And?"

"And, Charlie White, I'm unmarried. I've had to lie to the midwives, although I can tell they know."

She'd told them her fingers had swollen during pregnancy, and she'd had no choice but to take her rings off. He could imagine her doing that; she was so beautifully brazen.

"When's the baby due?"

"Mid-September. Just under two months."

"I'm out in five weeks. Let's do it then."

Maggie rolled her eyes. "How romantic."

Charlie immediately reached for her hand. He knew a young girl in her condition should be married, and he had been planning to do something about it as soon as he could.

"As soon as I'm out of here, I promise."

There was a few moments silence while Maggie studied Charlie's face, checking for sincerity. But Charlie never said anything he didn't mean.

"Can I start making arrangements then?" she asked.

As always, Maggie was impatient and clinical. Charlie smiled. Maybe this was why he loved her so much. Other girls would flutter their eyelashes and expect a man to psychically know what they wanted. But not Maggie. She didn't mince or sugarcoat.

Maggie waved her hand at him. "You haven't got me a ring yet."

Charlie grinned. "We can say it's being re-sized."

His warm sarcasm had tempered her enthusiasm. "How romantic," she repeated. "I'm sorry, Charlie. It's just… it hasn't been easy with the baby and you in here."

Her eyes brightened with tears.

She was right. Charlie need to fix this, put things right.

"Maggie Jones, I love you. I'll be out soon. Meanwhile, go and organise our wedding. I'll get some money dropped off."

She clapped her hands and laughed.

Charlie mused that Selfridges wouldn't know what had hit them.

CHAPTER 3

Maggie left the prison full of jubilation and relief. She was nineteen years old, about to have her first child, and was finally getting married. Her parents would be disappointed nonetheless. She was pregnant outside wedlock, which raised eyebrows and gave ammunition to the lips of gossips. In their eyes, Charlie had to marry her now; nobody else would. Not that anyone would dare say this to Maggie. Her tongue could be sharper than a butcher's knife, and besides, she didn't want any other man.

As Maggie stepped off the bus and walked the familiar route back to the narrow brick house that had been home since birth, she had a taste of freedom in her mouth. Maggie had mentally planned the registry office, the reception, and the short break they would take somewhere, anywhere, south of London. She was going to design her dress and get a seamstress to turn the pencil lines into something beautiful and in her case, appropriate. Her mother had taught her how a small alteration could transform a plain dress, or a few pins change a hairstyle, or how a simple accessory could alter an entire look. When you grew up counting pennies, you made those pennies stretch. She'd learned that from her mother too.

She was thinking about how much the wedding would cost as she put her key in the front door. The door refused to open and appeared to be jammed against something on the other side. Maggie huffed and gave the door a hard push. It finally opened and she stepped in to find a large brown paper envelope on the mat.

"Mum, are you in?" she called.

The smell of freshly baked bread meant her mother was either in or had recently gone out. She hoped it was the latter. She picked up the envelope and saw her name on the front in unfamiliar handwriting. Her heart began to race. As she carefully tore open the envelope, rolls of notes fell into her hand. She gasped and steadied herself against the wall. She had never seen this much money before. Charlie had told her he would get some money dropped off, but this much? And so quickly?

She stuffed the envelope into her bag, smiling to herself. She'd count it later. But she could already tell it was a considerable sum. She had no idea how Charlie earned his money. And she didn't want to know.

Maggie took off her shoes and placed them neatly in the cupboard by the door, a house rule her mother upheld vehemently. The hallway was narrow and dark, lit only by a small lamp on a nearby table. On a bright day, sunlight streamed in from the hub of the house: the kitchen. Maggie walked the few steps from the hall into the kitchen, and spied a loaf of bread cooling. A note next to it in her mother's scrawled hand told her she had gone to the greengrocer's. On the stove, a saucepan was still steaming, a sponge pudding simmering in its basin. Maggie hoped it was syrup. She knew she was lucky; there was always a decent meal every evening and homemade treats in the tin. On birthdays, her mum always made her a rich chocolate fudge cake complete with a chocolate flake crumbled on top. She usually had to get them from the ice-cream van, and they were Maggie's absolute favourite. As a child, she always begged for an ice-cream cone then only ate the flake. It was something of a family joke.

Her parents had worked in factories since they were both sixteen, always scrimping and saving. The same curtains had hung in the kitchen for as long as Maggie could remember, but the ugly brown frills and dull yellow flowers were homely to her. Every part of the kitchen was neat and functional, clean and necessary. But she couldn't imagine bringing her baby up here, his or her small hands stealing biscuits from the tin just as she had done.

"I haven't got the money to feed all the kids you know, Maggie Jones!" She could still hear her mother's voice even now.

She wondered what kind of a parent she would be. She couldn't imagine baking or sewing, braiding hair or spending hours washing and ironing clothes. It was perhaps the first time she realised how young she was to be having a baby, even though so many of her friends already had kids. She was also starting to feel nervous about the birth. The skin around her tummy had stretched and tightened, reminding her the time was getting closer. She was looking forward to having her body back, but equally dreading being a mother herself.

The responsibility felt overwhelming. Quickly brushing her anxieties aside, she got a pencil and paper and began planning the wedding. That was how her mother found her an hour later, as she heaved heavy bags into the house.

"Give us a hand, love. No, not that one it's heavy. I've got potatoes and onions in there."

Maggie took two smaller bags off her mother before Linda Jones pulled back a chair and collapsed on the cushion tied to the seat. She was exhausted carrying so many bags, but a trip to the greengrocer's was always better value at the end of the day when the fruit and veg were cheapest. Linda was amazingly resourceful and somehow managed to serve up mouth-watering meals from scraps. Mrs Beaton would have been proud of her. Living through the war years had taught her well, as had a mother with a will of iron.

"What are you up to?"

Linda peered at the paper her daughter had partially covered with her arm. She felt instantly uncomfortable.

"Mum, I went to see Charlie today."

Maggie rarely dressed her comments with pointless pleasantries. Linda held her breath, her eyes about to pop. It was impossible to predict what Maggie would say next.

"We are getting married."

Maggie waited for her mother to react. In her delicate position, she knew her parents couldn't object. Besides, they knew that once Maggie made up her mind, there was no changing it.

"I'm pleased for you, and it's the right thing to do." Linda nodded and gently patted Maggie's bump.

"Thanks, Mum. Will you help me, you know, get things sorted for the wedding?"

Linda stood up and began unpacking bags, mainly because she didn't want Maggie to see her crying.

"Of course, love. Now, do you want cream or custard with your syrup sponge tonight?"

Linda was on edge when her husband came home. It was impossible to anticipate his mood. Factory work was hard and he was so often exhausted. She watched him tear the foil off his dinner plate and eat in silence. He would only relax once he had eaten.

"I'll take my pud in the lounge," he said.

Linda had eaten with Maggie earlier. Maggie had then gone to see a friend a few doors down the street. She'd just had her first baby, and Maggie had promised she would visit, even though she wasn't sure she wanted chapter and verse on childbirth.

Linda followed her husband into the living room. Jim had put his feet up on the footstool and rested the paper on his lap. She put the steaming pudding bowl and a cup of tea on the table next to him. He smiled his thanks, expecting her to leave.

"Jim, Maggie had some news today."

She said it casually. Jim wasn't sure he had the energy to listen to gossip about someone on the street. He looked up, raising his eyebrows.

"Oh?"

"She's getting married."

Jim leapt off his chair, the newspaper flying.

"What! When?" Then the penny dropped. "Charlie White?"

Linda nodded. She heard him swear, which was rare. The last time an expletive left his lips, he had lost quite a bit of money on the horses.

The front door banged shut. Maggie walked into the living room and instantly guessed what had happened. Her father glared at her, his face almost disfigured with anger.

"Hi, Dad. Syrup pudding was lovely tonight, wasn't it?" Maggie said, deliberately keeping her tone light.

Both parents stared at her, shocked. Maggie proceeded to waltz into the kitchen as though everything was perfectly normal. Jim went to bolt after her, but Linda gently touched his arm. She didn't touch him very often, and the gentleness stopped him in his tracks.

"Leave her, Jim. Marrying Charlie is what she wants. And in her condition, it will give her and the nipper respectability."

Jim deflated like a balloon. He couldn't disagree. The last thing he wanted for his daughter was to entrust her to a wolf, but he knew he had no choice.

"What did we do wrong?"

It was all he could say.

Linda shrugged, wiser than she wanted to be.

"She reminds me of my mother."

Jim looked horrified, remembering what a tyrant his mother-in-law had been. Linda's lips curved into a small smile as she remembered all the times they had laughed together about her mother, Violet. Violet would argue black was white and was cantankerous and contentious even on one of her rare good days. On her deathbed, they had sat with her all through the night. She stirred once before she passed, only to complain about the weather. In fairness, life had been both hard and brutal for her; complaining was justified. Yet she had petrified most people she encountered, reducing them to tears with her sharp tongue. Maggie hadn't inherited all her grandmother's flaws, thankfully, but she had the same thick skin. As if to prove it, Maggie walked into the living room and pulled back the nets, grimacing as she looked outside.

"Looks like rain again, Mum. Bloody weather."

CHAPTER 4

The prison gates that had slammed shut behind him two months earlier yawned open and spat Charlie back out into the September sunshine. He was leaner than he had been; he neither liked nor trusted the slop served from the prison canteen.

Maggie wasn't expecting him to be released until the following week. But Bobby had an urgent job for him and there was a car waiting. Charlie opened the door and got inside. There was no need to ask where they were going. As they weaved through heavy traffic, he stared out at the historic landmarks, bustling market stalls, and crowds of busy people – a welcome relief from grey walls and steel bars. Charlie smiled happily. London was more than home; it was in his blood.

Half an hour later the car slowed down and Charlie got out. He knew exactly where to find the inconspicuous door tucked away down a side street. Out of habit, he scanned the street behind him, turned, then quickly walked down the nightclub steps. He had descended these steps a hundred times before. Usually with blood on his hands, scars on his soul, and loot tucked in his leather jacket.

"Welcome back, son."

Charlie took Bobby's outstretched hand. They hadn't seen each other since the night Big Joe had set Charlie up. They would never openly discuss what had happened, but Charlie knew Bobby wouldn't forget.

"How's that girl of yours? I heard you're getting married."

Bobby winked, pleased for him. Charlie recoiled slightly, feeling suddenly exposed. Charlie knew he hadn't told Bobby about the wedding, but he also knew every wall in London had eyes and ears. It was a timely reminder of just how threatening his world was. The fierce adrenaline that had been dormant in Charlie for months was beginning to spark again. Without it, he was doomed.

Charlie was acutely aware that Bobby's cold, calculating eyes were scanning him, searching for weakness. Had prison softened him or pricked his conscience? Holding back information about the wedding and the baby would imply that Charlie was scared. And fear was dangerous.

Charlie took a recent photo of Maggie out of his pocket, clearly showing she was pregnant. He handed it to Bobby, grinning.

"She's beautiful, isn't she?" he said. "The baby's due in a few weeks."

The photo captured everything that made Charlie vulnerable. He watched as Bobby appraised the picture, taking a little longer than Charlie felt comfortable with. He waited until Bobby handed it back, then calmly placed it back in his pocket. Simple as that, Charlie was back in the game.

Bobby explained the new job. Charlie listened, frowning. He was surprised Bobby would even consider a job like this. Bobby explained he had known the woman's father well. He had once lent Bobby a significant sum of money when no one else would.

Charlie had to admit, the story was intriguing. He had to get inside a large mansion and steal a painting. When Bobby outlined the details, Charlie whistled.

"Must be important."

Bobby shrugged; it was, but Charlie didn't need the specifics.

"It could be the most rewarding job you've ever done. If, of course, you don't get caught."

Charlie laughed and lit a cigarette. There was no way was he going back to prison.

He spent the next few days drinking strong coffee and smoking endless packets of Benson & Hedges, carefully planning the theft. It was an easy job – at least that's what Bobby had told him. But Charlie couldn't shake off the feeling that there was something more to this break-in, something that neither of them had anticipated – something that could throw everything off balance.

Three days after being released from prison, Charlie was ready. As the sky behind the grand mansion basked in the embers of evening sunlight, he crouched down low in the shade and waited.

The mansion resembled a Chateaux nestled in the Loire

Valley. Stunningly regal and romantic, it looked like the kind of fairy tale castle Cinderella might live in. Bobby had confirmed that the house would be empty; all lights inside and out had been turned off when the owner left earlier that day, leaving the building to naturally succumb to twilight shadows.

Charlie felt pins and needles sting his legs, encouraging him to finally move. He inched towards the house, his eyes scanning for anything odd. He knew the cameras had been tampered with, but he wasn't taking any chances. He wore a jumpsuit, mask, gloves, and protective footwear – the same outfit that forensics wore on a crime scene. The irony was not lost on Charlie.

The owner would be at the airport by now. She was travelling to France to stay with her son, according to the informant. She was elderly and suffered from dementia. It was unknown when she would return, as her illness had worsened recently. Charlie would have crept in even as the old lady slept upstairs, but it was less complicated this way. No hysteria or sudden heart attacks to worry about.

The surrounding estate was large, but the mansion, although spectacular, was tucked away from public sight. Its hidden beauty was both alluring and yet sad, like a forgotten jewel.

The mansion would be packed with valuables – a veritable sweetshop for criminals – but Charlie was intensely focused on the one piece of artwork. His plan was to enter the side of the house via the disabled access. He briefly considered breaking and entering one of the downstairs windows, but rigid frames and panes of glass took considerable time and effort to break cleanly. The resulting shards of glass were likely to offer up evidence too. The main entrance consisted of double, solid oak doors clad with cast iron. He was good, but he wasn't superman.

Inky darkness smothered the sky like a blanket, diminishing all light. Charlie stood underneath the drooping branches of a mature willow tree, a few feet from the mansion. A well-manicured hedge shielded him from behind, curving far around into a rose garden he could smell but not see. He inhaled the delicate perfume of old English roses clinging to the balmy air. Charlie was not impervious to the beauty of nature, especially after being cooped up in a prison cell.

A falcon swooped down low beside him. Mesmerised, Charlie stared at its glossy feathers. The falcon's beady eyes darted left and right, then the majestic bird left as soundlessly as it had arrived. Charlie was unnerved; it was as if the bird was part of the security team. He shook off the foolish fantasy. It was time to get on with the job.

Charlie moved slowly, anticipating each stone under his boot. He had to move quickly to limit possible exposure, yet cautiously not to trigger any unknown sensors. Reaching the side door, his fingers found the latch. His lock picking skills were rusty but adequate. It took him less than five minutes to open the door and step into the hallway.

Once inside, he paused, checking for unexpected noises or movement in the house. From here he would bypass the main part of the mansion and follow a spiral staircase deep down into the bowels of the house. There was a hatch that opened close to where the artwork was hanging. This strategy limited the time he would need to spend inside the main hallway once the alarms went off. He wouldn't have much time. He'd not had a dry-run but had to rely on careful calculations and informed guesswork. A shiver of fear sliced through him. What if the hatch into the main hallway wasn't precisely where he expected it to be? Servants had once used this entrance to transport bulky wine and food from the cellar to the main house, but it was a gamble. There was a possibility it remained bolted down.

Charlie crept slowly onwards. The spiral staircase was dark and narrow. At the bottom it smelt damp and cold. The hairs on the back of Charlie's neck began to tingle.

Something nearby rustled. He froze, listening intently. He hoped that whatever creature was moving near him, it was small. A mouse would be fine, whereas rats, especially large ones, made Charlie truly agitated. But not even the supernatural would deter him right now, although it might make him run faster.

There were no windows in the basement, so he took out a small torch and waved it quickly around the room. Nothing moved or looked out of place.

Charlie turned his attention to the hatch and prayed it was already open. He gave it a generous nudge and it pushed easily upwards. Exhaling deeply with relief, Charlie visibly relaxed.

He took a few long moments to mentally and physically prepare. As soon as he lifted himself up into the hallway, he would have to move fast. Alarms would trigger, flashlights everywhere would instantly turn on, and both private security and police would be on their way. Bobby had already paid off an insider to tamper with the main wires which had suspended the artwork for over forty years in the main hallway. It wasn't a large painting, but it was an original and of exceptional value.

Charlie felt his throat pulsate with adrenaline. Like a tight spring suddenly released, he pushed himself up and sprinted across the hallway. He didn't even blink as the darkness flooded with bright light, and the alarms began to wail frantically. He found the artwork, hanging high above a marble fireplace. He swore loudly; it was higher than he had expected.

The sirens crescendoed to a painful screech. Blocking out the sound, Charlie reached up and carefully tucked the tips of his fingers underneath the edge of the painting. It briefly swayed then tumbled into his hand. He closed his eyes for an instant as the prickly heat of stress evaporated.

Opening his eyes, he was about to turn and run, when something caught his eye on the marble mantelpiece below. A small pair of silk gloves had been pulled off and discarded. Sitting casually on top was a single stoned ring. Under the powerful light, the jewel flickered brilliant blue, momentarily paralysing Charlie.

With no time to think, he picked it up and put it straight in his pocket.

"Doesn't look like much, does it?" Bobby mused.

Bobby held the painting up, shaking his head. Charlie looked at the famous painting and shrugged. It was an original Renoir worth millions of pounds. Bobby pushed several rolls of tightly rolled-up notes over to him, as Charlie whistled.

Charlie took a deep breath and put the ring on the table. He watched as Bobby picked it up and raised an eyebrow.

"What is hell is this?"

A ring, Charlie wanted to say but didn't quite dare.

"It was on the mantelpiece when I went in. I don't know why, but I took it."

Bobby examined the ring carefully. He knew Charlie well enough to know he hadn't planned to take it. Bobby smiled, handing it back.

"Give it to your fiancé."

"I shouldn't have picked it up."

"Perk of the job. Anyone else would have ransacked the entire place."

"I'm not like the others."

"I know. And those bastards wouldn't have come in here emptying their loot like I'm running a bloody confessional."

Charlie grinned.

"It won't cause you a problem?"

Bobby shook his head.

"I don't care if it does. It's yours."

Charlie knew Bobby appreciated honesty. He returned the ring to a small pocket in his leather jacket and left.

The following day he received a message from Bobby with the name and address of a jeweller. The newspapers were rampant with breaking news about a high-profile burglary. Charlie leafed through the wafer-thin pages, fervently looking for clues that might implicate him. He lit up a cigarette and continued reading.

A piece of artwork had been stolen, but the owner had no idea what it was. Her husband had been the avid art collector when he was alive, but for some inexplicable reason, he had not insured this particular piece. To the relief of the insurance company, all the insured pieces were still intact. It was, however, the ring and not the painting that made headline news. A rare blue diamond was missing, also uninsured. The owner was convinced she had taken it with her to France, although the gloves she left on the mantelpiece confused her. The ring had spent almost five decades on her finger, yet she had no recollection why or if she had removed it.

The newspapers latched on to her dementia and strongly suggested she had probably lost the ring. They printed a photograph of her taken fifty years ago, in Paris. She looked vibrant and beautiful and had apparently been married to an exceptionally wealthy man.

Charlie remembered Bobby had known this man, and that his daughter had commissioned the theft. It didn't make sense to Charlie, but that didn't matter. It wasn't his job to analyse her motive. The job had been successful, he had been paid handsomely, and Maggie had an engagement ring.

Charlie looked at the address Bobby had given him, then glanced back at the newspaper photograph. It didn't take a master criminal to work out that the sooner the stone was in a new setting the better.

He took the ring out of his pocket and flipped it over and around his fingers, watching the colours inside the diamond shimmer and dance.

CHAPTER 5

The jewellery shop was wedged in-between a haberdashery and a bakery. The signage over the door had faded years ago and was barely visible, which Charlie suspected was deliberate. If the owner knew Bobby, it was likely he wanted the smokescreen of a regular high-street business.

A bell chimed loudly as Charlie stepped inside, making him jump. He swore under his breath; shop bells always caught him off guard. The owner appeared from seemingly nowhere and walked towards Charlie, his small hand outstretched. Charlie peered at the man, surprised by the mass of fluffy white hair which flopped to one side and large spectacles hanging off his elfin nose. He looked more like a hobbit than a shady jeweller who handled knock-off gear.

"Bobby sent you?" The man's voice was high-pitched and squeaky.

Charlie nodded. He swallowed the urge to laugh at this comical jeweller. The man flipped the sign on the door to closed, and turned the key in the lock before practically skipping back to Charlie, his eyes gleaming with mischievousness.

"Follow me," he said, gesturing for Charlie to follow.

Dutifully, Charlie followed. Tucked away behind the shop was a large workshop, carefully hidden from prying eyes. Here, the owner visibly relaxed and introduced himself properly.

"My name is Aleksander. I'm Polish," he announced, as though that explained something. Charlie didn't react, so Aleksander continued. "What do you have for me?"

Charlie assumed that Aleksander was used to seeing Rolex watches, jewel-encrusted necklaces, even tiaras placed on his workbench. His talent would no doubt stretch beyond simple repairs. He was clearly a master at transforming jewellery into something else – preferably making it disappear. As Charlie placed the blue diamond on the workbench, Aleksander gasped and exclaimed loudly in Polish.

Without taking his eyes off the diamond, Aleksander reached out for his monocular loupe. Charlie noticed the drama Aleksander extended to this simple task. With nothing to do but watch, Charlie waited. He became increasingly irritated hearing Aleksander mutter to himself in Polish, but he kept quiet.

Finally, Aleksander addressed him.

"Please, sit down. Here is a seat."

Aleksander waved his thin arm to the right of the workbench and Charlie sat down, visibly frustrated. The whole business was taking too long for him. He just wanted to get the ring set and leave.

"Can you re-set it?" Charlie asked abruptly.

Aleksander peeled his eyes away from the diamond and faced Charlie.

"Of course. But you must consider the setting carefully. This one is gold but in remarkable condition. Don't you think?"

Looking into Aleksander's eyes, it was obvious to Charlie that the jeweller was fishing to find out what he knew about the ring. It was an unspoken rule in their type of business not to ask questions. But Aleksander's excitement about the diamond was evident from the glint in his eye. Charlie's intuition kicked up a gear. Perhaps there was something more to this diamond than he first thought?

Charlie glanced down at a newspaper on the bench. His face was deadpan and his hand steady as he lit a cigarette. He looked up at Aleksander again, but not before registering the headline: PRECIOUS BLUE DIAMOND VANISHED.

For a second, there was an unspoken exchange between Aleksander and Charlie. Then Aleksander swung round and reached for two small shot glasses on the shelf behind him.

"Mr White, please have this," he said.

He poured a generous slug of neat Polish vodka into a small glass and handed it to Charlie. They clinked glasses and drank it straight. Charlie coughed and shook his head, feeling the heat of the neat alcohol ripple downwards.

"Tell me who will wear this ring," Aleksander asked.

Charlie relaxed slightly, as they talked about Maggie, and Aleksander sketched designs on a piece of paper. As he began to imagine the ring on Maggie's finger, Charlie leant forward in his chair, listening avidly to Aleksander as he spoke about the history of precious metals and diamonds. The topic was well out of his comfort zone, but he was genuinely fascinated. Aleksander had a small supply of platinum and was one of the few jewellers who would, or could, use it. For this diamond, it would be the ideal metal.

Aleksander talked him through the war years, when platinum was reserved mainly for military purposes, and how white gold eclipsed the demand post-war. The sixties began to change the trend back to platinum again.

Aleksander's enthusiasm and knowledge was contagious. Charlie was captivated by every detail.

"This diamond has a very high colour intensity, which is extremely unusual. However, what makes the diamond truly spectacular is the internal structure," the jeweller continued, bringing Charlie's focus back to the ring.

Charlie looked at him blankly. Aleksander poured another Polish measure of vodka into Charlie's glass, then showed him the diamond under magnification. Tiny, perfect darts of brilliant blue light reflected into Charlie's eye, like fragments of a kaleidoscope.

"It's beautiful," he breathed.

Aleksander nodded.

"More than beautiful, my friend. I am unable to find a single inclusion."

"What does that mean?"

"It means this diamond has no natural flaws, which is almost impossible to find, and the colour is very, very rare. It is also five perfectly cut carats."

"You mean it's a good size?"

"Precisely."

Both men sat back in silence.

The diamond lay innocently on the bench between them, waiting for its new beginning.

CHAPTER 6

Maggie stood by the window, twitching the net curtains. Charlie had reminded her twice not to be late, but she had been ready for hours. She had reapplied her lipstick several times. Her mother was driving Maggie mad, continually fretting over her beehive, spraying it with blasts of hairspray every ten minutes. The slightly arching conical updo was unlikely to move, even in a gale-force wind.

The evening was, fortunately, deliciously warm. Apart from two dainty straps, Maggie's neck and shoulders were bare, emphasising the skillfully cut dress. A band of narrow lace under her bust gave way to layers of opaque fabric which cascaded over her bump and swayed neatly just above her knees. She had struggled to find a maternity dress that wasn't drenched in pastel flowers, so had brought a regular dress one size too big and nipped, tucked and sewn it herself. Thankfully, her beloved heels had still fitted, although she could have easily afforded a dozen new ones.

Maggie had more pound notes stuffed in her drawers than she knew what to do with. It was a nice problem to have, but not necessarily when she was eight months pregnant. She'd already brought several styles and sizes of baby clothes and bedding in crisp white, luxurious lace, even though her mother was churning out blankets and booties on an industrial scale.

Her mother had more time on her hands recently. Maggie had been giving her handfuls of money for housekeeping, or just to treat herself. Their Sunday roasts no longer came from scraps that had to be stewed until they tenderised, their vegetables were bright green and sweet, and the milkman now delivered a variety of dairy products. Even the butcher and greengrocer had a home delivery service, for the right price. And Maggie always tipped generously.

Whenever her father began to grumble about accepting 'dirty' money from Charlie, Maggie reminded him he was also working fewer hours at the factory and spending more time frittering money away on the horses. Her father's bottom lip would clamp over his top lip in mute protest at this.

Maggie had been holding the edge of the net curtain back so long that pins and needles began to tingle up her arms.

"He's here!" she shouted.

The sudden outburst caused her parents to jump. Maggie jiggled excitedly and bent down to kiss her mother's forehead, leaving a distinct red lipstick mark. Pinned in his chair with nowhere to escape, Maggie kissed her father too.

"Don't wait up!" she sang as she skipped out of the room.

"Behave yourself!" called her mother.

Maggie paused briefly, knowing her dad would respond with a quip.

"It's a bit late for that."

And there it was. Maggie rolled her eyes and smiled.

Opening the door with bubbling excitement, Maggie threw herself into Charlie's arms. She inhaled the fresh peppery blend of spice and soap on his skin, feeling giddy. Charlie always had this effect on her, although hormones had dramatically intensified her sense of smell. She could even detect the slightly fruity hint of polish on his black leather shoes. Finally, she let go and looked at him.

His jet-black hair shone, as did the sparkle in his eyes. He looked debonair in a charcoal-black tailored suit and starched white shirt. No doubt about it, Charlie White was smoulderingly handsome. He was the first to speak, remembering his manners.

"You look beautiful, Maggie." He beamed at her proudly.

Her cheeks flushed pink, enjoying the compliment.

"Are you ready?"

She wasn't sure what she was ready for. Charlie had kept the evening a secret, heightening the thrill and anticipation. She nodded enthusiastically, taking his arm as he helped her into the car. Before he turned the key in the ignition, Maggie wound down the window and waved at her parents. She knew they would be peeking through the net curtains, and she grinned when she saw the fabric twitch.

As they drove, Maggie gazed out with fondness at the streets she and Charlie had grown up in. Sometimes, she dreamt of the countryside or living near the sea. But London was part of her soul; it tugged at her like a magnet. Even the air, heavy with noise and pollution, felt comforting. There was a vibrancy, energy, and urgency here that she had felt nowhere else.

Resting her hand on her bump, she felt immensely grown-up. Her world was changing and fast. She glanced at Charlie who was concentrating on the traffic, his dark eyes squinting. If other drivers didn't move quickly enough, he tapped his hands restlessly on the steering wheel and growled. Maggie knew Charlie was a fearless, dangerous man. It was a fact and fate she accepted. She also knew she loved him unequivocally. Having this baby – his baby – was like capturing a butterfly, part of the elusive Charlie White, forever hers.

The West End was always special, but tonight the magic was tangible. The evening sunshine felt like a warm blessing as they stepped out of the car and Charlie threw the porter his keys. The members-only, glitzy club greeted them with lavish, sprawling sprays of flowers at the entrance and live jazz drumming from inside. It was a stunning building, spread over several floors, in an exclusive part of town. Maggie's eyes rounded as she absorbed the opulent luxury, secretly praying no one suspected the necklace dangling from her neck wasn't real. This was a brand-new world to her; not even the cash she had stuffed in her drawers would stretch far here. They were guided to their table, like royalty. All around them beautiful people laughed, danced, and drank.

Charlie's voice dragged Maggie back from her reverie.

"Champagne?"

"Yes, please. Just a small one." She instinctively touched her stomach. They both watched in silence as the waiter poured the pale golden bubbles into chilled flutes, then sunk the bottle into a bucket of ice. They clinked glasses, smiling.

Maggie noticed Charlie was fidgeting. It was unusual and endearing at the same time. He lit a cigarette, inhaled, then concentrated on blowing a perfect smoke ring before quickly stubbing the cigarette out. He took another mouthful of champagne, seeming to savour the tiny bubbles racing down his throat. He waited as the glass was promptly re-filled, then lit another cigarette.

"Charlie, is everything alright?" Maggie asked.

Without further procrastination, he placed a small box on the table between them. Maggie stared at it, dumbstruck. Even though she had been expecting this, she was nervous.

"What if it doesn't fit me?"

Charlie laughed in response. Typical Maggie.

"Your mother sized your finger when you were asleep," he said, winking.

Maggie's eyes grew wide. She laughed.

"What if I don't like it?"

Maggie bowed her head slightly. Charlie gently took her hand.

"Close your eyes," he whispered.

Maggie did as Charlie asked. She would never forget the sensation of the cold metal on her skin as the ring slid onto her finger. Opening her eyes, she gasped.

The blue diamond sparkled next to her skin. Tears sprang to her eyes. She shivered.

"Charlie, I don't know what to say."

He nodded, understanding. The diamond had this effect on most people.

For a long time, Maggie simply stared at it, wriggling her fingers and watching the light catch against its brilliance.

Finally, she leant forward and whispered, "Where did you get a ring like this?"

Charlie laughed and raised an eyebrow.

"Rule number one," he said.

She nodded, suspecting as much. Rule number one meant: I'll tell you if you need to know. She didn't care; it was hers now.

"I'll never take it off my finger." She gazed at the ring as she made the solemn promise.

"It came from South Africa," Charlie said, recalling a recent conversation with Bobby. The same woman who had commissioned the Renoir theft had known about the diamond. Bobby had spoken to her again when the newspapers were hypothesising about the ring's demise. Her insight ultimately made the difference between the diamond vanishing or being re-set. Her father had purchased it in the early 1920s for his wife. His diligence at the time had been intriguing but posed no onward threat.

Bobby had challenged whether she had any interest in the diamond, which could complicate matters. Intriguingly, her answer had been simple: no. Her motive had been the Renoir, never the diamond.

She had confessed it was poetic justice the ring had been stolen from her stepmother. Neither Bobby nor Charlie had needed to understand why.

"Apparently it was stolen," he continued, filtering the information he wanted to share with Maggie.

Her eyes brightened.

"Who would have stolen it?"

Charlie smiled, toying with the truth.

"Who wouldn't?"

She laughed and nodded.

"How did it get from South Africa to London?"

"It travelled here sometime in the early nineteenth century, apparently. According to one source," Charlie leant forward so only she could hear, "it once belonged to the imperial family and was smuggled out during the revolution."

Maggie laughed out loud. Unlike most girls her age, she had paid attention at school and knew who the imperial family were. She didn't believe the story Charlie was whipping up. If it were true, the sheer value of the ring on her finger would be immense, even priceless. Dismissing Charlie's theory with a roll of her eyes, Maggie absentmindedly touched the surface of the diamond and encouraged Charlie to continue the story.

"What happened to my ring after that?"

Charlie waited for the waiter to fill his champagne flute and Maggie's with sparkling water.

"It was purchased in Paris during the early twenties."

Charlie shrugged, saying he'd told her just about as much as he knew about the ring's history. What happened to it before Paris was mostly guesswork and consisted of fragments of information pieced together and passed on like Chinese whispers over the decades.

Curiosity about the ring intoxicated Maggie and fuelled her imagination. She wondered about the other women who had worn it. Had they felt as she did now? What had their lives been like? Happy? Sad? She let her mind drift as she rested her hand on her tummy, admiring the ring. The baby kicked, and Maggie smiled. One day, this diamond would belong to her daughter. Taken slightly aback, she wondered why she was suddenly convinced she was having a girl.

Although Maggie suspected there was more to the ring's story than Charlie was willing to share, she didn't interrogate him about it. She had the inexplicable feeling this ring was both new and very old. It was fascinating to think it had travelled so far from its humble beginnings, uncut and undiscovered, in South Africa.

PART TWO

CHAPTER 7

South Africa, 1902

Long fingers of warm sunlight bathed the entire landscape as far as General James Murray's eyes could see. The temperature in South Africa that day had been unbearable. His skin prickled uncomfortably as the suffocating heat continued to blaze, making him curse this country even more.

James longed for the lush green grass of home, the snow in winter, the rain in spring, and even his wife, Marjorie. He reluctantly missed the petulant yet exquisitely beautiful girl he had married. Her long blonde hair, pretty blue eyes and creamy skin felt like distant memories to him now. She was so very different to the native South African women he had grown accustomed to.

James thought of Pearl, who he met several months after arriving in South Africa, and smiled. Her skin was warm mocha, her eyes gentle and untouched by make-up, and her hair the colour of ebony. She was the only sweetness he experienced in this war-torn country. He had been sincere when he whispered to her over and over that he loved her. She had replied with tears. James knew he couldn't expect more from her. It tormented him that their relationship involved the exchange of money; he was just one of countless other men that shared her.

In warzones, when every sunrise was a reminder that each new day could be the last, James knew moral compasses went haywire. His high rank did not exempt him from physical needs. But there was no point in deluding himself. Pearl meant more to James than mere physical relief. He had fallen in love with her, deeply. He also knew sometime, very soon, he would have to leave her.

The Second Boer War had left the country in political, physical, and emotional turmoil. Scores of immigrants poured in daily, like ants in desperate need of work. Opportunities existed in the mines, the chance to discover diamonds. Politics were dangerous, with parties and governments still vying for power, and Boer leaders resisting any union. It would come eventually, of course, as the British had already won the war; battle casualties were more likely to be victims of disease with only a few suffering the consequences of combat. James had fought through and survived the worst.

He had seen this country destroyed by political powerheads; the land and local people suffered the most. It was perverse that among the bloodshed and corruption, the mines offered prosperity. Immigrants received a shameful wage, but it was still money. Housing was inhumane, but it provided a physical roof. The food was inedible, but it was sustenance. Each man dragged his fractured, humiliated body through endless exhausting days. Harvested diamonds made the wealthy even more affluent, but rich or poor, the mining community and diamond business provided a means to survive. Natives from ancient tribes and villages were forced to succumb to an ugly reality, usually as slaves in the mines or workhouses. For these gentle, peaceful, and spiritual people, the shock and shame were unbearable.

Well-managed brothels housing up to ten prostitutes were permitted, providing their business was suitably discreet. In the shadows, hypocrisy was rife. Affluent businessmen and religious husbands would preach virtue and wholesome values, then slip under the shadow of darkness to visit their favourite nameless girl.

James knew what occurred in the soldiers' tents was even worse. If acts of brutality came to his attention, he would punish good soldiers for being bad men. These girls were not recreational playthings to be abused or tortured. Raging testosterone levels was no defense. General James Murray was unrelentingly strict when required, but always fair. If any man voiced a rumour that James was too soft, they would find a bayonet held to their throat.

The sun descended further over the horizon, its golden glow turning tangerine, then scarlet. Darkness followed instantly. James's legs dragged his tired, aching body along the familiar route. The parched and cracked ground was hard beneath his feet. He longed for a downpour of nourishing, cold rain. He recalled what it felt like to walk on the vibrant green, springy grass back home in England. And how it felt to inhale moist air after a rain shower, rather than choke on this hot, dry atmosphere. If he concentrated hard, he could almost taste the tart sharpness of a newly picked apple from his own orchard. He kept these memories fresh in his mind, mentally reacclimatising in readiness for the order to head home.

He wondered if his wife, Marjorie, would even recognise

him. His hair was shorter, his skin browner, his body thinner, and his eyes older. He didn't feel like the same man who left England to fight this war almost three years earlier. They wrote to each other, but the letters took weeks to travel back and forth. Recently her tone had been lighter and her letters shorter. Admittedly, so had his own.

As the white, single-story building partially hidden behind tall trees and fragrant hedges came into view, James slowed down. The heavy shutters were closed, signalling business was underway. A security guard paced doggedly in front of the brothel. Most of the men visiting this establishment were trained in combat and could kill him in seconds. The guard was, however, a useful deterrent for local inhabitants who were desperate to ransack the property for cash.

Rape was also rife here. The culprits were usually soldiers pushing sordid boundaries. Fear heightened the thrill for many men, especially if they didn't know if or when they were going to see their wives again. They were usually ratted on and always punished.

Some of the girls were waiting at the front door as James entered the building. Yet more girls were ensconced in bedrooms. They were all pitifully young with sad, pretty faces. Their skin was barely covered and their dark hair tightly braided; the madam insisted on this. His eyes searched the group of familiar faces until he found Pearl. She lifted her chin and he could instantly tell she had been crying.

The madam insisted the girls dropped their shawls to their waists until customers had chosen. James's heart twinged with tenderness as he watched Pearl stand up and pull her thin shawl even tighter over her shoulders. He admired her soft, luminous face that expressed just a hint of defiance behind dark eyes. She rarely spoke unless spoken to, although her English was excellent. James followed her along the dimly lit corridor to one of the vacant bedrooms. He could hear low moans from occupied rooms, an uncomfortable reminder of where he was.

When the door closed behind them, Pearl let the shawl drop to fully expose her body. A deep scar on her abdomen was her only physical imperfection, testifying that she had once been with child. James had seen the scar many times, yet it always made him wince. He gently pulled the shawl back around her shoulders and took her hand.

"Pearl? Are you alright?" he asked softly.

He loved her name and would often whisper it to her, which sometimes made her giggle. She had once told him her grandmother had chosen this name.

He felt her body relax at his touch.

"I'm sorry. You came here to feel happy." Her native twang was more pronounced when she felt at ease.

"Tell me what's happened," James persisted.

James knew she was reluctant to trust anyone, even him, and he didn't blame her. He watched her take a deep breath and sigh, as though she had no choice.

"I'm worried about Davu, my brother. He hasn't been to see me, and he usually visits every week. He works in the mines."

She had mentioned her brother to James before. He was the only family she had here. Everyone else had remained in their village north of the Cape. Pearl and her twin brother had been forced to find work, and in the end became desperate. Desperation could kill; James knew people often risked their lives over a tiny nugget of dirt on the slim chance it might turn out to be a diamond. He watched Pearl twist the threadbare fabric of her shawl around her fingers.

"Do you know where he might be staying?" James asked.

Pearl shook her head. The beads woven into her hair swayed like pendulums, clicking in quick succession.

"He *always* visits. Something has happened."

James sensed she knew more than she was telling him. He had heard twins had a sixth sense about one another. He decided to push slightly.

"Do you think Davu might just have got caught up in the mines? Maybe he's been too busy?"

She shook her head again.

"No. I can't explain it," she said firmly.

James wondered if what she really meant was that she *wouldn't* explain it. He tried to distract her with feathery kisses, but she was wooden beneath his touch. He gently pulled away.

"Try not to worry, eh?" He tilted her chin to better see her beautiful face. He wanted to absorb every feature, knowing their time together was always racing like sand down the hourglass.

James stood up reluctantly. Lamps burnt low in the small room, intensifying the heat. He unbuttoned the top of his shirt and ruffled his hair slightly, which would reassure the madam that Pearl had earnt his payment. Turning to the bedroom door, he noticed the small cross nailed to the wall. These crosses were in every bedroom, which always seemed ironic to him.

The cross was hanging at an odd angle and James reached

over to straighten it. But Pearl tugged on his shirt, abruptly pulling his arm away. Shocked, James stared at her.

"Pearl?"

"I'll see to it," she said, holding his gaze.

He frowned and opened his mouth to speak. A loud rap at the door stopped him. It would be the madam. Their time together this evening was over.

CHAPTER 8

Pearl straightened her shoulders and followed James outside. The madam scowled at this unusual extension of services – the girls were supposed to stay indoors – but the General paid well and had a privileged rank, so she let it go. Pearl relished these few rare, blissful moments when she could breathe fresh air.

She stood on the veranda and watched James leave until he disappeared into the shadows. She often wondered how she would survive without the comfort of his regular visits. She had become almost desensitised to the daily routine of the brutal and demoralising acts expected of her, but she prayed morning and night she would escape. Pearl suddenly remembered the cross. She had been careless and needed to fasten it securely to the wall before it drew any further attention.

She glanced at the night sky dotted with bright, sparkling stars. Pearl had an overriding sense that somewhere, sharing the same sky, her grandmother, mother, and brother were living and breathing. A sudden breeze tousled her shawl and chilled her skin. She had never shared her grandmother's supernatural gift, but tonight she felt her grandmother was close by. She rubbed her eyes, exhausted.

Back inside the house, the atmosphere was sweaty and damp as usual. Several customers had already been and gone, and more continued to arrive. Pearl sat down with the other girls, who also looked worn to a thread. The madam hovered nearby, but it wasn't yet time to blow out the lamps and send the girls to their rooms for the night. The front door opened, and the sound of a raised, drunken voice echoed down the corridor. The girls' eyes darted between each other uncomfortably.

Heavy boots made their way unsteadily along the wooden corridor and a man stalked into the room. The madam greeted him wordlessly. Several notes were exchanged. Satisfied, the madam waved over at the young girls who shifted anxiously in their seats.

The man stumbled towards them and stopped. He wasn't in uniform but was exceptionally well dressed, suggesting he was perhaps a businessman. Pearl guessed he was in his late thirties. She noticed he was unshaven, his clothes were encrusted with dirt, and his eyes were menacing. He was also exceptionally drunk.

"Take your clothes off," he ordered. There were seven girls in the room, including Pearl. They had no choice but to obey.

Pearl dropped her shawl in a well-practised movement, as did the others. She stared ahead, focusing on a single, tiny crack on the wall in front of her. The drunk man pulled at the girls' nipples with his long fingernails and yanked at their hair. Pearl felt herself being dragged forward along with another girl; they had been chosen.

Pearl took a shaky breath, trying to quell her rising anxiety and halt the nausea. She walked behind him to the bedroom, the other girl in front, as he jeered and swigged from his liquor bottle. They entered the same room Pearl had been in earlier with James. Her eyes sought out the tilted cross on the wall; her fingers twitched, wanting to straighten it but knowing that would be impossible now.

Pearl winced as the drunk man pulled her hair, forcing her to look up at him. She was repulsed by his nakedness. She shook her head in refusal as he pushed a new bottle of liqueur towards her. With a flash of anger, he landed an unrestrained blow across her cheek. The force of his attack sent her crashing into the wall, before she dropped limply to the floor. The other girl watched in horror. Pearl stood up shakily, wiping away a trickle of blood from the corner of her mouth. The man handed her the bottle again. This time she took it.

"More," he insisted, passing the bottle between them. Pearl's fear intensified. She knew men sometimes forced alcohol upon a girl in order to physically anesthetise and vocally subdue her. Pearl watched as the other girl retched uncontrollably on the floor. The man stomped over to her and gave her a desultory kick in the side. With no escape, Pearl curled up into a ball and was forced to watch him manoeuvre the limp girl onto her front. He raised her hips and mounted her. As he thrust himself deep into her back passage, she let out a low animal-like wail. Pearl clamped her hands over her eyes, inwardly screaming. The repeated thud on the wooden floor told her the girl's head was being smashed over and over again as the man thrust and thrashed inside her. Unable to control herself, Pearl was violently sick.

The noise of retching distracted the man. As Pearl composed herself she realised he had pulled himself out of the other girl, unconcerned by the blood seeping into the wooden floor around her. Pearl frantically glanced at the girl who lay motionless. Petrified, Pearl began backing herself towards the wall, pulling her legs close to her body. She clamped her eyes shut as her body was dragged across the room. The man dug his nails firmly into her scalp, pulled her jaw open, and forced himself into her mouth, laughing. She gagged; he laughed louder. Moments later, he released her. Her knees buckled and he picked her up like a ragdoll and punched her savagely several times across the head. She felt a tooth dislodge and blood fill her mouth. Her ribs throbbed with pain and it was difficult to breathe. She was vaguely aware that he had pulled her legs apart, using his fist to grind into her, clawing at her delicate flesh. Finally, he used her own hand to finish himself, covering her blood-soaked body with his mess.

Pearl saw him leave through one slightly less swollen eye. She couldn't hear any other noise in the house and had no idea how long it would be before someone found them. She mustered enough strength to raise her head a fraction and focus on the wall. The cross, although precariously lose, was still hanging on.

CHAPTER 9

James pushed past the security guard who futilely flapped his arms in an attempt to stop him. He had run all the way to the brothel, fuelled by adrenaline and fear. One of the girls had broken a window and fled in the night, risking her own life. A soldier had found her and brought her to James. The girl, visibly shaking, relayed what she'd heard through the wafer-thin walls. James listened in horror as she described the shouts of pain and the terrifying silence that followed.

He panicked when he saw the trail of blood on the veranda. He kicked down the front door, ripping the thin mosquito netting and throwing it aside. The madam stood at the entrance to the hallway, glaring at him, but the rage in her eyes was no match for his, and the venom in his voice would have made hardy combat soldiers cower.

"Where is Pearl?" he spat.

The madam refused to speak. Blinded by rage, James took out his gun and fired it at the ceiling.

"In her usual room!" she quickly replied.

Taking two steps at a time, James thundered down the

corridor. The putrid smell of vomit mixed with the warm, heavy air made him gag as he stood at the door and closed his eyes briefly. He wouldn't be able to rewind what he was about to see.

James was aware the madam was hovering just behind him. It occurred to him she must not have gone in the room herself yet. He scowled at her with disdain, and she shrunk back slightly. Pushing his hand down on the handle, he walked briskly inside.

Daylight throbbed through the torn blinds. James squinted, momentarily blinded. His vision cleared and he saw a girl on the floor, naked and motionless. He reached down and pressed two fingers against her neck. She was dead.

Bile rose in his stomach and choked him. Flies buzzed in the rancid air, vying to land. He pushed them away with angry, flailing arms. Turning, he saw Pearl.

She was curled up in the corner, her legs tucked under her in a tight ball, her head flopped at an awkward angle on the floor. James tore a blanket off the rancid mattress and gently covered her with it before scooping her into his arms. Relief washed over him as she made a soft, almost inaudible moan.

"Pearl, it's James," he said tenderly. "You are safe. I'm here… I'm here."

He laid her on the bed and quickly assessed the damage. His hands shook with pent-up anger. He counted slowly in his head, his breathing unsteady. Feeling slightly more composed, he straightened the blanket around her. He had seen enough. She desperately needed a doctor, but he knew no medic would set foot over the door of a brothel. He barked orders at the madam to bring fresh towels and warm water. His imagination tortured him as he gently bathed Pearl's wounds and kissed her eyes. It was too painful to imagine the evil that had gone on in this room. Pearl stirred occasionally, raising his hopes for her recovery, then sank back into unconsciousness. She seemed to be teetering on the edge of life itself. He had to pull her back.

Pearl woke to the sound of a man's voice. She fought her drowsiness as she strained to listen. She should have been feeling deep physical pain, but trauma had replaced the agony with shock and numbness.

Her twin brother, Davu, consumed her thoughts.

It had been a week since she'd seen him, and she had no idea where he was or what had happened to him. The contents of her mind twisted and turned. There was something she had to remember. Something important. The thought drifted away from her like a rare, white butterfly fluttering to and fro. She tried to focus. With a sharp intake of breath, she remembered.

Davu had stolen a blue diamond from the mine.

Pearl pictured Davu's face the last time she saw him. His eyes, identical to her own, had been wide with excitement.

"This will buy our freedom! We will go home soon," he said.

"What are you talking about?"

Pearl would never forget the first sight of the rough diamond as he slowly opened his clenched fist. Despite being covered in dirt, she could see it was sparkling.

"It's blue!" she said, awed.

Even she knew blue diamonds were exceptionally rare.

"It's quite big too," Davu added proudly.

Pearl felt nothing but panic; her brother could have been killed. She knew the miners were watched like hawks and subjected to humiliating, invasive inspections to verify nothing had been inserted or swallowed. She nibbled at a nail as her brother explained how a fight between a handful of other miners had distracted the guards. Miraculously, he had walked straight out through the gates with a large blue diamond in his pocket. The simplicity of the theft had been uncanny – more than just luck.

"But what if there hadn't been a fight, Davu? They would have caught you," Pearl said, distressed.

Davu nodded.

"When I found the diamond I knew it would be our only chance. I had to take it." He shrugged.

"You are a fool, you know that?" Pearl leant forward, taking his hand. "But thank you."

Pearl looked at the diamond in her palm, wondering what they should do with it.

"We have to keep it somewhere safe," she said.

Davu looked terrified. "*I* can't take it. It's too risky," he said, shaking his head.

Pearl reluctantly agreed. She would have to deal with it.

Later that night, she carved out a small hole behind the cross hanging on the wall of her usual bedroom. She wrapped the diamond in a thin cloth and buried it inside the wall. She stuffed the chalky debris back in place and positioned the cross over the top.

She had no idea what else to do with a priceless diamond.

Pearl held on vehemently to the image of her brother's face, trying to pull the memory of him closer. She remembered how she used to chase him through their village, darting in and out of huts, ignoring their mother's warning. But when their grandmother appeared, hands on her hips, they *always* stopped. The look she gave them was more effective than a scolding from their mother.

Childhood memories continued to play out in her mind, offering comfort. Pearl conjured up an image of her grandmother, remembering how she had felt her nearness the evening before. She lifted her head off the pillow a fraction, detecting a sweet, woody scent burning nearby. She recognised it: Cape Snowbush. Her grandmother would often tie plants and herbs into bunches and hang them over the embers of a fire, allowing the smoke to permeate the room for medicinal or spiritual benefit. Pearl remembered watching the tiny white flowers of the cape snowbush as the scented petals drifted down into the glowing embers.

Her grandmother was the most respected sangoma in their village. She had a gift that enabled her to communicate with their ancestors. Her ability to allow her mortal body to become a channel of wisdom was undisputed and widely celebrated. She relayed ancient cures, specifying the name and often location of a particular plant. The medication was then crushed, rubbed, burnt or infused. More often than not, the ailment, whether emotional or physical, was completely cured.

Pearl breathed in as deeply as she could, trying to draw the smoke closer. Her grandmother had told her branches of cape snowbush had been burning in the room on the day the twins were born. Pearl had arrived into the world first, quickly followed by Davu.

Their births had been foreseen by the ancestors. Pearl remembered her grandmother telling her the tale as she grew up.

"Your lives will be part of a great journey. The name 'Davu' means 'the beginning'. It is significant for your brother's destiny."

"What about my name?" Pearl had asked, irked that her brother's name seemed more important than hers.

Her grandmother had sat back in her seat, smiling, a twinkle in her eye.

"Your name is even more special, Pearl. The spirits will reveal their reason, child… all in good time."

Their grandmother had given the young Pearl and Davu bracelets made up of dark blue beads interspersed with five pearlescent ones. The twins had worn them ever since, although Pearl now wore hers on her ankle to avoid notice by the madam – no one looked at the girls' feet in the brothel. Each bracelet was a gift passed down from their ancestors, a talisman to honour and prosper their native bloodline.

Pearl could remember touching the pretty pearlescent beads and asking her grandmother why there were only five of them.

"These five beads are symbols of our ancestors' wisdom, child. Davu and you are beginning a special journey. You are connected to others, like stars in the sky. You stand alone, but time and the universe have woven your souls into an intricate pattern."

The words of this prophesy came back to her now, as she recalled childhood nights spent stargazing with her grandmother.

Her mind suddenly switched to thoughts of Davu and the diamond. She pictured the blue gem nestled in his hand. Its colour was reminiscent of the dark blue beads in the bracelets her grandmother had given them.

Pearl writhed uncomfortably. She managed to touch her ankle with her toe. She felt the hard beads twist around, then dropped her foot. It was too exhausting to move. She was conscious James was there, still talking to her and holding her hand. Her eyes almost opened, fluttering briefly, but she drifted back into her thoughts as further memories summoned her.

Hours passed. Pearl floated in and out of consciousness before once again becoming aware of James's voice. Her body ached and she flinched. There was a beautiful light somewhere, gently beckoning, encouraging her to draw near. She heard his voice again.

"Pearl? Can you hear me?" His tone became insistent. "Pearl? *Pearl?*"

She forced herself to try and move. Her fingers barely flickered, but that was enough for James who grabbed her hand tightly. "Pearl I felt that! Try and speak to me!"

In her head, she could hear a drumbeat slowly getting louder. Growing up, there was always music in the village, cheerful singing and the regular rhythm of drums. Pearl turned her head slightly, listening to the familiar sound.

James's voice interrupted her again.

"Pearl?"

Irritated, she growled. She wanted to follow the music, but his voice kept pulling her back. The drumbeats slowed and then faded.

Forcing herself to concentrate, Pearl opened her left eyelid until she saw a slither of the room. The other eye was too swollen to open.

"That's it, Pearl, look at me," James urged.

She mustered what remained of her physical strength to turn to where she knew the cross was hanging.

'There,' she croaked.

The word was barely recognisable. She saw James trying to follow her gaze. The room was so bare it wasn't difficult. James cried openly as he yanked the cross off the wall and tucked it gently by her side.

"You have it now," he whispered.

"No!" She forced the word out.

She managed to lift her wrist off the bed and point with a single finger at the wall again. James went back to the wall and picked at a previously dug-out area, no larger than a coin, with his army knife. Something fell out, wrapped in a thin piece of cloth.

"What is it?" he asked.

She tried to communicate with her eyes, but he looked back at her, confused. He unwrapped the thin cloth and gasped.

"Is this a… a… diamond?" he stuttered.

She nodded.

Her eye closed again as her head began to throb.

"Can't keep it safe. Take it," was all she could manage to say.

Pearl slumped back against the pillow, exhausted, and relieved. She could hear James talking, but his voice was rapidly fading. Her body began to feel weightless again, floating effortlessly as it drifted towards a warm, ethereal light.

Pearl became aware of a palpable shift in energy and the sound of her grandmother's hands clapping to evoke the ancestors' spirits. The earthy, floral aroma of spiritual smoke that had welcomed her at birth surrounded her again. Pearl inhaled long and deep, drawing the smoke into her lungs. With one final exhalation, her spirit left her physical body and followed the beat of the drum.

PART THREE

CHAPTER 10

ENGLAND, 1902

James lifted his chin up to the dark, wintry sky and savoured the cold rain spitting on his face. He closed his eyes, struggling to remember the South African peach-gold sunrises and scorching heat that had consumed his existence for almost three years. Raindrops mixed with tears of relief; he was finally home.

The journey had taken several weeks. Every man aboard the British Army vessel had been pushed beyond measure. The rough sea had been unrelenting, illness rampant, and living conditions dire. Several people had died, leaving many survivors feeling death would be a relief.

James had been one of those men.

He had replayed the horror of discovering Pearl over and over in his mind, distracted only by having to repeatedly hurl his stomach contents over the edge of the ship. Vomiting was commonplace; most men aboard suffered from constant motion sickness, severe infection or virus.

Two weeks after pearl died, James received his order to leave. The Treaty of Vereeniging had been signed six months before, securing peace and victory for the British. The bloodshed was over, but James knew the sun-drenched earth he left behind would take many years longer to heal. As would his own heart.

James steadied himself against the familiar wrought-iron gate. His father had built it when James was just a child; he remembered it well. A sturdy fence embraced the perimeter of the estate as far as his eye could see. Two maybe three acres of fertile land surrounded the farmhouse. Beyond, dense woodland stretched across a vast landscape. James could remember darting through the trees as a boy, usually on horseback.

Breathing in the moist, cold air, James smiled. The sight of his home reignited a spark of vivacity. He raised his shoulders and marched forwards, his heavy boots squelching through wet, sloshy mud. It was a twenty-minute walk from the gate to the farmhouse if he walked fast.

James forced himself to think about his wife, Marjorie. He had written to her weeks ago, but there was no guarantee his letter would have arrived before he did. He realised with wry amusement and a twinge of anxiety that his arrival would likely be a complete shock to her.

The farmhouse came into view long before he reached it. For a moment, he stood perfectly still. Even though it was only five o'clock in the morning, smoke puffed out of two large chimneys, and lamps shone through the kitchen windows. He had left behind several loyal members of staff and was especially eager to see Peter who had been like a father to him for the past thirty years. James frowned, thinking how fractious Marjorie could be with Peter. He hoped he'd still find the old man in his employ.

He stood outside the front door. To the left of the knocker, a name was chiselled into the thick stone wall. He ran his hands over the letters: Murray Farm. James grinned at the irony. They had never had a single farm animal on their land. His father had insisted it *used* to be farmland and would be *ideal* farmland, but the truth was they had never used it as such. James's father had made significant wealth from stocks and shares in London then retreated to the countryside to enjoy early retirement. The family kept several horses instead. James listened for the familiar unison of snorts and neighs coming from the stables just beyond the farmhouse. He couldn't wait to see his beloved Irish Draught stallion, Prince.

He inhaled a deep breath of the fresh air until his lungs fully inflated, then released it. He couldn't put it off any longer. He lifted the heavy iron door knocker, then quickly let it drop. What if Marjorie had changed?

James had no choice but to wait as the door would surely be bolted. After a few minutes, he heard footsteps and the door opened a few inches.

"Who's there?"

James recognised Peter's voice.

"Thief, coming to steal your wears," James joked.

He heard a frantic shuffling as Peter no doubt scrabbled for his gun, which probably wasn't even loaded.

"Peter, it's me, James. I'm home!" James called through the door.

After a brief silence, the door was pulled wide open.

Tears poured unashamedly down Peter's face. James stepped forward and embraced the older man.

"You fool! I could have shot you," said Peter, grinning.

"You were always a lousy aim, even at this close range." James ducked as Peter swiped him affectionately.

"It's good to have you home, son."

The words made James ache for his father. Peter read the emotion in James's eyes and pulled him into a warm embrace. Father and son had been inseparable for twenty years. James's mother had died giving birth to him and Joseph, James's father, had never re-married.

"Where is Marjorie?" James asked, pulling away, his eyes beginning to dance.

"In bed, I imagine. It's still early."

"How is she?"

James's eyes searched Peter's face. He knew Peter and Marjorie clashed. He had once overheard Peter telling the cook Marjorie was a twisted, spoilt and vicious tyrant.

"Same as always," replied Peter with a shrug.

James untied his heavy, soiled boots and kicked them to one side. They reminded him of his long journey home and he would throw them on the fire later. He took in the wide, open hallway; it looked identical to the day he left three years earlier. The wooden seat still had the faded cushions scattered on top, and the fireplace had the same fire irons hanging from the wall. His father had nailed them there when James was a boy.

He turned and walked up the staircase, wincing at the familiar creak of the third and seventh step. His lamp cast shadows across the whitewashed walls and low ceiling. It surprised him how dark and eerie his childhood home suddenly felt as he crept upstairs.

As his hand touched the handle of his bedroom door, he was startled by the sound of footsteps on the wooden floorboards scuttling towards him. A small hand snatched his arm.

"No, sir, please. Mrs Murray will be so angry if she is disturbed this early. Please, let me wake her first."

The young maid who was trying desperately to wriggle between James and the door hadn't even had time to dress fully. Her apron was undone at the back and her hair unbrushed. It was, however, the wild panic in her eyes that alarmed James. Something was very wrong.

He pushed her away from the door. "I'm her husband, for goodness sake, and this is my bedroom."

"Please, no. Your room is down here," she said, pointing down the corridor.

James ignored the young maid. Enough was enough. He pushed down hard on the door handle; the door sprang open. The maid gasped and retreated unsteadily backwards as James pushed her aside.

Heavily lined curtains enveloped the room in darkness. James took a few steps, but he could see nothing. He stalked over to the window and yanked back the curtains, allowing faint sunlight to spill into the room. Allowing his eyes to focus, he saw her.

Marjorie sat bolt upright in bed, her long beautiful blonde

mane falling across her naked chest. James found her face and then her blue eyes, raging with horror and shock.

Beside her, a man stirred.

For a moment, James's eyes were transfixed. Remembering to breathe, he forced himself to take in gulps of air. His legs shook violently beneath him.

He reached inside his pocket and pulled out a loaded pistol. Aiming it at the man's head, Marjorie screamed.

"James, no!"

They all heard the trigger click.

"Get out of my house!" James thundered.

The naked man nodded frantically, holding his hands up. He spoke rapidly in hysterical Russian as he quickly grabbed his clothing and bolted out of the room.

James went straight to the window and dropped the latch. He pushed his gun through the gap and waited for the unwelcome visitor to appear. Aiming at the sky, he squeezed the trigger. The noise echoed backwards into the room. James collapsed to his knees.

"James?" Marjorie's voice pulled him back to the cold bedroom.

With horror, James thought of Pearl. Had his own behaviour been any different to this man he had just chased?

"You will never see that man again. Are we clear?" His tone was quiet and even.

Marjorie hesitated then nodded. She began to cry, pulling her knees up to her chin defensively. They had been apart for years, and she was a beautiful young woman – it wasn't unreasonable that she had been as lonely as he had. But her blatant unfaithfulness in his house was unforgivable. Most men would have horsewhipped her, but he was not most men. James watched her for a long time. He needed time to think.

"Get dressed. We will talk then."

She turned to look at him, her eyes bright blue and as wild as ever. They reminded him of the cornflowers which grew in the fields every summer.

"What are you going to do?" she asked.

James felt a stab of disappointment. It was clear she was referring to her lover.

"First, we need to talk. I'd prefer to do that when you are decently dressed."

"Please don't hurt him."

Her words triggered something monstrous inside him. He leaned forward and grabbed a handful of her long hair, twisting it tight around his fist. She yelped, but her eyes remained steadfastly cold.

"Don't you dare tell me what to do. You are lucky I don't beat you!" he spat.

"But he is a Russian count!"

The revelation of his status, as though that somehow warranted any justification or leniency, was the last straw for James. With one hand he held onto her hair and with the other, he pulled his belt free from his trouser loops.

"James, please, I'm sorry!"

But he could not stop. Marjorie had pushed him too far, and he struck her several times. She clutched her stomach defensively, trying to curl into a ball.

"James, I'm with child!" she sobbed.

He stopped, frozen. He pulled away the covers to expose

her full nakedness.

    Marjorie lowered her eyes to her stomach.

    James followed her gaze and clearly saw a small, rounded bump where a baby was growing.

CHAPTER 11

James tipped the bottle upside down, watching the caramel coloured liquid splash into the glass. He gulped the drink down, wincing as the alcohol burnt his throat. Quickly, he poured another.

He rested his head on the desk in his father's study. Above him, a portrait of his father hung on the wall. It seemed as if the old man was looking down on him. The painting was extraordinarily lifelike; it always unnerved James.

Peter appeared in the doorway with his head bent low. James ushered him in and offered him a glass of whiskey.

"How long has this been going on under my roof?" James asked calmly.

Embarrassed, Peter frowned.

"I don't honestly know when it started. It became apparent a man was being, how can I put it… being sneaked inside. Two maids lost their jobs over it."

James looked despondent. "Why didn't you tell me?"

"I didn't want to lose my position either, not until I knew for certain that you were coming home."

James nodded, believing Marjorie would be capable of blackmail.

"She's pregnant," he said quietly.

Peter gasped, shaking his head.

"I'm sorry."

They shared several whiskeys in silence. James had been carefully evaluating the options. The first: let the baby be born and accept everyone knowing the child was not his own flesh and blood. The second option: abort the child now.

His mind settled firmly on the second option, but he needed Peter's help. He knew there were women, witches, who could stop a pregnancy using herbal concoctions. In South Africa, he had seen far more barbaric procedures. James thought of Pearl, and the scar that had been carved deep into her stomach.

James felt his shoulders collapse with relief as Peter assured him he would help. There was a witch, well known for her exceptional powers, living on the edge of a nearby village. Peter fidgeted uncomfortably in his seat as he talked about her.

"Is she so fearsome, Peter?" James asked.

"The locals say she can read your thoughts," he replied.

James shook his head and laughed. "I doubt that."

"And she can cause someone pain just by thinking about them," Peter continued earnestly.

James paused and considered this sinister claim. He remembered in South Africa there were spiritual people who reportedly had similar abilities. He had brushed their otherworldly theories aside; only a gun was truly effective in his world.

"Can you find her?" he asked.

Peter swallowed slowly. "Yes."

The small cottage was located at the end of a long entrance of tall trees, craning towards each other like arching bodies. Peter shuddered. The hairs on the back of his neck bristled uncomfortably. Wind chimes were suspended from the branches, creating a sharp melody even though there seemed to be no wind. He walked slowly to the cottage, his eyes darting left and right anxiously. Smoke swirled from the chimney. Someone was home. A window was open and he stopped abruptly, breathing in the surprising wafts of delicious home cooking.

Peter tapped gingerly on the front door. His scarf suddenly felt too tight around his neck and his coat uncomfortably hot and heavy. He quickly chided himself for letting nerves get the better of him. His eyes were wide and fixed on the door as it opened.

"Can I help you?" the woman asked blankly.

Peter didn't move. His gaze flickered just beyond her head, searching for the witch. Was she holding this young woman hostage? He shook his irrational thoughts aside. Looking down at the small, dark-haired woman, he raised his eyebrows.

"I'm looking for Sylvia," he whispered.

She cocked her head and studied his face then leant towards him.

"I am Sylvia," she whispered back.

"You are?"

Peter couldn't mask his surprise. He had been mentally preparing for a woman who advertised her black arts with a bent back, straggly hair and warts on her face. The woman staring back at him was young and incredibly pretty.

"How can I help you?" Sylvia asked cheerily.

Peter hung his head, unsure how to explain. It was a delicate situation.

"A woman who is with child needs help to…" He faltered.

"Did her husband send you?"

Peter nodded.

"Wait here."

Sylvia partially closed the door and disappeared back inside her cottage. Peter focused on one of the windchimes by the door and tried to calm his breathing. He jumped as Sylvia reappeared. She handed him a piece of reddish-brown bark wrapped in linen cloth.

"Soak a small piece of this in a cup of cool, boiled water for at least three hours, but ideally overnight. Then make sure the woman drinks all of it before I arrive. Putting it in tea usually helps."

Peter sighed with relief.

"When will you arrive?" he asked.

"First thing tomorrow morning," Sylvia replied. Her tone was businesslike, but Peter felt reassured by the warmth in her eyes.

Peter thanked her and tucked the mysterious bark into his coat pocket. As he walked brusquely away from the cottage, he prayed Marjorie would be oblivious to what was about to happen to her and her unborn baby.

◈ ◈ ◈

Marjorie watched with scathing eyes as the new maid filled the large copper tub the following morning, her head bent low.

"I didn't ask for a bath," she snapped.

The maid turned, unmoved by Marjorie's tone. Mrs Day was sixty years old and did not need this brash young girl to bark at her. She was quite capable of barking back, which was why James had hired her that morning. She was fully briefed with the gruesome reality that lay ahead.

"Master James did."

"I am not a child," Marjorie replied tartly.

Her response was met with cool silence.

Marjorie watched as Mrs Day sprinkled a few drops of lavender oil into the hot water. The smell was lovely, comforting even. Marjorie decided a bath might be a good idea after all. Perhaps it would stop her feeling so wretched. Mrs Day held up a towel, which was Marjorie's cue to undress and step into the swirling, steaming bath. Marjorie obeyed, sinking deep into the relaxing water.

Afterwards, she held her arms up, relishing the coolness of her nightdress as it fell over her head. Marjorie's hair was dried and brushed until it was tamed. She looked pretty and demure as Mrs Day tucked her back into bed with promises of fresh tea and toast. For the first time that day, Marjorie managed a half-smile. This hard-faced woman had a way of taking control and to her surprise, Marjorie rather liked it.

She had felt like a prisoner since James returned home and was desperately worried about Vladimir. Only the day before, she had shared the news of her pregnancy with him. He had frowned, his dark eyes telling her nothing. In the early days of their love affair, he had begged her to go to Russia, and she had been swept away by that romantic notion. However, in recent months he had been colder. He said it wasn't practical, she was married, and now the baby complicated the situation between them.

His English was excellent; however, he reverted to Russian when he was stressed. Marjorie's love for him was at the same time unreasonable and deep; it was destroying her.

When Mrs Day put the tray on her bed, the smell of toast made her head feel dizzy and her stomach clench. She started to cry.

"Come on. You need to at least drink," Mrs Day said, offering up the cup of tea.

Reluctantly, Marjorie tilted her head back and drank the cool tea.

She instantly pulled a face. "That tastes funny."

"Nonsense. I made it myself. Probably just your taste buds, dear."

Marjorie nodded and eased herself back against the plump, fluffy pillows. She yawned, exhausted. Pregnancy was draining the life out of her. She closed her eyes and felt her muscles relax.

Mrs Day checked the cup where the reddish-brown tea had been stewing. It was empty.

CHAPTER 12

Sylvia tied her horse, Star, to the hardy English elm and patted the mare's silver-grey neck. Heavy, dark clouds above them signalled rain; she'd need to ask someone to walk Star to the stables for her. Sylvia fastened her cloak tightly around herself as a feisty breeze whipped her cheeks and caused her long hair to fly. She quickly tied her hair in a loose knot and tucked it underneath the hood then unhooked the bag attached to Star's saddle. Before leaving home, she had checked several times she had packed all necessities. Once they got started, there would be no turning back.

She knocked on the farmhouse door, glancing back over her shoulder to check on Star. Sylvia knew the next time she saw her beloved mare she would climb back up on her saddle emotionally and physically drained. This procedure was rarely easy and always difficult to witness. Usually young, unmarried girls called upon her for resolving unwanted pregnancies, or ageing married women who already had a full flock of children. It was unusual to carry out this procedure on a healthy, married woman of childbearing age.

Except, when Sylvia had swirled the tea leaves around in her cup that morning she had understood why.

Sylvia was about to knock again when the door opened. James greeted her with a solemn frown.

"Mr Murray?" she asked.

"Yes?"

"I'm Sylvia."

Sylvia tactfully ignored his look of surprise. She quickly absorbed every detail: his unshaven face, dishevelled hair, and crumpled shirt. She accurately guessed he hadn't slept the night before. But his eyes looked desperately sad, which touched and troubled her. "May I come in?"

James composed himself and opened the door fully. He barely spoke as he walked her to the bedroom where Marjorie was sound asleep, although he brightened when she mentioned her horse.

Sylvia knew he was fearful; she could read his thoughts. She was used to people expecting to see an old hag arrive on their doorstep carrying a smoking cauldron and magic broomstick. It only upset her when people were cruel to her face, which inevitably some were. Their fear of the unknown often turned them into fanatics, mocking her beliefs and sabotaging her practice. She had a powerful gift but, nonetheless, she knew not to misuse it or waste it on frivolous revenge.

James and Sylvia stood outside the bedroom door. James gently touched Sylvia's sleeve.

"Will it hurt her?"

Sylvia was unable to lie. Besides, it would be evident soon enough.

"It is not an easy procedure, but she will heal. Be prepared for the sadness women suffer when they have lost a child." And a lover, she almost said.

"Afterwards, will she be able to have more children?" James asked tentatively.

"I believe so."

James nodded with relief.

Sylvia observed his reaction, becoming aware that the temperature in the hall had just dropped. Boldly, she looked deep into his brown eyes.

"Mr Murray, who is Pearl?" she asked.

He began to speak, but words failed him, and he stood, swaying slightly, his jaw slack.

Sylvia quickly put her hand up. "No need to explain."

James sunk to the floor in shock. Sylvia knelt beside him, her hand on his arm. She felt the skin between her eyes tighten. She took a handkerchief out of her pocket and handed it to him; it was sprinkled with calming lavender oil. She urged him to breathe deeply.

"How do you know about her? About Pearl?" he asked hoarsely.

"I can see what she gave to you."

Open-mouthed, he stared at her.

"How?"

"I see the most beautiful colour blue," she said gently, closing her eyes.

As her mind reached out to a higher plane, Sylvia could see fast-moving images: a man's hand, his skin dark, holding something in a tightly clenched fist. The soft brown eyes of a young woman, his sister, smiling and radiating peaceful energy. In the distance, the sound of staccato drumbeats.

Then she saw the most spectacular colour blue again shimmering like ice on fire.

With a jolt, Sylvia opened her eyes. She quickly pulled her hand away from James's arm, breaking the link. She could feel the taut skin between her eyes tingle and slowly return to normal.

"Are you alright?" James asked, anxiously.

Sylvia nodded.

One day she would be able to tell him what else she had seen.

In the bedroom, Sylvia watched Marjorie sleeping. Her hair was fanned out around her face and her eyelids were closed peacefully. Mrs Day stood nearby, her chest puffed out defensively, her arms crossed.

"Did Mrs Murray drink the tea?" Sylvia asked softly.

"I soaked the bark all night, as instructed. Mrs Murray drank it all this morning with breakfast. She's been asleep since then," replied Mrs Day, frowning.

"Good," said Sylvia politely.

Mrs Day raised her eyebrows, secretly impressed.

Sylvia turned to James, whose fear had turned to awe. "Mr Murray…"

"James, please," he interrupted.

Mrs Day tutted, expressing her disapproval at such

informalities.

"James," continued Sylvia, pointing to the door. "I think it may be easier if I took over with Mrs Day now."

She was aware Mrs Day lifted her head in staunch approval. James left without any resistance, and Sylvia closed the door firmly behind him. She turned to Mrs Day who had changed her apron, tied back her hair in a fierce bun, and scrubbed her hands. Sylvia knew she was expecting instructions.

"We will need towels and warm water, but not for a while yet," Sylvia said as she carefully unpacked the contents of her bag.

Mrs Day scrutinised every item with eagle eyes.

"What are those for?" Mrs Day asked, pointing to a pestle and mortar.

Sylvia tore the leaves off a twig and ripped them into small pieces, scattering them into the mortar. She then ground them with a well-practised wrist until the invigorating aroma began to rise.

"These wonderful leaves will help keep us alert for as long as we need until the towels and water are required," she said.

Sylvia breathed in the scent, feeling her senses awaken. Mrs Day gave a little huff of scorn and busied herself folding sheets.

Sylvia closed the curtains and dimmed the light. "The softer lighting will relax Mrs Murray," she explained.

"But she's fast asleep!" retorted Mrs Day.

"Tell me, Mrs Day, do you feel more comfortable sleeping in dim light or bright daylight?"

Mrs Day fell silent for a moment. "What was that bark

you told me to put in her tea, anyway? She's been away with the fairies since she had that."

Sylvia bit back a smile, enjoying the romantic notion of fairies. The bark was powerful, kept only for procedures such as these, but it was tricky to get the balance right. If Marjorie had too much, it could be difficult to wake her, but too little, and she could be conscious. If nature were kind, as was difficult to predict, she would be mostly unaware until it was over or at least unstoppable.

Sylvia placed her hand on Mrs Day's shoulder and looked her squarely in the eyes, measuring the older woman's nerve.

"Are you ready to begin, Mrs Day?"

Mrs Day nodded.

Sylvia seemed satisfied and removed her cloak, revealing a simple black dress. She tied an apron on securely and pushed stray wisps of hair away from her face. Closing her eyes, she began to whisper the words she had been taught long ago. Marjorie responded with unintelligible murmurings, moving her head slightly left and right. Sylvia paused to mix powders and grind special spices. As she did so, she glimpsed Mrs Day, who looked ready to gather her skirts and bolt.

"Mrs Day, please could you turn your wrist towards me," she asked the maid.

"Why?" croaked Mrs Day.

"Here," Sylvia replied, holding out a dark brown ointment on the tip of her finger. "You twisted your wrist, and I know how painful it is for you. This will help."

Shocked, Mrs Day obeyed, detecting a pungent scent of clove.

Sylvia turned her concentration to various small pots in

front of her, aware that Mrs Day was now more intrigued than sceptical.

"We need to wake Mrs Murray slightly to encourage her to swallow this," Sylvia said, shaking a small vial of watery liquid. "I have more of the tea to send her back to the fairies afterwards."

The two women, united in this unpleasant yet necessary task, shared a moment of unspoken compassion.

Sylvia whispered to Marjorie as she stirred, then lifted her gently in her arms, dripping liquid from a pipette into her mouth. Dropping her gradually back against the soft pillows, ensuring Marjorie was once more asleep, Sylvia carefully lifted the bedsheets. Tenderly, she examined Marjorie's abdomen.

"Can you tell how far along?" Mrs Day braved the question.

Sylvia had pressed her hands upon many pregnant midriffs, and she knew this one was further along than first thought. The medicine was effective whatever the number of weeks; however, it was usually more complicated for the mother later in pregnancy. This herbal concoction also aided childbirth when the mother was struggling to deliver.

Sylvia dropped her head, recalling a problematic birth she had attended, using this same medicine to induce the baby. The expectant mother, thirteen years old and only a child herself, had been abandoned in end-stage labour near her home. The girl's family had cast her out, leaving her to the mercy of wolves or witches. Sylvia had found her writhing in agony and carried her back to her cottage.

The girl's hips had been too immature for childbirth, but

Sylvia's powerful medicine worked. Finally, the baby came. Afterwards, Sylvia had sewn the girl's torn flesh, chanted healing spells, and nursed her diligently.

A few days later, the girl died, broken emotionally and physically by the vipers who raped her. The girl's parents came for the baby, disappearing back into the shadows to raise him.

That same night, Sylvia had summoned the blackest of magic, pushing boundaries she knew she shouldn't. There would be a price to pay. But she had spent hours staring at the dead girl's body in silent rage, fixated on the child's long matted hair which fell down her back like angel's wings. Sylvia was willing to accept the terms, whatever the cost.

She had gathered candles, secret plants and herbs, and began the potent spell. The candle flames stretched four or five inches high, licking the air and fizzing with tiny sparks of strange colour.

Sylvia lit logs which hissed and whistled in the firepit as she cast her powerful ingredients into the flames. She shut her eyes, chanting the sacred, ancient words over and over.

As the first rays of sunlight filtered through the windows, the spell was complete and Sylvia opened her eyes. Her final task was to prepare the young girl's body for burial, which she did according to traditional custom.

The news ricocheted fast, creating a stir among the local villagers. A raging fire had ripped through one of the houses, taking the lives of a man and his son. Miraculously, a woman and a newborn baby had survived. Sylvia had trembled when she heard the reports. Her spell had been successful. She had taken the souls of those who had abused the young girl. It was payment in kind.

Sylvia lifted her head and prayed her gift wouldn't let her down now. She cried silently as she looked at Marjorie, still thinking about the young girl. But her tears were also for the unborn life that was about to be taken. It was already too late to stop the procedure.

She still hadn't answered Mrs Day's question about how far along the pregnancy was. "I believe several weeks further than we originally thought," Sylvia said.

"I wish there were another way," Mrs Day replied.

Sylvia was touched to discover the maid was in tears too.

Sylvia had been agonising over the same sentiment. It was wrong to deceive a mother, yet the rules of marriage were steadfast and non-negotiable. This child was a bastard, and neither mother nor child could survive without James's support. It was honourable he was even willing to keep her.

All the two women could do was minimise the trauma this procedure would inevitably cause.

"What now?" Mrs Day whispered.

"We wait. How is your wrist?"

Mrs Day wriggled her wrist. She gasped. "The pain has completely gone."

Sylvia nodded, pleased. They sat together mostly in silence as the hours slowly passed and night-time fell. Suddenly, Sylvia noticed a change in Marjorie's face and leapt to her feet.

Marjorie clenched her legs to her stomach, groaning.

"We need towels and water now, Mrs Day," she ordered.

There was a new assertiveness to Sylvia's voice that hadn't been there before. Mrs Day quietly obeyed. She handed Sylvia the clean towels and turned to fetch the water.

There was no way of knowing how fast this next stage would progress. The two women stood either side of Marjorie in silence. Tension filled the lavender-infused air.

At last, Marjorie woke fully; her blue eyes darted from Mrs Day to Sylvia. "What's happening to me? Who are you?" Her voice was shrill, but before anyone could answer, she screamed as an excruciating pain ripped through her body.

Sylvia frowned, bracing herself.

Marjorie's arms flailed around uncontrollably. In her torment, she swept the bed covers aside, revealing a patch of bright red blood. Sylvia hastily covered the worst with a towel, but Marjorie had seen it.

"My baby! Get me a doctor, quickly!" Marjorie shrieked. She clutched her abdomen, frantically grasping at the bedsheets in panic. "I'm bleeding!"

Sylvia knew there was no time to waste. "I am here to help you, Mrs Murray," she soothed.

"NO! I need a doctor. Who *are* you anyway?" Marjorie spat, looking in horror at Sylvia.

"She's the only option we have, dear," said Mrs Day. "It is best for everyone if the doctor doesn't come."

Sylvia watched defeat register in Marjorie's eyes.

"Can you save my baby?" Marjorie asked.

Sylvia shook her head, knowing her medicine had sealed

the child's fate hours before.

Marjorie let out a loud, painful wail and tugged fiercely on Sylvia's dress, pulling her close. "I know you have special powers. Do something!" she said through gritted teeth.

But before Sylvia could find a reply to mollify her, Marjorie pushed her head back against the pillows and clenched her legs together tightly. Sylvia closed her eyes and began to recite a prayer. As Marjorie thrashed and screamed, the flame in the oil lamps dotted around the room stretched higher and glowed brighter. Sylvia rested her hand on Marjorie's shoulder, continuing the prayer.

On the crest of an almighty scream, Marjorie's body collapsed, and the cry descended into a mournful wail. The oil lamps suddenly extinguished, and the entire room was plunged into darkness as Marjorie's child was abruptly expelled from between her legs.

CHAPTER 13

James clamped his hands tightly over his ears as Marjorie's screams reverberated through the walls. He sat at his desk in the study, praying the last scream signalled it was finally over. Peter poured him another whiskey with an unsteady hand. James necked the liquor without flinching. By then, his throat was well anaesthetised.

The house fell silent, and James began to breathe normally again. Every minute that dragged by mercilessly felt like an hour. He felt dutybound to stay in the house, although he longed to take the reins of his horse and canter hard. He remembered Sylvia's mare, which was sheltering in the stable alongside his horse, enjoying plenty of fresh, sweet hay.

Sylvia was entirely different from the person James had been expecting. She seemed familiar to him somehow, and in the strangest, most bemusing way she made him feel at ease. Yet he was confident they had never met before. It would have been impossible to forget such a beautiful face.

It had unnerved him when she mentioned Pearl. He had spoken to no one about their liaison; not even his men in South

Africa knew Pearl's name. There was no doubt in James's mind – Sylvia's gift was real.

His fingers reached inside his pocket, ferreting for the small leather pouch where he kept the diamond. He tipped it out onto the table, watching as it tumbled and sparkled.

He'd forgotten Peter was also in the room.

"What's that?" Peter asked.

James stopped the momentum of the diamond with his finger and turned to Peter.

"A diamond. From South Africa," he replied.

"Can I see it?"

James nodded cautiously, feeling protective of Pearl's diamond. He watched as Peter examined it curiously, squinting as though trying to peer inside.

"It looks like a beauty, but my cousin could tell you for certain."

"Is he a jeweller?" James asked with sudden interest.

"No," Peter answered casually, then burst out laughing. "He's a diamond cutter. He's based in London and about to cleave a large diamond on behalf of the Crown."

"*That* diamond?"

Peter nodded.

James had read about it in the newspaper. An unusually large diamond, over a thousand carats, had been discovered in South Africa the previous year. It was going to be presented to Edward VII, once cut. Other diamonds would also be cut from it and made into world-famous jewels.

James shook his head in disbelief. "Another whiskey?" he asked Peter.

"I think we should," Peter replied.

There was a small tap on the door. James pushed back his chair, steadying it quickly. He felt the effects of too much whiskey rush to his head, making little lights flicker behind his eyes.

Composing himself, he walked assuredly to the door. Sylvia stood on the other side. He immediately noticed how exhausted she looked. Stray strands of hair had fallen from her tight braid, and the skin under her eyes looked swollen.

"Come in, please," he said.

Peter put down his glass and with a polite nod at Sylvia, left them alone.

"It's over now," began Sylvia in a hushed tone. "Your wife is resting."

"How is she?"

"Tired. She's been through a great deal. Mrs Day is with her."

"It sounded awful."

James didn't mean for the words to come out, but he couldn't help it. He could still hear Marjorie's screams vibrating in his eardrums. He suspected he always would.

"It's over now," Sylvia repeated.

A few moments of silence passed. Then James cleared his throat. "You look very tired, Sylvia. Can I get you anything?"

"Tea would be nice."

James quickly disappeared and returned a short while later with a small tray. Sylvia had fallen asleep on the window seat. He watched her for a moment, admiring her prettiness. Before he could wake her up, her heavy eyelids fluttered open.

"Ah, tea. Lovely," she said wearily.

He felt her watching him as he poured tea through the strainer.

"May I?" she asked.

She removed the strainer and poured the tea mixed with tea leaves into her cup. James watched, fascinated.

Sylvia held the cup in her hands, savouring its warmth. He couldn't take his eyes off her as she swirled the cup around and around, peering inside.

"Would you like some more tea?" he asked.

"No, thank you." Sylvia paused, frowning. She looked inside her cup then back up at James; her startling blue eyes searched his face. "It isn't a coincidence."

"What isn't?"

"You need to make a change to something, and soon. But it isn't a coincidence, as you think. It was always planned this way."

He knew she was referring to cutting the diamond, but chose to say nothing. Instead, he simply nodded. He'd had the same feeling himself.

◆ ◆ ◆

James accompanied Sylvia to the stables. It was damp and bitterly cold outside, but thankfully dry. She gently took Star's reins and encouraged the horse out of the warm stable. She heaved herself up onto the saddle while James helped to fasten her bag.

"Thank you, Sylvia," he said.

She smiled in response, pulling left on Star's rein and

nudging her horse forward. The sound of hooves clattering on the hard ground changed to a rhythmic thump as she reached the grass, and the farmhouse slowly disappeared from view.

She would never forget the vision she had seen earlier as she swirled her tea leaves. Her heart palpitated at the thought of it. As her eyes fully adjusted to the dark, she took in her surroundings and accepted that she would return here one day.

She lifted her face and searched the midnight sky as her horse picked up pace. She counted five stars, distinctively iridescent like shimmering pearls, and acknowledged them with a reverent nod.

CHAPTER 14

The tall trees beyond the farmhouse stood like proud soldiers, their heads touched by the morning sunlight. Mist rose around their trunks, where the warmth met the chilly forest floor. A stream flowed to one side of the dense forest, rolling to a river in the nearest village. The tinkling sound of running water was the only noise to be heard.

When the sunshine was as bright as it was today, Marjorie felt as close to happy as she possibly could here. Her daily walks into the forest provided her with her only sanctuary, somewhere she could escape the claustrophobic heavyset stone walls of the farmhouse. And somewhere she could meet Vladimir.

She pulled on her boots and fastened her coat. Excitement was reflected in the glow of her cheeks as she shut the farmhouse door behind her, relishing the fresh air upon her skin. No one would query her going out, not even if it was raining; she regularly walked around this time. For months Peter had kept a close vigil as she wandered through the forest, eventually leaving her to her own devices. Even Mrs Day no longer interrogated her.

Four months had passed since she lost their baby. Her recollection was strangely foggy, although she would never forget those final moments of excruciating agony. She ticked off the days mentally; her baby would have been born any day now.

Marjorie trampled through a cluster of wild snowdrops as her head grappled with the pain still throbbing in her heart. Vladimir's visits were her only solace. They were taking a phenomenal risk meeting like this, but she no longer cared.

After James returned from South Africa, Vladimir had kept his distance for several weeks, sending Marjorie spiralling into an unshakable, hormone-fuelled depression. She yearned for her lover, though the hope that he would ever come back to her diminished with each passing day. But he had returned, finally. They could, of course, no longer meet in the comfort of her bedroom, but seeing him here for just a few precious moments was enough to sustain her soul.

Marjorie ambled alongside the stream, casually checking the pathway behind before ducking her head and disappearing into the forest. Branches fanned out overhead, letting in slivers of sunlight. It would take her as long as thirty minutes to reach their meeting place, but she couldn't risk being caught or followed. Her long blonde hair tumbled freely down her back, swishing left and right as she walked briskly.

A twig snapped beneath her foot, making her jump. She paused, scanning the panoramic rows of tree trunks. Satisfied no one else was there, she continued, increasing her pace.

Vladimir was leaning against a tree, waiting. Abandoning all caution, Marjorie ran to him, laughing. She flung herself into his arms, and he twirled to stop her falling.

"Hello, my love," he said.

She breathed in his familiar scent. He tipped her chin upwards and parted her lips slowly. His gentle kiss soon became fervent. She collapsed in his arms, her heart thumping hard in her chest.

"You are crying!" she said, feeling the moisture on his cheek.

Marjorie pulled away, panicked. She had never seen him cry before.

"My love sit with me a moment," he said.

But she couldn't move. She watched as he laid his coat on the ground and beckoned her to sit. She shook her head. Vladimir tugged the corner of her dress and pulled her gently to him. Reluctantly, she sank down next to him.

"Where is your husband?" he asked nervously.

"He's gone to London."

James had been in an unusually buoyant mood when he'd left, which had unsettled her. But that was irrelevant now. All she cared about was why Vladimir was upset.

"Marjorie, I have to go away for a while. I cannot visit you anymore."

She took a small sharp breath and snatched his hand.

"Why?" she asked, although she suspected she knew the answer.

He shook his head, murmuring in Russian. "It isn't safe. Someone will catch us."

"I don't care," she shouted.

"Your husband will shoot me! No, I can't take the risk anymore."

"Vladimir, please, I can't go on without you."

Marjorie hated how weak she sounded, begging him. But she couldn't take another loss; it would break her for good.

"You must," Vladimir said. "I will come back one day…" He paused. "But not for a very long time, I'm afraid. Goodbye, my love."

He stood up, leaving her slumped on the damp ground. Marjorie sat there for a long time until her legs were numb and the cold had penetrated her body.

She wasn't sure how long she remained there before a faint rustle nearby roused her. Lifting her head, a beam of sunlight caught her eyes, making her squint. She saw movement and her heart lurched; maybe it was Vladimir returning. She stood up, scanning the trees. Standing in-between the trees in a small clearing was a large stag. It had white tipped antlers and was steadily watching her.

Silently, the stag turned and vanished.

Marjorie was jolted back to reality. She got up and brushed the loose dirt off her dress, focusing on the flakes of dirt as they tumbled to the forest floor. She dragged her feet back towards the farmhouse, knowing her dishevelled appearance would raise concern. She would say she had fallen if pressed.

As it happened, there was no one to question her when she arrived back at the house. At first, she didn't see James's handwritten note left by her bedside. She sank heavily onto the bed, burying her head in the pillow to stifle her sobs. But her tears came silently. Her grief no longer had a voice.

Reaching for a handkerchief, her hand found the note. She scanned the words, blurry with tears, then scrunched the paper up into a tight ball and flung it with all her strength across the room.

◈ ◈ ◈

James found the address tucked away down a narrow side street in the heart of London, a short walk from Tower Bridge. He disliked London, especially this particular area. Construction on the bridge had been completed eight years ago. But in more recent years, the Tower Subway had closed, driving pickpockets and prostitutes onto the walkways between the towers. Even with military training, James did not feel comfortable taking this route, which most sensible pedestrians avoided.

He walked past the same door several times, eventually convincing himself it must be the right one. There was a single window to the left, but it was boarded up and barred. The place looked derelict and forgotten. James banged the knocker several times and waited, patting down his coat thoroughly to check the contents of his pockets. A hundred sets of hungry eyeballs must have followed him across that bridge, scanning for an opportunity to steal something from him.

James knocked again, louder. Dusk was settling over London, and he was tired from travelling. Not even the lure of staying at Claridge's appeased him. He had fleetingly entertained the idea of bringing Marjorie, but she was still convalescing, and besides, he wanted to see the diamond first. He hoped the ring would lift her out of the depression that was slowly crushing her. Maybe it would symbolise a new start between them.

He'd written her a brief note to that effect before he left.

He said he would be home from London the following day with a special gift for her.

At last, the door opened, and Peter's cousin, Edward, greeted him with a flurry of excitable smiles and flailing arms.

"Don't stand out there! Someone will have that coat off your back!" he said, laughing.

James suspected he wasn't joking. They exchanged a formal yet comfortable handshake as James walked quickly across the threshold. Three small rooms sprouted off the hallway; these seemed to be Edward's living quarters. Another door, rather like an under stairs cupboard, revealed the entrance to a steep, staircase spiralling down to the basement. James's eyes grew wide in wonder as several workbenches, rows upon rows of pristine tools, and specialist machinery came into view as they slowly descended. This was where the blue diamond had been for the last two months, gradually being transformed.

"The facets are divided into corners and bezels before ensuring the diamond is perfectly round and smooth. All sixteen main facets are then polished. Only at that point can you add and polish the stars, pavilion and crown halves, before checking for perfect symmetry," Edward said.

But James wasn't listening. He was thinking about the blue diamond and what it would look like cut and set. He was also thinking about Pearl.

Aware that Edward was staring at him quizzically, James shook his thoughts free and turned his full attention to the older man.

"I'm sorry. It's just been a very long day," James said.

"Would you like to see the ring?"

James nodded, feeling his pulse race a little faster as Edward invited him to sit down.

Without further ceremony, Edward handed him the ring.

James breathed heavily as he focused on the breathtaking transformation.

Edward had shaped the diamond into a brilliant round, emphasising the inner fire and maximising its original size.

"It's magnificent," James spluttered.

"What do you know about this diamond?" Edward asked.

James wasn't sure how much information to part with. He had a feeling Edward was too knowledgeable to buy a fabricated version of the truth.

"Not much, I'm afraid," he offered.

"I couldn't find a single inclusion, you know," Edward said.

"What does that mean?"

"It means, dear fellow, it is flawless."

James looked blank.

Edward continued, exasperated. "Inclusions are generally solids, liquids or gases that were trapped as the mineral formed. This usually affects the structure of the diamond itself, creating imperfections such as tiny cracks, for example. The number, size, colour, location, and visibility all make a difference. You need suitable magnification to see them. The point is, I couldn't see them."

"Which means?"

"Which means this diamond is exceptionally rare and extremely valuable. It is quite literally a fluke of nature," Edward pronounced proudly.

James stared at it. He had kept it in his pocket for months.

It had travelled with him across turbulent seas. Before that, it was wedged inside a hole in the wall, with just a few bits of chalky plaster and a cross preventing its discovery. It had side-stepped danger, out-manoeuvred risk, and defied all odds to get here.

He twisted the diamond around, marvelling at the sparkling blue light. For some reason, he was reminded of Sylvia's eyes.

CHAPTER 15

James couldn't settle at Claridge's. Ordinarily, he would have been in awe at the sheer splendour of the building's architecture. But he couldn't concentrate. Inside, the hotel dazzled guests with sparkling chandeliers, high ceilings, and beautifully polished floors. James was eager to get to his room and rest. After a few hours sleep, he felt restless again. He splashed cold water on his face, shaved hurriedly, and changed clothes. The noise, heavy air, and pungent smells of the city weighed on him like a heavy coat on a hot day. He decided, after a quick nip of brandy, to leave.

The journey home was arduous but uneventful. James fingered the ring box in his pocket. He felt uneasy knowing its true value. While the truth about the diamond thrilled him, it also peppered him with guilt. This diamond could have changed Pearl's life if she had survived. The thought plagued him for the rest of his journey.

By the time he got off the train, he was drunk-tired and negotiated a higher than fair price for a ride back to his farmhouse. As the cart pulled away, he saw her: a tiny figure concealed by a long slender cape. The evening had brought with it a chill breeze, and she looked dishevelled as the wind tousled her hair.

"Sylvia!" he called.

His voice was lost on the wind. She had already turned away. Disappointed, he nodded for the driver to continue. Sylvia was standing perfectly still and James watched until he lost sight of her and the sound of the horses hooves lulled him to sleep.

James crept into their bedroom as streaks of sunlight brushed the horizon like watercolours on canvas. He glanced out of the window, shivering. It was surprisingly cold. Mist clung low to the ground but could not obscure the beauty of the landscape for him. This was home.

Marjorie was curled up on the very far side of the bed. He peeled off his clothes and eased in beside her, feeling like an intruder. The image of the Russian still occasionally flashed through his mind, but he thought of him less and less as the weeks went on. He reached out for Marjorie and pulled her to him, feeling her stiffen.

"James?" she asked hesitantly.

He wanted to ask who else she had been expecting. She was like a wooden doll in his arms. He could smell the fresh scent of chamomile as he kissed the top of her head. Releasing her, she recoiled back into a ball. It had been months since he returned home; how long was it going to take? Frustrated, he watched her pretend to sleep and thought about the diamond in his coat pocket.

When he woke a few hours later, Marjorie was gone. He didn't see her again until dinner that evening. The sleep had done him good. He felt more human.

He stepped into a deep, steaming bath in front of the fire, and relaxed. He had missed having a bath when he was in South Africa. Shaving his rough stubble and splashing cologne over his smooth skin, he was conscious he was making an extra effort. He desperately wanted to put an end to the chill between him and his wife; the ring would be the icebreaker.

James dressed for dinner, feeling optimistic. A delicious smell of stew wafted through the house. He sent the cook to fetch one of the better red wines to accompany the meal, hoping it would help relax his uptight wife. He found Marjorie in their small library. She put her book down as he walked in. He bent down to kiss her, seeing the cheek she offered.

"You look lovely," he said.

She responded with a thin smile.

They shared a small sherry but did not speak. There was no conversation during the meal either; only the clink of silverware and the tick-tock of the grandfather clock broke the silence. He could sense Marjorie was irritated by the noisy clock as she pushed her food around the plate. James, however, loved the sound of the grandfather clock. He recalled hearing it as a boy, sitting at the same table, family chatter ricocheting around him. The house brimmed with happy chaos and laughter most of all at Christmas. It was why he wanted children now; they would change the energy of this place. Turn it back to what it once was.

But getting close to Marjorie was like trying to embrace

spikes of glass.

"You are drinking more wine than usual tonight," Marjorie said, interrupting his thoughts.

Her tone was flat and critical. Undeterred, James nodded.

"I'm celebrating," he said.

She arched an eyebrow. Even now, with her face as stony as an etched cameo, her loveliness was unquestionable. She wore an old dress and her hair had barely been brushed.

She sighed. "What are you celebrating?"

"I picked up something rather special in London. For you," he replied.

At last, the merest hint of interest sparked in her eyes.

"Can I see it?" she asked.

She showed less enthusiasm than he'd hoped. He had imagined her clapping her hands, her eyes dancing. He wondered whether even the diamond could stir her. He held it out, his hand shaking.

"Is it real?" she asked, her face still expressionless.

He laughed, remembering what Edward had said about the diamond.

"Very much so. It's been on quite an interesting journey."

She waved her hand, uninterested. She fanned her fingers and took off her other rings, slipping the blue diamond onto the fourth finger of her left hand. She clasped her fingers tightly together and stared.

"It's… beautiful," she said, her gaze never leaving the diamond. "Beautiful," she repeated solemnly. "I will never take it off my finger."

Watching her closely, James started to fill her wine glass.

"No, thank you," she said, reaching out a hand to cover her glass.

Crushed, he stopped pouring and took a deep breath.

"Tell me, Marjorie, what will it take to win your affection back?" The muscles in his jaw clenched as he fought to hide his frustration.

Marjorie's shoulders dropped.

"James, please. Let's not spoil the evening with silly questions."

"Silly questions! It's an important question," he said, his voice raised now.

Marjorie rolled the diamond around towards her palm and clenched her fist until it visibly indented her skin.

"I'm sorry, James. You are right, I've found the last few months very difficult."

"A man can't be patient forever."

She nodded sadly.

"I'd like to feel as though you don't hate me when I come close to you. But either way, I want children."

"I don't know how I feel about having children anymore."

Her voice was barely louder than a whisper.

It was as though she had pulled the pin and thrown the grenade. James picked up his wine glass and smashed it into the fireplace, making Marjorie jump. The alcohol hissed and erupted in an outburst of flames. James's eyes became dark, his expression demonic as he grabbed her arm, forcing her to face him.

"Yet you were quite content to have a bastard child," he hissed.

It was a cruel thing to say, but correct.

"James, please. We should not talk this way," Marjorie replied.

"Why not? Does it offend you, Marjorie? Good. You deserve to be offended, just as I was when I came home to find you in bed with *him*!"

He had finally said it. Months of keeping it bottled up inside, months of torturing himself with mental images of the two of them intwined.

"Keep your voice down! The servants," she said, yanking her arm from his grip.

James laughed bitterly.

"You weren't bothered about the servants when you snuck your lover into my bed, were you?"

Disgusted, she stood up to leave.

"I'm going to my room," she said quietly.

"*Our* room," he replied.

She froze.

She gathered the skirts underneath her dress and stalked out, slamming the door behind her.

James watched her leave, then began pacing the room, explosive energy raging through his veins. He wanted children; it was the only reason he was willing to put up with her now. Without further contemplation, James gulped down the rest of the red wine, followed by a shot of brandy, wincing as it burned a path down his throat. He blew out the lamp; he didn't need directions to their bedroom.

Marjorie was already in bed, her back turned. She was still fully clothed. He climbed into bed and forced her to turn and face him. Her eyelids and hands were clenched tightly closed, and her body was rigid. He knew she did not love him, but love was not what he needed from her anymore.

"James, please no," she whispered.

He wasn't listening. Memories of returning home that day and seeing her naked and in bed with another man overwhelmed him. He pulled roughly at her dress, loosening the ribbons at the back until they gave way. Several buttons pinged off, and the stitching ripped. He did not care. She began to fight, her fists punching his arms as her anger rose to match his. Her eyes looked wild as she slapped him hard across his face. He recoiled, shocked. She was breathing heavily, trying to cover her exposed breasts whilst pushing away clumps of matted hair stuck to her face. James watched her, feeling nothing.

He reached forward and with a single movement twisted her long hair around his hand until she could not move. Suspended in misery, they were both transported back to the moment when he had found her with Vladimir.

James opened his fist and let go of her hair. With uncompromising decisiveness he took the rest of her clothes off. She lay before him motionless, her eyes empty. James pushed her legs apart and she looked the other way. He didn't care anymore that she felt nothing. If this is what it took to bear him a child, this was what he would do.

Afterwards, he swung himself out of bed and lit a cigar. He took a couple of deep puffs and threw it into the fire. His head was spinning and his hands shaking as he tugged on his clothes, grabbed his boots, and left in silence. But the following night he would do the same. At some point, she would bear him a child.

CHAPTER 16

After several months continuing with this loveless nightly routine, Marjorie finally became pregnant. Her hatred of him was undisguised by then. She avoided him when possible, snarled when he spoke, and viewed her pregnancy like an affliction. Ironically, as the weeks went on, she blossomed; her hair took on a glossy sheen, and her skin glowed.

As the baby's due date approached, the tension between them increased. James took every opportunity to step outside and breathe in the crisp, fresh air, desperate to escape the atmosphere in the farmhouse. He watched bluebells and tulips give way to wild geranium, which pushed up through the hard soil, creating a carpet of colour. Every morning, he wondered if this would be the day he became a father. Whenever he caught a glimpse of Marjorie, he longed to touch her swollen belly, but she would never allow it. He accepted that.

Late spring merged into early summer. The first hint of colour from tightly closed rose buds started to appear, climbing up the side of the farmhouse. James was watching a wild rabbit dart across the grass and disappear into the hedgerow when he heard the shout.

"Master Murray! Master Murray!"

He turned see Mrs Day racing towards him, her skirts gathered under her arms.

"Is it time?" he asked, already starting to walk to the house.

"We need to fetch the doctor… urgently," she puffed.

"Why, what's happened?"

Mrs Day's face was ashen. She was out of breath and struggled to speak. "I've seen it once before. Headache, sickness, swollen ankles..."

"What does it mean? What are you talking about, woman!" James snapped.

Mrs Day shook her head. "It can be dangerous for the mother," she said, "and the baby too, if it isn't delivered quickly. Hurry, we need the doctor."

James pushed past her and ran inside, bolting up the stairs to the bedroom. He flung the door open. Marjorie lay on the bed quietly, clutching her head. She'd been sick again, judging by the smell in the room. Her face and feet were puffy; she looked desperately unwell.

"How long has she been like this?" James called back to Mrs Day who was struggling up the stairs, panting.

"Since just after breakfast, sir," she said, finally reaching the bedroom. "It came on very fast."

"Send Peter out for the doctor. Now!"

Mrs Day nodded and left the room. James heard the front door slam and a short while later the horse's hooves pounding on the ground outside.

Peter returned within the hour. He left the horse untied

outside and ran upstairs to deliver the bad news.

"The doctor is in London, we think. He might be back tonight… but he might not."

James shut his eyes, reviewing the options. He looked at Marjorie, who by now was almost unconscious.

"We don't have until tonight," he said.

He prayed he would be able to find help before it was too late. He ran to the stables and heaved himself up onto his stallion's back, grateful to find the horse still saddled from a recent ride out. James pushed his weight deep into the saddle, squeezing his legs as tightly as he dared either side of Prince's barrel. The stallion, recognising the gesture and sensing the urgency, cleared the stable and accelerated into a gallop. James gripped the reins tightly with bare hands and encouraged him to go faster.

The sound of the wind chimes told James he had reached his destination. As he neared the cottage, he saw her in the garden. She turned at his approach and put down her basket which appeared to be filled with herbs.

James slid off his horse and rushed towards her.

"Sylvia, please help. It's Marjorie and… the baby. Our baby." His voice trailed away as he wondered whether she already knew that his wife was pregnant again.

Sylvia held up her hand.

"How far is she gone?"

"The baby's due any day."

Sylvia gathered her skirts and beckoned him to follow her inside. He did so without hesitation, leaving Prince tied loosely to a gate.

His eyes followed Sylvia impatiently as she gathered various items and dropped them quickly into a basket. Her kitchen was a neat haven of sweet-smelling flowers crammed into vases, freshly baked bread, and tiny pots stacked into towers. High above the fireplace, plants and herbs hung in bunches, gently crisping. She grabbed several handfuls and added them to her basket. On the stove, something was bubbling in a copper pot, which she quickly removed. It struck him how tranquil the cottage felt, and how well loved. It was a stark contrast to his own home.

"James?" Sylvia pressed him.

"Yes?"

"Can your horse carry two? My horse is in her stable and not saddled-up."

James nodded. His horse was almost sixteen hands and a thoroughbred black Irish stallion. The animal didn't even flinch as James pulled Sylvia up onto the saddle behind him and instructed her to hold on tightly. The unfamiliar warmth of another human made him feel slightly giddy. The wind whipped around them, as the horse pounded towards the farmhouse, taking vast, steady strides. James glanced down and saw the knuckles of Sylvia's small hands were raw red with the wind chill. He reached down and cupped his own hands tightly around hers, feeling his fingers tremble with adrenaline, fear, and something indescribably new.

Mrs Day was pacing outside the bedroom and was inconsolable by the time they arrived.

"She's much worse, sir."

James stood at the edge of the room, redundant. He could only watch as Sylvia examined Marjorie, pursing her lips tightly in concentration. She shrugged her cape off, and James sprung forward to take it from her, desperate to help.

"Are you going to stay, James?"

Sylvia's voice was soft yet assertive.

He knew he couldn't leave; last time the waiting had almost driven him insane.

"I'll stay, yes," he said.

Mrs Day gasped. "Mr Murray, I really think…"

"We will need all the help we can," interrupted Sylvia.

"Tell me what you need," James said.

"Tepid water and cloths," Sylvia replied.

He was grateful for the distraction of fetching and carrying. Most of the time, he sat at the back of the room, trying to be invisible. His nerves were in tatters, but his eyes were transfixed on Sylvia as she darted around his wife, applying ointments to her feet, forehead, and wrists. Pulling back the curtains, she opened the window to allow fresh, clean air to mingle with the potent medicinal aromas. Brilliant sunlight flashed into the room.

James leant forward on his chair, desperate to see what was happening as Sylvia began pressing her hands gently upon Marjorie's bulging stomach. Up until now, Marjorie had been silent, but she began to wail like a snared animal, pushing Sylvia away.

Sylvia spooned a dark brown liquid into Marjorie's mouth and said something indistinguishable to her. A few minutes later, Marjorie was calmer, and Sylvia returned to her examination.

James's fingers clasped the edge of the seat, and his nails dug into the soft wood. He turned his head, desperately afraid of what Sylvia might find.

"I felt a kick!" Sylvia said, almost laughing.

The baby was alive! James leapt to his feet and rushed over, but Sylvia gently pushed him back.

"We need space, James. There is a long way to go yet."

He nodded and took small, backward steps. But for the first time, there was hope.

"Marjorie, as soon as your baby is born, you will feel much better. You need to work hard now to make that happen," Sylvia said assertively.

Marjorie became slightly more responsive, and James felt sorry for her. He had put her in this situation. He felt a sharp stab of shame – what would Sylvia think of how he'd treated his wife? And why, he asked himself, did that bother him so much?

Marjorie was saying something, but he couldn't make out her words. He craned his neck forward.

"You were here before… when," Marjorie began.

"Yes, but there is no need to…" interjected Sylvia.

"My baby died!" Panic began to enter Marjorie's voice.

"Marjorie, *this* baby will not die," Sylvia said firmly.

Marjorie turned her head away. Her left arm flopped over the side of the bed, revealing the diamond ring.

James noticed Sylvia's eyes focus on the ring; he was surprised she hadn't noticed it before. She gently picked up Marjorie's hand, mesmerised. He watched as her eyes closed, the skin puckered between her brows in concentration.

Marjorie yanked her arm away. Sylvia stumbled

backwards, and her hand caught the edge of a water jug, sending it crashing to the floor. Water soaked into the rug. James rushed over to steady Sylvia.

"Sylvia?" he asked anxiously.

"I'm fine… I'm… fine," she whispered.

She quickly composed herself as Mrs Day helped clear up the broken ceramic and mop the floor.

◈ ◈ ◈

Over the next hour, Marjorie visibly deteriorated. The various potions and chants had quietened her mind, but things were not as they should be. Sylvia explained in hushed tones that Marjorie's body was not prepared for childbirth, but the baby needed to be born, and quickly.

"Is this our only option?" asked James.

He watched as Mrs Day and Sylvia exchanged an uncomfortable glance. Sylvia nodded. "It would be dangerous for your wife not to deliver soon."

James noticed how strange it felt when Sylvia referred to Marjorie as his wife.

"I can give her something to deliver the baby, but she isn't in natural labour. I will have to assist her," Sylvia said and raised her eyebrows at James.

James strongly suspected that involved something a man shouldn't witness.

"Should I leave?" he asked.

"Yes… but it is up to you," she replied.

James didn't want to go; he would end up drinking

whiskey in his study, trying to drown out screams as before.

Sylvia quickly returned to her duties. She dripped the clear liquid into Marjorie's mouth before making a small incision in her stomach with a sterilised knife.

Marjorie cried out in pain. Wincing, James turned away, holding a hand over his mouth and squeezing his eyes shut.

Every few minutes, when Sylvia pressed down on Marjorie's stomach, pressing and kneading after another tiny cut, Marjorie screamed. After about an hour, the responses from Marjorie became faint even though the pressure Sylvia applied was more intense.

"Pass me the pipette please, Mrs Day," Sylvia said.

There was a rustling then spluttering as Marjorie coughed.

"Quickly, the towel!" Sylvia demanded.

Sylvia's voice was no longer calm. James squirmed in his chair, twisting left and right. He opened his eyes to see a whoosh of water and Sylvia lunge forward. This time, he heard Mrs Day screaming. Unable to stand it a second longer, James ran to the bedside.

The baby lay lifeless on the bed. He watched in horror as Sylvia lifted it upside down and slapped its back. A plug of mucus flew out, followed by a tiny gasp, then a loud, furious wail. Sylvia quickly cut the cord and tied it, freeing baby from mother at last.

James was immobilised by what he had just seen. Sylvia presented him with the wriggling, pink baby.

"Your son," she said, beaming.

James reached for the baby, laughing.

Mrs Day did not hold back her tears as she admired the surprisingly perfect baby, covering him with a blanket.

"I'll go and tell the others!" she called and ran from the room.

James nodded his thanks without taking his eyes off his son.

With deft hands, Sylvia turned and carefully stitched Marjorie's wounds and gently bathed her skin. Marjorie mutely stared ahead, rigid with detachment.

"Marjorie, would you like to see your baby?" Sylvia asked softly.

Marjorie shook her head. Sylvia glimpsed James out of the corner of her eye. He held the baby close to his chest and scowled at Marjorie with contempt. Sylvia smoothed the blankets over Marjorie and returned to James.

Sylvia suggested another blanket and together they carefully wrapped the baby, who made soft cooing noises as he settled contentedly. Instinctively, James reached out and tucked a stray lock of hair behind Sylvia's ear. She leant away from him slightly, her blue eyes puzzled.

"Thank you, Sylvia," he said.

Seizing the moment, he leaned forward and kissed the top of her head, feeling the silkiness of her hair against his cheek.

This time, to his overwhelming delight, she didn't pull away.

CHAPTER 17

Sylvia knew she should have resisted James's kiss. Yet suspended in that exhilarating moment after the baby was born, she felt dizzy with relief. She chided herself – what she felt had been more than relief. As his lips touched her hair, she had felt a fluttering deep in her chest.

She studied the way James cradled the baby tenderly in his arms. She was moved by how he gently stroked his son's velvety cheek, swaying rhythmically to soothe the baby. Sylvia swallowed the lump in her throat and peeled back the blanket to admire the baby's face.

"What will you call him?" she asked, attempting to lighten the atmosphere.

She saw him glance briefly again at Marjorie.

"I would like to name him after my father, William James Murray," he said.

Sylvia moved closer and touched the infant's delicate fingers.

"I think it's perfect. William…" Sylvia repeated the name, slowly moving her fingers to encompass James's hand. She felt her breathing become more rapid as their eyes locked.

"Sylvia, I…" James began.

The door swung open, and Mrs Day burst into the room.

"A fresh jug of water!" she chirped.

She held the jug up victoriously and placed it carefully on the table. Sylvia withdrew from James, quickly averting her eyes. Mrs Day seemed to be unaware she had interrupted their moment of intimacy. The maid fussed over the baby, and Sylvia distracted herself by pouring a glass of water.

As she sipped her drink, she recalled the vision she'd had at first sight of Marjorie's ring. She closed her eyes; her mind was filled with a blue shimmering light. But the image was still cloudy, as if opaque layers of fabric were draped over it. The light became more intense, the blue deeper, until she could see everything clearly.

She could feel her hair being tousled by a sea breeze and the taste of salt in her mouth. She could see Marjorie standing in a crowd of people, her pretty blonde hair tied back beneath a hat. Her left hand was high in the air, waving. Sylvia could see the diamond on her finger. Marjorie turned; her face was radiant with joy. In the background, Sylvia could hear the melodic sound of violins and cellos playing in exquisite harmony. The musical notes drew her onwards, towards Marjorie, like a magnet.

With a suddenness that sent goosebumps coursing up her skin, the violins and cellos changed tone, descending into a mournful melody. Sylvia felt chilled to her core and had the strange sensation of water beneath her feet, almost as if she was standing in the pool of water that had been spilled from the jug earlier. Marjorie's hand reached out urgently to Sylvia, her fingers grasping at air. Sylvia's eyes were immediately drawn to the diamond on Marjorie's finger. Spikes of brilliant blue and dazzling white light burst out of the jewel, blinding her. She shielded her face and forced her eyes to open.

"Sylvia!"

James steadied her just before she lost balance. He cautiously put an arm around her shoulder, guiding her to a chair.

"I'm sorry. I don't know what happened… I… I…" she stuttered, grateful for the solidness of his body against hers.

"You are exhausted, Sylvia," he replied tenderly.

She shook her head. "No, I saw Marjorie… she was…"

As if in response to the sound of her name, Marjorie stirred and clutched her stomach, murmuring something incomprehensible before quickly falling silent.

Mrs Day raced over to the bed. "I'll make sure she's alright," she offered. "You need to get some rest, my dear."

Sylvia was grateful for the affection in the older woman's words and nodded her thanks to her.

"I'll take you home," said James assertively.

Home was not where Sylvia wanted to be right now. Given the choice, she would rather have been curled up in front of the fire here, with James, cuddling the baby. It would be a wrench to leave. She glanced at Marjorie and felt envy tinged with sadness – how could this woman feel nothing for her newborn baby? And, stealing a sideway glimpse of James, how could she feel nothing for this wonderful father and husband?

James's stallion, Prince, glided at a softer pace on the journey back to Sylvia's cottage. It was close to midnight, and their pathway was cloaked in darkness, lit only by the crescent moon. Sylvia closed her heavy eyelids and let her body bounce in time with the natural rhythm of the horse's hooves.

The wind chimes were silent as they approached her home. She opened her eyes, wondering why. She noticed the sunflower heads were swaying gently to and fro.

James jumped down and held out his hand to Sylvia. She took it and slid gently off the horse, her feet landing on the soft grass. She felt his fingers tighten as he pulled her to his chest.

"Thank you, Sylvia," James said.

Her throat turned dry.

"You have a beautiful son," she replied.

"You saved him."

Her voice was a mere whisper. "It was meant to be."

As James leaned forward, she felt his breath on her lips. Arching her face towards his, she closed her eyes. She felt his soft bristles touch her skin, then the touch of his lips and gentle probing of his tongue. Her mouth responded unreservedly, feeling years of loneliness drain away.

Just behind her, the wind chimes began jingling.

PART FOUR

CHAPTER 18

Southampton, 1912

Marjorie eased on her coat and slipped her feet into a pair of sturdy shoes. The dimly lit lamp beside her offered the only light, making her movements clumsy. Her arm caught the bag on the chair next to her, and it tumbled noisily onto the wooden floor. She winced, holding her breath. If her escape backfired now, she would never get another chance.

She picked up her bag, praying the clasp would hold. Her wrist shook under the weight, but she gritted her teeth and continued along the edge of the corridor. She had rehearsed this route for days and knew the noise every floorboard was likely to make.

She stopped outside William's bedroom. He was almost nine years old and was the image of James, apart from having Marjorie's blue eyes. It always unnerved her to see her own eyes staring back at her, although she avoided the child most of the time. She had survived the past nine years by focusing on thoughts of Vladimir. She had continued her regular walks through the forest where they used to meet, aching to see him, desperate for news of his return.

Marjorie knew her son would be better off without her. His eyes lit up whenever he talked about Sylvia, as did his father's. Marjorie was no fool; she knew James and Sylvia were in love. She knew exactly where James spent his waking hours. She didn't care.

The farmhouse door closed quietly behind her. She inhaled the spring air. Sudden panic choked her. She rapidly scanned the trees – what if he wasn't there?

Every step she took into the forest brought her further from her dark and depressing existence of the past decade.

Leaning up against a tree stood Vladimir, waiting for her.

She crept forward gingerly at first then started to run. Throwing herself into his arms, she laughed and cried.

Vladimir kissed her fiercely then pulled out of the embrace. "We must go, my love," he urged.

She nodded, taking his hand, not daring to look back over her shoulder. Even if someone caught her escaping now, she knew she couldn't go back.

A carriage was waiting for them on the other side of the trees on a dirt track. As the two horses at the front led them away, Marjorie felt so exhilarated she could barely sit still. By the time James found her short note on her dressing table, Marjorie and Vladimir would be long gone.

"Will you miss all this, my love?" Vladimir asked cautiously, looking out across the pretty landscape.

"No. I never want to see it again," she replied and closed her eyes.

Heavy mist gathered around their carriage, like untold spirits of the forest. Marjorie shuddered, wishing they could move faster. Vladimir reached for her hand, resting it on his lap and ran his finger over her ring. He had told her they were going to his home in Russia. He had not yet told her he intended to sell her ring first.

Marjorie finally relaxed as they arrived in Southampton the following day, Wednesday the 10th of April, 1912. The weather was mild, and only a soft breeze teased the air. The majestic ship stood proudly in the dock, waiting for its passengers to board. Flashbulbs went off like exploding fireworks as the press eagerly tried to catch glimpses of anyone famous. The *Titanic* would be on the front page of every newspaper the following morning.

The atmosphere was electric as the time approached noon when the ship would begin her maiden voyage towards Cherbourg, then Ireland the following day. It would finally arrive in New York exactly a week later.

Marjorie and Vladimir boarded just after ten o'clock. Marjorie held onto Vladimir's arm tightly as they searched for their second-class cabin. He had told her the cost of their tickets had wiped out all his savings. Unperturbed, Marjorie had pilfered some silver from the farmhouse; sale of this silverware would sustain them handsomely for some time.

But she would have fled with nothing but the clothes on her back if she'd had no alternative, as long she could be with Vladimir. When she'd read his handwritten note two weeks earlier, saying he was leaving England and begging her to join him, she hadn't hesitated. She didn't know his wife had recently died in childbirth, leaving him with no reason to stay. Neither did she know her ring was legendary among the village folk. It would pay for her freedom but also his own.

Aboard the *Titanic*, second-class cabins were typically four berths; however, Vladimir and Marjorie had been given a two-berth cabin, most likely because many other second-class passengers were sharing with family. Marjorie was pleased. It would give them privacy to rekindle their passion.

The beds fitted into the walls, which were dark mahogany. A bright white enamel sink stood in the corner. The rooms were pristine and clearly brand-new. There was a small seating area, and although it was impossible to move in the cabin without bumping into one another, it was theirs. Marjorie sat on the bed, feeling overwhelmed. For years she had dreamed of a moment like this. Her heavenward pleas came daily, whether she was sitting soaked in the cold rain, walking with snow under her boots, or feeling the abrasive English wind on her face. Every day, every season she prayed. And now, finally, he had rescued her.

She pressed her face against the tiny porthole and watched as passengers hurried aboard, dragging suitcases and children behind them. The excitement was contagious, and she longed to feel the fresh, salty air on her face as the ship eased away from shore.

"Can we go up on deck?" she asked.

Vladimir had been unpacking and shrugged his agreement. They gathered up their warm coats, and Marjorie secured her hat with two pins. As they shut the cabin door behind them, Vladimir pointed at the small brass number.

"At least that's an easy number to remember," he said, laughing.

Marjorie turned and looked up at the small plaque above their door. They were in cabin E-55. She frowned, feeling a peculiar sense of déjà vu. The relevance of the number seemed significant, but she was puzzled as to why.

Up on deck, Marjorie adjusted her hat to keep it steady in the breeze. Crowds of people were gathered along the shore, waving frantically. Marjorie lifted her left hand and waved back. She turned to Vladimir; her cheeks flushed with happiness.

In the background, the melodic sound of violins and cellos started playing. The elegant music swelled as the ship pushed off from the harbour. Marjorie glanced down at her ring, its blue light mirrored in the ocean that awaited them.

CHAPTER 19
St Petersburg, 1913

Almost a year after Vladimir and Marjorie stood on the freshly painted deck of the *Titanic*, waving goodbye to the vast crowds of well-wishers on the Southampton shoreline, Vladimir finally arrived back home, in St Petersburg.

He climbed out of the carriage and looked up at the pale blue building, unsure if it was just another dream. The grand white pillars looked as regal as they had when his great-grandfather built them over a hundred years ago. He wondered if the neatly clipped trees lining the driveway were in fact taller, or whether he was just feeling small these days. Flashbacks and memories of the *Titanic* clung to him like ghosts, and the lump in his throat hurt. The relief of arriving home was overwhelming.

The driver had already gone, discarding Vladimir like an orphan with only a thin bag by his feet. It was dark and bitterly cold, although not even the harsh sub-zero Russian winter was as cruel as the icy North Atlantic, the *Titanic*'s final resting place. Vladimir's hands were marked with frostbite scars, and his disfigured fingers limply grappled with the door knocker.

Before the *Titanic*, he had visualised this moment very differently. He closed his eyes, transporting his thoughts back to the image he had created as he wrote Marjorie the letter, begging her to join him. He had pictured himself wearing a suit that had been tailormade in New York, pinched to his lithe frame. His hair would be groomed, slicked to one side. Marjorie would have been stood by his side, wearing a fashionable dress and draped in jewels. Minus, of course, her diamond ring.

Yet here he was, filthy and threadbare.

When Alexei Derinsov opened the door, he narrowed his eyes and frowned at the thin, dishevelled boy standing on his doorstep. He didn't recognise his own son.

It was only when Vladimir slowly lifted his head, feeling every notch on his vertebrae ache, his father recognised him. Without speaking, Alexei reached forward and pulled Vladimir into the house like a rag doll, pinning his son's head on his shoulder and rocking him like a baby.

"You are home... thank God you are home," he sobbed.

Hearing his father speak in Russian caused the tiny thread of strength that had been holding Vladimir together to snap. He felt his knees buckle as Alexei caught him, supporting his weight as Vladimir's body convulsed with exhaustion and emotion.

He had never allowed his father to hold him in his arms. As a child he had wriggled free, eager to seek out his next adventure. The same insatiable spirit had driven him from his family home years ago, desperate to find his own fortune. He had returned broken and shattered. His plan had backfired and almost cost him his life.

Vladimir had been on a journey through hell and high water, in a painfully literal sense. After disembarking in New York, he had stayed in America for several months, refusing to set foot aboard another ship, but the reality was there was no alternative. In the end, his journey home had involved several vessels across the Atlantic, travel on foot, horseback, and train, and always heading north. It was a cruel irony to travel back over the route the *Titanic* had taken, with lead in his heart instead of hope.

He numbly followed his father along corridors he remembered racing around as a child. A door to the left opened into the living room, and for the first time in months, the corners of his mouth curved upwards. A fire roared contentedly, filling the room with smoky warmth. His father encouraged him to settle on the seat nearest the fire, helping him to shed the layers of wet, dirty clothes. A kafuffle at the door made his father curse as he stepped aside to deal with whoever was there. Vladimir heard female voices speaking in rapid whispers to his father. His response was swift and uncompromising; Vladimir was home and needed rest, not fuss.

He knew he had a stepmother and stepsister he had never met. Only now could he feel any potential compassion towards them. His mother's death sixteen years earlier had caused him to spiral into a raging depression, fuelling unbridled anger and resentment. At whom, he was never certain. When he left Russia the baggage he carried was mainly emotional, weighing down heavily on his heart. He had never replied to his father's letters informing him he intended to remarry, or that his sister had been born.

"Take this, son."

Alexei wrapped a heavy blanket around Vladimir's shoulders. Vladimir watched him pour clear liquid into two small glasses. Father and son clinked glasses and swallowed the neat vodka straight down their throats, as was customary. Vladimir winced, feeling the alcohol burn. He flopped his head back against the sofa and shuddered. Was he really home? If he closed his eyes, he could find himself back on the *Titanic*. He appeared to have no control of his memories – they controlled him.

His eyes focused on the flames in the fireplace as they reached like twisted fingers towards him. He let out an agonised, high-pitched cry, oblivious to his father's panicked concern. Vladimir's eyes remained riveted to the fire.

All his father could do was watch in horror.

Vladimir would never forget the moment his foot first stepped onto the *Titanic*. The smell of the fresh paint was exhilarating, like electrical wires touching. He marvelled at the mix of passengers: people festooned in jewels smiling at reporters whose cameras flashed repeatedly, and those less upmarket, though no less excited passengers, vetted for lice before being directed towards steerage. The *Titanic* had been a unique colony of very different classes, yet in the end, none of it had mattered. Rich or poor, most ended up at the bottom of the icy

North Atlantic. When the *Titanic* hit the iceberg at 11:40 pm on the 14th of April 1912, a circus of blind panic and deranged chaos could only describe the scene aboard the unsinkable ship as she began her descent to the bottom of the freezing ocean, dragging the souls of innocents with her.

Vladimir remembered those raw, savage and final moments where everyone, including himself, had to make heart-wrenching decisions. Some chose selflessly, others selfishly. It was a matter of hideous logic: a choice of certain death or the slim chance of survival.

Every tiny detail of his own choice tortured him.

On the 18th of April when Carpathia soberly reached New York, he looked up to see the Goddess of Liberty, holding her torch above her head, and he dropped his head in shame. He could feel the stony blaze of the Goddess's eyes upon him even when he pulled a blanket over his head and turned the other way.

He knew he would never be liberated from what he had done.

He felt his father shake him gently.

"Vladimir, son, please talk to me."

The long, red fingers from the fire retreated.

"I'm sorry… I… I'm so tired." At last, tears glazed his eyes. "I should never have left Russia. I was a fool."

"No, you were just young. I was that headstrong once, but my mother always stopped me."

They both smiled affectionately at one another, remembering mother and grandmother well.

"I should never have left," Vladimir repeated.

"Did you find what you were looking for?" Alexei asked.

It was a good question. Vladimir thought of the young girl he had married, who had died in childbirth. Then of Marjorie.

"I'm not sure yet," he replied.

His father poured them each another vodka.

"What does that mean, son?"

Vladimir focused on his father's face so he wasn't tempted to look into the fireplace again. He heard the fire spit and pop, challenging him. But he would not be drawn back to look at the flames.

"I intended to sell something when I reached New York, but I never did," he told his father.

"It was a miracle you reached New York yourself."

Vladimir nodded. In truth, he never expected to, but he wasn't ready to talk about that.

Vladimir reached into his pocket and put the blue diamond ring on the table between them.

Alexei picked it up, blinking. "How much vodka have I had?"

Despite himself, a faint chortle escaped Vladimir.

His father leaned forward. "Is it stolen?"

"No." Vladimir shook his head slowly, looking away as he spoke. He had stolen it, but not in the way his father inferred. He hadn't rampaged into a bank, forced a safe open at gunpoint, or held someone to ransom. His crime was *far* more sinister.

"What will you do with it now?" Alexei asked.

"I *need* to sell it."

Vladimir was convinced the diamond was a bad omen. Ever since he heard about the ring, his luck had turned sour. He wasn't stupid enough to fling it overboard, although once on the perishing journey home he had considered it. His thoughts had been dangerously dark and he had climbed as high as the last bar on the ship's handrail. The wind had whipped his hair, and the black waves below had soared then crashed, seducing him to join them. But he had jerked backwards onto the deck, more afraid of who might greet him in the afterlife than facing the life before him.

Alexei waved his hand in front of Vladimir's eyes, bringing him back from his reverie.

"Do you remember me telling you about Albert, Natasha's godfather? I wrote to you, but you never replied…"

Vladimir lowered his head, struggling to remember. The name triggered something in his memory – Natasha was his stepsister. Or perhaps his stepmother?

"Never mind…" His father brushed the awkwardness aside with his hand. "I will take you to meet Albert tomorrow. Be sure to bring that ring."

CHAPTER 20

The House of Fabergé in St Petersburg stood tall and proud, boasting several floors of glass windows. Vladimir and Alexei stood looking up at the landmark building, which represented strength and prosperity to the Russian people. The economy was buoyant, and the Romanov dynasty had celebrated its 300th anniversary; on the surface, Russia was positively booming. The political underbelly, however, was turning slowly cancerous.

A fresh thick blanket of snow had fallen overnight. Dozens of dim lights glowed from within the iconic building. Snowflakes danced in the air, making the scene look like something out of a fairy tale.

The notion of fairy tales continued inside, with jewels made into tiaras for real princesses. The Fabergé family were renowned for their world-famous craftsmanship and special appointment to the Imperial Crown, dating back to their very first commission in 1885. Imperial Easter Eggs were exclusively made by Fabergé for Tsar Nicolas II, with 'Winter' a gift from the Tsar to his mother that same year in

1913. There were other Fabergé Eggs, including commissions for Rothschild and the Duchess of Marlborough, but none quite as unique or elaborate as those commissioned for the Imperial Crown.

Alexei was thinking about the Imperial Eggs as he stood outside with Vladimir, easily imagining the blue diamond in Vladimir's coat as a centrepiece on one of them. It was undeniably beautiful, although he had to admit he knew very little about diamonds. Vladimir, however, wasn't thinking about Imperial Eggs.

The freezing air caught in Vladimir's throat, making him wheeze and cough. The moment of truth was here. He would soon find out whether Marjorie would have the last laugh, and the diamond would turn out to be worthless. He shivered from both cold and anxiety.

"Son, are you alright?" Alexei asked.

Vladimir nodded curtly. They walked across the road and through the famous arched doorway.

Albert Yezhov had worked for the House of Fabergé all his adult life, catching the eye of Peter Carl Fabergé personally at an amateur art and design award presentation. By some miracle, Fabergé was one of the judges. Albert's passion was metalwork, especially gold. He had been just seventeen years old when he started welding, bending, heating, and re-shaping metal. Never gold, of course; he couldn't afford to work with such precious material. What he had done, however, was somehow create an exceptionally delicate broach out of scrap metal on a minuscule budget. His drawing, a flower broach with a polished gold stem and fragile leaf skeleton, was filled with intricate jewels, and in the centre a brilliant pink gem. To the right of the flower, a small butterfly had landed. Its delicate wings were encrusted with tiny jewels, yet it looked feathery light. It was a piece of jewellery that both shouted and whispered, and Peter Fabergé heard.

The broach earnt Albert an apprenticeship at the House of Fabergé and he never left. He worked on several of the Imperial Eggs, and his craft and integrity was highly respected.

His wife was a close friend of Alexei's second wife, Misha. It had been an obvious choice for them to choose the couple as Natasha's godparents. Alexei was a warm and amusing character and they had been friends for many years. His heritage was fascinating to Albert, who had been raised as an underprivileged Russian. Alexei, on the other hand, had inherited the title of Count from a long line of nobility, descending through the male line. History intrigued them both, usually over a bottle of vodka as their wives talked. It was a pastime both parties could indulge in for many, happy hours.

He had been surprised when Alexei asked to see him so urgently. He had been waiting in the elegant lobby when he saw his friend together with a young man arrive through the doors, and rose to greet them. As they approached, he was startled by the remarkable resemblance between Alexei and his young companion.

"It's like seeing double," he teased affectionately. "Vladimir,

I presume?"

Vladimir nodded. Albert glossed over the obvious discomfort the young man displayed as he shook his hand. He seemed withdrawn – his handshake was limp and he didn't make eye contact. Albert had known Alexei's son had survived the *Titanic*; the aftermath of trauma perhaps explained the strange behaviour he was witnessing.

"What brings you here today, gentlemen?"

Albert, conscious they were meeting inside working hours, wanted to focus on the business at hand. Alexei had been insistent they meet today which made Albert more than a little curious.

Vladimir rummaged around in his pocket, pulled out the diamond ring and handed it to Albert.

Albert adjusted his spectacles until they were on the very tip of his nose and squinted, holding the ring up to the light. His face was deadpan. "I may have seen this work before. The brilliant round is a very modern cut. There is one particular cutter in London with the skillset to achieve such a remarkable polish. Would that be correct?"

Vladimir stared at him blankly.

"I don't know," he replied quietly.

Albert frowned, disappointed not have his hunch confirmed. "It appears to be an exceptionally beautiful diamond." He examined the diamond again but had long since mastered the art of containing his excitement handling extraordinary jewels. Once back in his workshop, he would be able to confirm whether his professional instinct was correct. He suggested they return again the following day.

♦ ♦ ♦

Albert ushered them into a private room. He still wasn't clear whether Vladimir wanted a valuation, or to sell the diamond. Albert diligently explained the clarity of the ring, the cut, and colour. It was rare to find that exact combination of all-round perfection. Albert had never actually seen such flawlessness before, and he saw many remarkable jewels. He felt compelled to be honest with them, although it was clear neither of the two men before him had any comprehension about the actual value of the diamond in his hand. In many ways, it was priceless. It was, however, transparent that Vladimir was only interested in the monetary value of the diamond.

Albert decided to cut to the chase. "What price did you have in mind?"

Vladimir slipped a piece of paper across the table towards him with a figure written on it in black ink.

Albert adjusted his spectacles and peered at the numbers. "A considerable valuation, indeed. You realise there is no paperwork and no guarantee this is yours to sell."

He noticed Vladimir flinched.

"Everything went down with the ship..." Vladimir's voice trailed off.

Albert decided not to push. He already had a buyer for the diamond. "A receipt would be necessary to prove the purchase," he continued.

"For the full amount?" said Vladimir.

Albert nodded and pushed the paperwork across to Vladimir. The sale would be binding and non-retractable.

For the briefest moment, Albert felt guilty. He had been given significantly more wriggle room to negotiate with if necessary. The buyer had been unable to resist such a rare acquisition and had indicated he would pay a staggering sum to the House of Fabergé. The second the diamond became the official property of the new buyer it would become infinitely more valuable.

The diamond was immediately placed in a small box lined with crushed velvet. Later that afternoon, the famous gates with gilded double-headed eagles yawned open, allowing the diamond to be delivered to its new owner. It was rehoused on top of a large wooden desk surrounded by pictures, books, pens and calendars. Each item had been carefully and thoughtfully arranged. On the back wall opposite the desk hung a collection of paintings of the Romanov Dynasty and others of their cousins, the British Royal family. Antiques, books, and many other valuable treasures were crammed into the room.

The custodian of the blue diamond was now The Emperor of Russia, Tsar Nicholas II.

CHAPTER 21

Back home, Vladimir slumped against the padded cushions, allowing his body to sink into the chair. It was the same seat to which his father had gently steered him when he arrived home the night before. Vladimir had since eaten a hearty stew with potatoes and meat, taken a hot bath, and sold the blue diamond for an astonishing sum of ruble.

He felt and looked like a different man.

Vladimir threw chunks of wood onto the fire and distributed them among the flames. He watched the red embers envelop the wood, causing smoke to rise. Vladimir looked directly into the flames, daring them to provoke the demons in his mind. He'd already drunk almost half a bottle of vodka on the journey home, and his nerves felt sufficiently anesthetised.

The ring was now gone. He needed to know whether the ghosts that had been clinging to his conscience like weights had also gone.

He poured himself a double measure of vodka and recalled the shudder that woke them that fateful night on the *Titanic*. He knew now that the jolt happened at the exact moment when the ship's starboard side struck the iceberg. He closed his eyes, seeing a replay of the panic as mothers began crying, babies in their arms and children clinging to their skirts. Men brandished fists or guns in a desperate attempt to get into a lifeboat. Other men handed over rolls of cash. The crew members pushed it back – what use was the money to them now? Flashbacks raced through his mind in random order, like a movie playing out of sequence. His conscience could not escape the torment after all.

Vladimir swilled the neat vodka around in his mouth, feeling his gums sting, then he swallowed.

He remembered walking past a small cluster of musicians still playing their violin and cellos. "Come, quickly!" he had said, waving his hands towards the upper deck.

One of them shook his head, and the other lifted his bow, turning sadly to face Vladimir. "Go where?"

"To a lifeboat!" Vladimir shouted.

Vladimir would never forget the look in the musician's eyes as he gracefully lowered his bow onto his cello and played a deep, harrowing note in acceptance of his fate. Shaking his head, Vladimir had pulled Marjorie towards the staircase leading to the upper decks.

Marjorie.

Vladimir poured more vodka.

The flames in the fire now engulfed the wood, stretching upwards and outwards as they flickered towards him. He closed his eyes and felt himself begin to sway. Dizziness and nausea overwhelmed him. He reached out his hands to steady himself but felt his body slipping. His arms tried to grasp onto something, anything. He fell to the floor, feeling his teeth smash upon impact. His eyes sprang open then clammed shut.

He could see her face so clearly, staring at him.

"I'm sorry, Marjorie… I'm so sorry!" He knew he was screaming. She was standing too far away, and he couldn't be sure she heard him.

He felt someone slap him hard across the face. A man's voice pierced through the noise and silenced him. Someone rolled his body over as the toxic contents of his stomach and mind emptied onto the floor. He reached out, begging Marjorie to come back.

He *had* to know she heard him say he was sorry.

He was aware of being lifted onto a flat surface, presumably a bed. He heard voices but couldn't decipher them.

All he could think about was the dress he had just seen Marjorie wearing; it was the same one she had worn to dinner that night on the *Titanic*. The night he killed her.

Unbeknown to the passengers aboard the *Titanic*, throughout the day on 14th of April 1912 several iceberg warnings had been received. Regardless, the unsinkable ship's engines continued at full throttle, and she sailed her mighty bow defiantly and proudly onwards.

Marjorie had managed to pack several evening dresses. She'd chosen her favourite one that particular evening, pulling it over her corset and smoothing it over her shapely figure. It was cream and gold, falling in elegant layers all the way to her feet. She had unrolled the hair pinned to her scalp and scooped the springy curls into a fashionable updo. She finished by tying a gold scarf with feather plumes around the middle.

She had taken his arm and followed him into the dining room. There was no silverware or extra courses, which they had in first-class dinning; however, in their dining room on D Deck, there were oak-panelled walls, elegantly upholstered chairs, and a beautiful piano. Even without the opulent frills of first-class there was a sense of luxury. Vladimir and Marjorie enjoyed a wonderful dinner of spring lamb with mint sauce, green peas, and roast potatoes, followed by plum pudding. They retired to their cabin early and were fast asleep when the ship shuddered at around 11:40 pm. Stirring only briefly, they drifted back to sleep. Around twenty minutes later, frantic footsteps and voices woke them again. Vladimir sat up and shook Marjorie. He quickly pulled on his clothes and opened the door, stopping a steward.

"What's happening?" he asked.

"Captain wants all passengers up on deck," the steward answered.

The young boy looked pale and anxious but didn't offer any further information. Vladimir shut the door and urged Marjorie to hurry.

"Quickly, wrap up warm. It must be some sort of drill."

She nodded, still sleepy. She pulled her coat over her nightclothes and tugged on her boots. They made their way up one of the two designated staircases for second-class passengers. In the nearby smoking room, other passengers gathered together, puffing cigars and cigarettes as they discussed the situation. There was no urgency or panic, even though in another part of the ship, the captain had just received the solemn information they would only stay afloat for a couple more hours. Twenty-five minutes after the shudder that woke most passengers from their slumber, the crew received an official order to uncover the lifeboats. In those horrific, panic-fuelled moments it became apparent there were not sufficient lifeboats for all passengers. The *Titanic* would sink, and most of the souls on board would not survive. Once the iceberg had struck, the fatal time bomb had started ticking.

Around an hour later, the very first lifeboat was lowered, holding twenty-eight passengers, not the sixty-five people it could have saved. Yet in those life-changing milliseconds, the condemned crew were forced to make frantic decisions, and all rational thinking morphed into sheer panic: that, and the fact the class system had been perversely applied to a life or death emergency.

As lifeboat number seven began to drift away from the ship, the first distress rockets were fired into the calm, clear sky. By then, Marjorie and Vladimir were among hundreds of hysterical, disorientated people still trapped on board the *Titanic* as she began to slip beneath the water. They held onto the railings, watching as others jumped, fell, or stood frozen with indecision and fear.

Pumped with terror and adrenaline, Vladimir knew their death was inevitable. He could feel his heart beating faster as his body began to shake. He looked at Marjorie – her skin had taken on a white glow.

The ship was at an angle, tilting the remaining passengers towards the sea. Vladimir clasped his arm around the railing, holding onto Marjorie's waist with his other arm. He could hardly move his muscles and shivered violently. It was difficult to focus, and the chaos around him seemed to move in slow motion. He felt Marjorie slip from his grasp and grabbed her hand, pulling her towards him.

"We are going to die…" she cried. Her voice trailed off as she began to sob.

He noticed her lips were tinged with blue. "No! We are *not* going to die!" he yelled back. He felt her body stiffen and slip out of her coat. He frantically grabbed her arm with numb fingers as she screamed.

"Don't let me go!"

He lunged forward and reached for her left hand, just as she slipped again. Her right arm swung wildly around, pulling her body weight with her. His arm shook as he dug his fingers into her wrist, feeling his own weight begin to slide.

It was then he saw the blue diamond sparkling on her finger. Her eyes followed his.

"No…" she said hoarsely.

The lights on board the ship had already gone out. Vladimir felt exhausted, confused and unbearably weak. A surge of energy forced him to concentrate.

Marjorie was screaming. Vladimir knew he couldn't hold her. She was seconds away from falling, and there was nothing he could do. He was still gripping onto the railing, but his arm was peeling slowly away, and her weight was going to pull him down with her. He still had hold of her wrist. With his right hand, he lent forward and clinched his frozen fingers around the ring. He had just about enough strength to pull it swiftly from her finger. As he did so, he released his grip from her wrist, and she fell.

He turned away as her body dropped to the icy ocean below. But he would never forget the final look of horror in her eyes or the sound of her scream as it descended into silence.

Alexei stayed with his son all night, not daring to leave his side. As dawn washed the dark grey skies of St Petersburg with pale sunlight, and new snow began to smother the city again, Vladimir slept. At last, his body was still, the torrent of words and broken phrases had finally ceased.

Alexei now understood Vladimir had been with a woman called Marjorie on board the *Titanic*, and the ring had been hers, but she had not survived. He wondered what she had been like and how she had met his son. Had they been happy together? Was the diamond a family heirloom, or a gift from an admirer?

He would never find answers to these questions. His son would not speak about Marjorie again, or the diamond. Memories of them would always lurk deep in the shadows of Vladimir's mind, but over the next few years those memories would become fainter until the demons in his dreams eventually ceased to wake him in the early hours.

It would have shocked and unsettled Vladimir to know the ring was still in St Petersburg. It remained in the famous study but was tucked into an inconspicuous section of the wall with only the most valuable items, untouched for almost four years. Only once during that time was it taken out of the safe, to be sketched, weighed and expertly designed. It would form the centrepiece for a special commission Fabergé was creating for an Imperial Egg the following year. The drawings were stunning and possibly the most spectacular design ever attempted.

By early 1917 the toxic politics had fed unrest in Russia, which had spiralled into a revolution. The Tsar and his family were placed under house arrest, sending shockwaves throughout the palace. The family were later evacuated to protect them from the rising tide of the revolution. But the Bolsheviks were gaining political power, and their momentum was gathering unprecedented speed.

As the Romanov family were led away, an inconspicuous girl watched from an upper window. The Tsar's study was several floors below her and along a long corridor. Inside a concealed safe, there was a pouch containing various jewels. The young girl, Alena, felt too numb to cry. She remembered what her mistress had said to her before she left. A ship was leaving St Petersburg that afternoon and taking white émigrés abroad. If she snapped out of her shock and moved quickly, she would have just enough time to find the jewels and board the ship.

CHAPTER 22

Alena lowered her head and walked hurriedly away from the palace, not daring to look back. She had kept her servant's uniform on until she was clear of the gates, then stopped in an alleyway to untie her apron and unpin her hair. All Alena carried with her was a small bag. Her fingers shook as she fastened her coat buttons, trying to hurry; she knew she didn't have much time. She gently patted her chest, checking that the velvet pouch was still there, hidden beneath her layers of clothes. She hadn't yet had the courage to look inside the mysterious bag she had taken from the Tsar's safe.

She repeated her mistress's words over and over in her head. Her mistress was a fierce woman who wore her thick black hair in a tight bun, making her skin taught. Alena had always feared her, but that morning she had pulled Alena into her arms. She was leaving with the Romanov family, and they would never see one another again.

"You must leave today. Don't stay here, Alena." The older woman had squeezed her eyes shut, crying despite herself. In the only gesture of softness Alena had ever known her mistress to show, she pulled Alena's hand towards her heart. "You are a good girl. Take what is in the safe."

Alena gasped, shaking her head. "I can't!" she protested.

Her mistress gripped Alena's chin, forcing them to look into each other's eyes. "You must. Take it before those bastards take it all."

She told Alena where to find the safe and how to open it. And with that, the Romanov family were gone. Alena had no family or friends here, and no reason to stay.

Her legs felt like jelly as she began to run. She was desperate to reach the ship on time but also to escape the memories she had left behind. Hair whipped her sore, red cheeks, but she continued to run, picking up pace. A few people shouted at her as she brushed past, but she couldn't stop now.

She stumbled as she slowed down, almost crashing into an older woman waiting to board. "I'm so sorry," she muttered, pushing past. The old woman growled in response as Alena began to merge into the group of other white émigrés. She was no longer out of breath, but her chest ached from running so fast. Alena looked up at the ship with wide eyes. She had heard the ship might eventually dock in France, Poland, or Germany. She didn't care.

The air felt bitterly cold as she queued behind a line of people waiting to board. She rubbed her shoulders with bare hands to try to bring some warmth to her skin. She'd had no time to prepare for the journey. A young mother, with a little boy clinging to her skirt, handed her a thick blanket, tucking it around her shoulders. The act of kindness made Alena melt into sobs of exhaustion and fear. She felt the young mother take her in her arms, holding her for a few moments. Alena pulled away, afraid the pouch could be detected through her clothes.

Finally, the ship pulled away from the harbour. Alena huddled on a wooden bench, her head bent low. She didn't look up to see the land slowly fade behind the grey mist, but she did feel the damp wind sting her face, reminding her of the harshness of the country she was leaving behind. Alena squeezed her eyes shut, trying to recall happier – warmer – times. She didn't want the bitter, wintry skyline to be her last memory of home.

A few hours into the journey, she locked herself in the tiny room used as a lavatory and pulled the needle and thread from the hem of her coat. She'd had the sense to take it from her room before she left. Someone banged on the door, making her jump. Panic rose from her stomach and clenched her throat; she only had minutes to finish.

Tugging the pouch out of her brassiere, she reached her fingers deep inside and pulled out a long string of perfect pearls intertwined with small, dazzling diamonds. A single, much larger pearl pendant dangled from an elaborate diamond bow cluster. Alena felt her heart summersault, instantly recognising the necklace – it belonged to the Empress of Russia. Guilt stabbed at her conscience. Her mistress's words rang in her ears again – *Take it before those bastards take it all* – forcing her to reach inside the pouch again. She found the matching earrings, which were equally exquisite. The set was unmistakable, and a precious reminder of home. But these jewels were famous. Perhaps, she considered, they would be *too* famous to sell.

Alena was so distracted by the pearls that she almost didn't check the pouch was completely empty. She tipped it upside down, gasping as the ring fell into her lap. She knew she had never seen the ring before; she would have remembered. A ceiling lamp gently swayed above her head, moving to the swell of the ocean, and Alena held the diamond up to it, watching the blue colours sparkle.

There was another bang on the door, this time accompanied by swearing and unveiled threats. Alena threaded the needle with deft fingers and stitched the jewellery tightly into the hem of her dress, going over and over the stitching as many times as she could. She'd already unpicked the hem earlier. Her haberdashery skills were exemplary; it would be impossible to tell the hem had been tampered with unless someone deliberately unpicked it or squeezed the edges.

Alena unbolted the door and stepped outside, apologising quietly and giving the excuse that she'd been ill. The woman who had been banging on the door looked at her angrily, complaining that she didn't *look* sick. Alena lowered her head and returned to the wooden bench on deck. She pulled the blanket over her lap, folding it neatly under her feet.

This young maid, although she tried to blend in among the other refugees, stood apart from everyone else – she had devoted her life to serving the Emperor and Empress of Russia. She had seen some of the world's most dazzling, priceless, and irreplaceable jewellery, and had even helped to fasten some of the pieces on her employers' clothes. Yet none of the jewels she had seen draped over the Grand Duchess's arms, or around the Empress's neck, or upon the Tsar's head, had been as singly bewitching as the blue diamond she had just sewn into the hem of her dress.

PART FIVE

CHAPTER 23

Paris, Christmas Eve, 1919

Rita Brienne was not remotely intimidated by the incessant car horns of frustrated drivers as they frantically negotiated the undisciplined roads around the Champs-Élysées, Paris. She adjusted her hat and pursed her bright red lips together, dismissing every driver in the path of her Rolls-Royce Silver Ghost with a kid-gloved hand.

It was Christmas Eve, the first in five years when they could officially celebrate peace following the Treaty of Versailles which had been signed earlier that summer in June 1919. To the vibrant young woman driving through the streets of Paris, the treaty was just something she remembered the men discussing at dinner parties. Thankfully, they always withdrew to the drawing-room to continue debating such boring topics, although she wondered how they even saw each other through the thick cigar fog. That said, she wasn't keen on the women's discussions either; they bored her even more. Many of them had volunteered for the Red Cross during the war, wrapping bandages and making cups of tea. It was hardly trench work, she ruminated; not a strand of lacquered hair had been put out of place by their volunteering efforts, unlike some of the 'real' volunteers who got their hands properly dirty. Rita struggled to conceal her frustration during their tedious conversations.

She killed time during endless afternoon teas by checking her nails, applying a little extra lipstick, twirling her hair around her finger. The other women would stare at her indignantly. But Rita didn't care. She knew they'd have to put up with her, regardless. Rita's husband was one of the wealthiest men in France, lending the couple significant status in these times of recovery. Other women's husbands needed Henri Brienne, but more than that, they respected him. The wives had to sharpen their claws behind closed doors, which they did often. In their opinion, Henri Brienne was wrapped around Rita's little finger. Rita would have laughed out loud if she had heard them say that. And she would have been quick to confirm how right they were. Henri would have chastised her then kissed her. Maybe they had a point.

Rita honked her horn, enjoying its powerful blast. Several people walking nearby jumped, and she gave a wicked grin of satisfaction. Filled with a delightful Christmas spirit, she wound down the window and started singing 'Jingle Bells' at the top of her voice.

She recalled this song had been initially composed for jingling ice in glasses at parties. Perhaps it was a stiff drink she was subconsciously thinking about as she opened her lungs fully and belted out the lyrics. Passers-by glared at her as though she were inebriated. If only, she mused.

She lit a cigarette and puffed hard on it, balancing one hand on the steering wheel while pressing a dainty leather boot hard on the throttle, all of which took impressive coordination. Finally, the traffic inched forward. La Résidence Brienne was only a few streets away, but it was taking forever to get there in this wretched traffic, even though the six-cylinder engine was keen to please. She teased the accelerator, just because she could, and was amused when the exhaust spluttered an unnecessary backlash. She overlooked the fact her beloved car was named Silver Ghost to emphasise its quietness. The more drama, noise, and fanfare, the better, according to Rita Brienne.

It was ironic that Rita had married a quiet, unassuming man, but not a coincidence he was extraordinarily wealthy and arguably the most influential man in Paris. Many criticised the twenty-two-year age gap, but never to her face.

During the war, Henri had relocated them to the French countryside where it was safer. Rita had been restless and bored. As soon as the war was over, they had returned to Paris, where by some miracle La Résidence Brienne had been left untouched. Henri was too old for active service and had no sons to send to the front lines, but he did have property and money.

Rita knew he was already supporting several new businesses as part of the recovery effort, providing work for the men and women who had survived. He interested her with his controversial views on women's rights, which she advocated wholeheartedly. She teased him that he praised Nancy Astor for becoming the first woman to take a seat in the House of Commons in England, while locked in his library with only men who clinked brandy glasses and puffed on fine Columbian cigars, congratulating one another on their forward-thinking. Except, Rita knew Henri was genuine. England was technically as much home to Henri as Paris, as his mother had been English, but it was Paris that thrilled his soul. Rita longed to go back to England, but for now she would indulge him with their Parisian lifestyle. Nonetheless, she was not prepared to relinquish her ultimate goal to return to England.

As she swerved round the final corner and hurtled through the ornate iron gates, she thought about England. She had been so excited to leave and explore the world with Henri six years earlier that she had never imagined she would feel nostalgic or homesick. Perhaps she was getting soft in her old age. Christmas had a particular way of stirring emotions and memories. She suddenly missed carols sung in English, church bells ringing out in quaint little villages, holly studded with red berries, and the scent of warm cinnamon, red wine, mistletoe, and fresh pine.

Rita strolled into the grand entrance of her Paris home and stood under the extravagant crystal chandelier. It stretched outwards like an angel's wings, sparkling brilliantly. She briefly admired the dazzling shadows it created on the shiny marble floor. Glancing to the left, she saw that fresh holly had been wrapped around the staircase. Henri must have organised this festive gesture to remind her of England. It was just like him to be so thoughtful.

She started to sing again, this time 'Good King Wenceslas'. The servants stifled giggles as they picked up her fur coat and recovered the heels she had discarded on the staircase like Cinderella.

"Is Henri home?" she asked, startling one of the maids.

"Monsieur Brienne is in the drawing-room, Madame. With colleagues from the bank, I believe," the maid replied.

"On Christmas Eve? Well, thank you for the warning. It sounds tedious. Be a darling and run me a bath will you?" Rita gave the girl her brightest, loveliest smile. "And see if you can sneak the bottle of brandy from the library, as it's Christmas Eve. If anyone asks, tell them it's for me. They'll believe you, don't worry."

The girl grinned despite her excellent training. It was impossible not to find her mistress's mischievousness contagious.

Rita sunk into the rose-scented bubbles, a glass of warm brandy perched on the side of the bath, and started singing again. Fortunately, she had an exceptional voice. This was how her husband found her, this time singing 'O Come, All Ye Faithful'.

"Someone is feeling festive," he said with a chuckle. He gestured towards the brandy; she was an impossible minx.

"Hello, darling," Rita crooned.

They shared a long, lingering kiss.

"Are you looking forward to the party tonight?" he asked hopefully.

She rolled her eyes.

"Not really."

They were going to The Ritz for dinner. It meant a glitzy dress and no doubt a divine meal, but for Rita it also meant an evening in the company of yet more dull women. She would prefer to spend Christmas Eve at home alone with Henri.

Henri gave her a mock stern look. "Could you at least *try*

to behave? Pretend to enjoy yourself, maybe?"

She smiled sweetly.

"I can only promise to try."

He sighed. "That means no. I've heard that promise before… many times."

"The women think I'm rude," Rita said, pouting.

"You are rude, my darling," Henri said. "But also, enchanting."

"I'd say I was honest rather than rude. I simply tell them what I think."

Henri laughed. Rita took a swig of the brandy, enjoying its inherent warmth. She cocked her head and looked at Henri carefully. His moustache was twitching, and he was trying to avoid eye contact.

"What are you wearing tonight?" he asked casually.

Rita arched an eyebrow suspiciously.

"Interesting question, Henri. It's unusual for you to ask what I'm wearing. Any particular reason why?"

She knew him well, of course.

"No, my darling. I'm just curious."

She didn't believe him, but fortunately for Henri, Rita loved surprises.

Henri was waiting for her in the main hallway an hour later when she emerged in a cloud of exotic perfume. Layers of navy satin floated around her knees, and an elaborate bow was fixed to her right shoulder. Her shoulder-length curled hair was scooped to one side and decorated with plumes of white feathers and sparkling jewels. Her cheeks were heavily rouged and her lips painted bright red. Several diamond bangles snaked up her left arm, and around her neck she wore both long and short strings of pearls. Dangling from her ears were the diamond and pearl drop earrings that Henri had given her the previous Christmas. She adored these particular earrings and wore them as often as she could.

Henri felt his heart skip. "You look wonderful," he breathed.

She glowed with his compliment as he helped wrap a white fur around her arms. The clasp had been handmade with her initials 'RB' in diamonds, which he carefully fastened. She looked like a Snow Queen, although many would have tartly retorted Ice Queen was more appropriate. She didn't gel naturally with other women, possibly because they were jealous, but likely because Rita stuck her nose slightly in the air. It certainly didn't help that other women's husbands struggled to take their eyes off her. Everyone expected her to be wildly flirtatious, especially given how many younger men watched her adoringly, but she was devoted to Henri. It made other women despise her even more.

Henri, however, felt like the luckiest man alive. Despite being almost sixty, he had never married before Rita. His life revolved around business and politics. There had been women, of course, but the ladies in his social circles saw him as a prize, not a man. While it was true that Rita was spoiled, she cared nothing for gossip or social acceptance.

Yet Henri often felt he was walking around with an

unpinned hand grenade by his side. The Prime Minister's wife had once spotted Rita at a ball and made the mistake of raising an eyebrow. Rita had been wearing a long red gown, which was her favourite colour.

"You don't like red?" Rita had pointedly asked the Prime Minister's wife. The woman spluttered awkwardly in response. Henri had held his breath, then reminded himself he was the government's most significant financial contributor. He was certain Rita was well aware this gave her immunity from criticism.

"On *you* dear, it's very fetching," the Prime Minister's wife gushed.

Rita appraised the other woman's sombre grey dress. "Thank you. Red is such a delightful, happy colour. I just can't resist it. I'm quite convinced we wear colours which best reflect our demeanour." After a pregnant pause Rita offered a bright smile. "I hope you have a pleasant evening." And with that Rita drifted off, leaving the woman slack-jawed in her wake.

Henri thought back to that particular exchange now as he kissed the top of her head, grateful the Prime Minister's wife would not be at the party tonight. Not that Rita would have given more than a shoulder shrug if she had been, although she might have laughed if the woman had turned up wearing a red dress. As they walked towards the waiting car, Rita turned to Henri. Something had been on her mind all day.

"Have you sent anything to Sophia for Christmas?" she asked.

A shadow fell across Henri's face. It pained him to hear her name. He nodded, feeling the stab of fresh guilt. Sophia was eight years old by then, born to a woman – a maid – who he had taken into his bed for several years but could never marry. The maid was possibly the prettiest girl Henri had ever seen, but when she fell pregnant, the affair had to end. He had ruined her for all others, with a bastard child no other man would accept. Life would be extremely difficult for a young woman with a baby and no husband. It was even worse for the baby, who had no family name and no legal right to parentage. Henri didn't agree with men disowning their responsibilities, even though many of them did. He ensured both Sophia and her mother had financial security. They had a pretty house on the outskirts of Paris, Sophia went to a private school, and her mother had enough funds to support them amply.

At Christmas and on Sophia's birthday, he always sent gifts. It was up to her mother whether or not she gave them to Sophia, although a simple thank you letter usually arrived a week or two later. This year he had sent Sophia a pretty pink dress, matching shoes, and tiny diamond-drop earrings. He always signed the card 'LH' for 'Love Henri'; he felt he had no right to sign 'Papa'.

He had told Rita about Sophia before they married, and she had reluctantly accepted the situation, providing mother and daughter remained safely ensconced on the outskirts of Paris. Henri kept several photographs of his daughter tucked into the pages of one of his favourite books in his study. Sophia was the mirror image of her mother, with a halo of pale blonde hair and lovely brown eyes. It tore at Henri's heart that he had missed her growing up.

At some point, Henri wanted children with Rita. Recently,

he had been thinking about it a lot more. As they drove through the familiar streets of Paris, Henri leaned over and kissed her cheek.

"You seem thoughtful," he gently probed.

"You know me so well."

"Will you tell me?"

She gently patted his hand. "Maybe later."

"I'd better supply you with plenty of champagne then," Henri teased.

When they arrived at Hôtel Ritz a short while later, Henri took her hand and laughed as Rita squealed with delight.

The world-famous hotel sparkled with thousands of lights, both to celebrate Christmas and to remember César Ritz who had died a month before the war officially ended in 1918. Inside, it was as though a fairy godmother had sprinkled her magic everywhere, reinforcing the over-the-top unrivalled luxury of the hotel. Exquisite decorations adorned every surface and created a fairyland of lights, ribbons, and festive holly. The atmosphere was both magical and electric. The relief that war was over was tangible; emotional, economic and political recovery was underway.

The 'can do' ethos of The Ritz was legendary. With a graceful nod, staff could bring together a dinner party for several hundred people with only a few hours of preparation time. They could locate, deliver, and find time to polish a sought-after piano just because a famous guest wanted to play it that evening. It was the only hotel where the seemingly impossible could be provided, always with smooth timeliness and elegance. Famous people, writers, artists, and businessmen were drawn to the hotel to absorb the auspicious energy it emitted. Of course, the pre-requisite for being a guest was a hefty bank account.

Henri and Rita ate a sumptuous meal and drank exquisite champagne. Afterwards, everyone gathered around the grand piano to sing carols. The pianist had to play as loud as he could to dampen the more enthusiastic vocalists. Rita and Henri were among them, enjoying every moment of the festivities. Dancing followed and every guest was on their feet, swinging and swaying. Henri left his wife in the arms of a well-known poet on the dance floor. He felt tired as he eased himself into one of the velvet chairs and watched his wife. Rita looked ravishing and positively radiant as she waltzed. She glanced over at him and blew him a kiss, all the while keeping her footwork impeccable.

Henri thought about his Christmas gift to her that year, and also what he wanted to ask her. He felt distinctly nervous, knowing how headstrong she could be. He would never force her to agree to his request, of course. If she said no, he would be disappointed but accept her answer.

The song finished and she walked back towards him, negotiating the other tables with caution, doing her best not to reveal how tipsy she was. She collapsed in the chair beside him and giggled. "No more champagne! I can see double." She shook her curls, laughing.

Henri took her hand and kissed it. "Happy Christmas, my darling."

"Is it officially Christmas?"

"Yes, you danced straight through midnight."

"I'm not Cinderella then," she sighed.

"I should hope not. Your shoes cost more than glass slippers, so thank goodness you didn't lose one."

She rolled her eyes, grinning.

"Henri, there is something I want to discuss with you," she said.

He twitched his immaculately clipped moustache and briefly wondered if it was the same thing he wanted to speak to her about.

That was highly unlikely.

"You can tell me anything," he said encouragingly.

He watched as Rita took a deep breath and exhaled with a flurry of fast words. "Henri, I want to go home. To England. To live."

He had not expected this revelation, and yet he had learnt Rita was often full of surprises. Moving to England was neither simple nor straightforward – their life was in Paris – but he knew his wife had never truly settled here. She was an English rose through and through, complete with sweet petals and sharp thorns.

He sat back in his chair, contemplating the idea. It may, he decided, compliment his own request. It was time to place his cards on the table.

"If we did that, would you consider starting our own family?" he asked.

She sat up straight, suddenly sober.

"Darling, we already have a puppy. Why would you want another?"

He knew she was teasing. It was typical of her to use humour to deflect, especially when she needed time to digest her thoughts.

"You know perfectly well what I mean. I'd like a child or maybe several," he said.

"I need more champagne," she said quickly, looking around for the waiter.

She was perhaps jesting, but he raised his hand to attract the waiter's attention. Neither spoke as a bottle of chilled Dom Pérignon promptly arrived. It was an exceptional vintage, which had taken refuge during the war years in a cave used for Champagne storage. Henri had whispered to the waiter that they were celebrating.

Henri watched the bubbles burst in the thin crystal flutes for a few moments before turning to his wife once more. "Would that be acceptable to you, Rita, my darling?" he asked gently.

Rita paused. "Yes, Henri, I believe I am ready. But there is a condition."

He felt his heart race. Whatever her demand was, he didn't care; he was desperate to start a family with her. He nodded thoughtfully, a pose he used whenever he was about to strike a business deal that was not yet entirely sealed. Rita sat up very straight, her legs crossed, her eyes fixed upon him.

"Before we start our family," she said, "I'd like to be settled back in England."

He felt immediately crestfallen given the impact such a move would have on his proposed timescale for fatherhood. But it wasn't an unreasonable suggestion. It was sensible to be firmly settled in their new home, wherever that was to be, before raising a child.

"I agree to that condition. It does mean, however, we

will need to move fairly swiftly," he said. "I'm not getting any younger." He winked at her.

Rita threw her arms around him, almost knocking the chair over, screeching with delight.

"Hold on." He pushed her away slightly. "I have a condition of my own."

Rita sat back in her chair looking uncomfortable. Henri leaned forward, taking her hand in his own. "You must wear this always to remember tonight."

Bursting with pride, he placed a ring on her finger. It fitted perfectly. At first, she simply glanced at it, so used was she to receiving jewellery from him. A second look caused her to leap up and attempt to steady herself against the chair. She held her hand out and splayed her fingers wide, staring. Her eyes glistened.

"I will never take this off my finger," she whispered.

Surprised by the effect the diamond had on her, Henri quietly congratulated himself. It took a lot to impress his wife, but he had succeeded. He would tell her later how he had come to acquire such a jewel; it had been more through luck and fate than from any intention to buy it. He had been intrigued by the diamond's history, which he had investigated with the utmost discretion. Amazingly, every part of the astonishing story was correct. The diamond was arguably priceless, and he had given the young female refugee a staggering price for it in return for her discretion. It would be wise never to tell another living soul this diamond had once belonged to the imperial royal family, especially as it was entirely feasible Fabergé could produce a receipt. The young girl had agreed eagerly.

Henri turned back to his wife. For once, she was speechless. He watched as she turned the ring around her finger, lost in her own thoughts.

The ambience that evening was magical. Henri glanced around the room, savouring the glittering lights on the Christmas tree, the sound of glasses clinking and the noise of jovial banter. A lone violinist was playing the most exquisite piece of music he had ever heard. It was ethereal and strangely captivating.

"It's beautiful, isn't it?" Rita said, breaking his reverie. She waved her hand around proudly.

He'd never seen her look so enchanted.

"The ring or the music?" he asked.

She frowned at him.

"The ring, of course! Although the music is lovely." She rested her chin on her hand, steadying her elbow on the table, listening. "It feels like I've heard it before, but I'm quite sure I haven't."

"Strange…" muttered Henri.

They clinked glasses again. Henri glanced down at Rita's hand and admired the ring on her finger. It amazed him this jewel had once belonged to Tsar Nicholas II. Knowing that the entire imperial family had been executed the previous summer, the diamond felt infinitely more precious now, as though it was infused with secrets.

Henri had been able to discover the link to Fabergé very discretely. It was suggested this ring had survived the sinking of the *Titanic* and had originated from South Africa. The latter was guesswork, based on an expert who believed he recognised the original craftsmanship. It was questionable how such a gem had travelled under the radar of official experts, sanctioning the theory it had not been legitimately mined. As there were only a few locations in the world capable of producing such a jewel, South Africa seemed most likely.

Henri couldn't help thinking how extraordinary it was that this diamond was now on his wife's finger.

CHAPTER 24

England, Christmas Eve, 1919

The wind howled and battered the farmhouse door, causing the wreath of holly and mistletoe to sway. Rain pelted sideways, attacking the figure running from the stables towards the front door, his head bent low, his boots squelching through puddles. He'd been worried about his black Irish stallion, Prince, and his wife's silver gelding, Star. The horses were getting old and bad weather unsettled them these days.

James heaved open the front door. He stood in the hallway, shaking the rain off his hair. He peeled off his coat and hung it up, smiling at the line of smaller coats on the lower pegs.

The smell of sweet pastry baking had filled the house with cinnamon, cloves and citrus. Over the years he had learnt to recognise the distinct fruits and spices. He could hear some kind of commotion coming from the kitchen. There appeared to be an argument taking place concerning the portion size of pie being allotted. A soft female voice was trying to resolve the issue diplomatically.

"You can have mine," came William's voice. At nearly sixteen, he was almost a man. He had a softness to him that his mother, Marjorie, had never possessed. In the years after she left, James had watched their son blossom. The child had grown up surrounded by constant warmth and love, as opposed to the cold, negative energy offered by his mother. Her rejection of him from birth left him with a scar that would never heal, but William appeared to use it to remind himself how fortunate he now was. James could not be prouder of his firstborn son.

It had been a shock when Marjorie had left seven years earlier. James had woken up to find her handwritten note on his bedside table. His impulse had been to set out on his horse and search until he found her, but he knew she could have boarded a train in any direction. The end of his marriage did not bring him heartache, but he did, however, crumple to the ground and howl when he realised she had taken Pearl's diamond.

He had eventually tracked down information revealing Marjorie had been on board the *Titanic*. He'd read about the ship's terrible fate in horror, scanning down the list of passengers. Suddenly, he spotted Vladimir's surname and knew instantly that Marjorie had gone with him. The coincidence was too uncanny not to be a certainty. He had hung his head in sorrow for the cruel end she had endured. And because Pearl's diamond was now lost at the bottom of the North Atlantic Ocean.

James walked along the warmly lit corridors until he reached the main sitting room. Above the large fireplace, the children had already hung their stockings on hooks, ready to be filled. Beyond the sitting room, he could see the dining room had already been laid for lunch the next day. There was an impressive centrepiece constructed with pine cones, holly, bundles of cinnamon sticks and dried oranges. Tall candles stood in the middle of the display, waiting to be lit. James gave a sigh of contentment. Sylvia had thought of everything.

"Are the horses alright?" Sylvia asked.

James turned at the sound of her voice. Her long black hair fell down her back, her brilliant blue eyes glowed, and her cheeks were flushed a bright rosy pink.

"They are fine," he said. He arched his shoulders back to see her face. "I love you, Sylvia Murray."

She reached up on tiptoe to kiss him. Their embrace was interrupted by four rowdy children bounding into the room. The children were used to seeing their parents kissing, and they carried on creating chaos, dropping biscuit crumbs and chasing the family cat.

James and Sylvia snuggled on the sofa, enjoying the lively scene. James felt strangely nostalgic. He was thinking about how lucky he was and how much had changed since he returned from South Africa seventeen years earlier. Time had diluted but not erased the horrors of finding Pearl in the brothel. He wished so often he had not given her diamond to Marjorie. It irked him, although Sylvia always said the diamond was where it was meant to be.

He was mulling over the injustice of the situation, when he felt a small hand tug on his arm. Anna, their five-year-old daughter, was staring at him. She had the same beautiful blue eyes as her mother.

"Daddy, it didn't sink," she said.

James felt his heart almost stop. Sylvia sat bolt upright.

"What didn't sink?" James asked gently.

"Whatever you were thinking about," Anna replied. She shrugged and wandered off, distracted.

"Were you thinking about the diamond?" Sylvia whispered.

James nodded. "Is our daughter a…" He lowered his voice to an almost imperceptible whisper, "*witch*?"

He was only partially teasing. Anna's words had had a profound effect on him. Sylvia also had the strangest feeling her daughter had some supernatural knowledge about the diamond.

"I believe her," Sylvia said.

"So do I," James agreed.

How could Anna have known the diamond didn't sink with the ship? It was impossible, yet James knew in his heart that the diamond had survived. Sylvia had told him a long time ago she had seen it on the finger of a woman far in the future, long after their natural lifetimes had ended. James had secretly questioned her vision when he found out Marjorie had been on the *Titanic*. But now, it would appear, his incredibly gifted wife – and daughter – were right.

CHAPTER 25

ENGLAND, 1920

Henri drove Rita's beloved Rolls Royce slowly underneath the canopy of arching trees, their branches interlacing like fingers, beckoning the way towards the couple's new home. Wild bluebells lined the winding road, still vibrant in colour. Rita leaned out of the window and breathed the fresh, crisp air deep into her lungs, then exhaled. Turning back to face Henri, she grinned excitedly.

"Henri, it's beautiful!"

He flicked his cigar out of the window and smiled, swerving the car in the direction of the newly laid road. It had been a mammoth feat to renovate the mansion and grounds in less than six months. Rita had remained in Paris during the extensive work – today she would see the sketches come to life for the first time.

The original building dated back to the seventeenth century but had been extended over the years. The previous owner had finally run out of money and energy to maintain its upkeep, making the house ripe for buyers. Henri was generous with an offer, providing the sale was swift. The owner hadn't hesitated, and within weeks architects, builders, designers, and craftsmen were drafted in to restore the dilapidated building and transform it into a glorious mansion. Bathrooms were ripped out and replaced with marble ones; walls were either painted or covered with luxurious wallpaper, and floors were polished or newly carpeted. Antique furniture was placed in every room, either shipped from Paris or acquired at auction. Framed canvases hung on the walls as though they had been there for centuries – many of them worth eye-watering amounts of money. Henri had a particular passion for art and was well known for his extensive collection of originals. Rita, however, was blasé about the whole thing – if she liked the colour and general scene that was all that really mattered.

In the library, an impressive selection of books was neatly stacked on shelves, including several first editions. The dining room was elaborately dressed to welcome guests; the silver gleamed, and the linen had been perfectly folded.

Henri's rooms were finished in rich chocolate brown and moss green, with dark mahogany furniture and fine Egyptian linen. In contrast, Rita's rooms were adorned in peach silks, delicate gold, and heavy cream satin. Their belongings had already arrived from Paris, and the maids had spent days unpacking. Henri had personally made sure Rita's shoes were in neat rows in her dressing room, that her dressing table had all her favourite powders and bottles in position, and her slippers were by her bedside.

As the car pulled up outside the house, Rita fell silent in awe. The turrets either side of the grand entrance made the mansion look like it belonged in a fairy tale. She cocked her head as Henri studied her reaction.

"What are you thinking?" he asked, unable to veil his enjoyment.

"That it looks like it belongs in a storybook," she said, smiling. "Is this really where we live?"

They got out of the car and Henri put his arms around her, pushing her curls gently to one side. "You should see the horses," he teased.

"We have horses?" she spun around, shocked.

"Sort of."

He took her hand, and they followed a pathway which veered around the back of the property. They stood at the top of perfectly aligned steps leading down to a well-manicured garden. Rita's hand flew over her mouth. A statue of stone horses galloped through an expansive, shallow pond. Henri was especially proud of the final effect, although he was still reeling from the vast sum of money he'd had to part with at auction to secure the purchase. He practically had palpitations while watching the workmen lever it into position.

"There is a rose garden over there," he said, pointing to the left. "I've already hired a full-time gardener," he added.

Rita's curls bounced as she clapped her hands and laughed. "I *love* it!" she squealed.

"Would you like to see inside?" Henri asked.

She nodded, pushing her hand through his arm. He noticed her complexion glowed and the snug cream dress she wore clung to her shapely figure. He wished he could photograph how beautiful she looked right now, and how happy.

Inside, Rita stood beneath the crystal chandelier hanging

in the entrance. "It's just like the one in Paris," she remarked.

She twirled around slowly and took in her surroundings, wrinkling her nose at the smell of fresh paint and complaining that it irritated her sinuses. Henri laughed; he had ushered the workmen out a few hours earlier. He *knew* there would be something she would pick up on. She was in a wonderful mood though, as she kicked off her shoes and ran through the rooms like a child. Henri followed the shrieks of excitement.

"Have you seen this dining table?!" she squealed.

Henri caught up with her, finally. "Yes, darling, I saw them trying to get it in through the door. In the end, it had to come through the French windows."

"Henri, you are amazing. How did you do all this?"

"While you were sipping champagne in Paris, you mean?"

He was teasing her, and she knew it.

It took her hours to explore every room, although Henri ended his tour in the study and lit a cigar. He watched her through the windows as she strolled in the garden and thought he had never seen her look more radiant. It was the right decision to move here if only to see her look this happy.

Rita found him in his study a short while later. She collapsed on a Louis XV sofa next to him, exhausted yet exhilarated from her tour.

"We could fit a swimming pool in the garden!" she marvelled.

"Does this country even get warm enough for that?" he mocked.

She shrugged; he had a point. Besides, they planned to stay on the French Riviera every summer.

"Henri, I love it here. Thank you."

She snuggled up to him and let her head rest on his shoulder. Their life was idyllic. Since Christmas Eve it had been a romantic whirlwind of dreams coming true. He offered her a glass of champagne to celebrate.

Surprisingly she shook her head and with a shy smile whispered, "No thanks, I shouldn't."

Henri had been travelling backwards and forwards between England and France for weeks and hadn't even noticed she was no longer drinking. Rita looked up at him with shining eyes. She seemed unusually nervous.

"I think now would be the perfect time to tell you we are going to have a baby," she said.

He paused to digest the shock of her news then burst out laughing.

"When?" he asked.

"The doctor thinks it could be a Christmas baby," she said and joined in his laughter.

"That's incredible!" he exclaimed, pulling her swiftly into his arms.

They both happily agreed – fate had fast-tracked their wishes.

♦ ♦ ♦

Henri and Rita settled like proverbial lovebirds in their new nest well before Christmas. In the gardens, classic English roses, lavender, tall delphiniums, hydrangeas and wisteria had been freed from weeds and walls so they could climb the following year. The gardener had painstakingly planted countless bulbs deep in the ground, ready for spring.

The mansion received its finishing touches in early summer, including a shipment of artwork from Paris, as well as delivery of Henri's cars. A new garage now housed several classic and brand-new cars, although Rita's Silver Ghost was usually found parked at an odd angle in-front of the mansion's front steps.

They stayed at home, in England, for summer. Usually they went to the French Riviera, but Rita was too enchanted with the mansion to leave. Also, she reluctantly confessed, pregnancy was exhausting.

By Christmas Eve 1920, Rita was bored and restless. She stood in the drawing room, daydreaming as the afternoon collapsed into the dark winter evening. The ground was frozen, the trees painted white with frost, and the woodland beyond the mansion glistened ghost-like. A fire crackled nearby, filling the room with warmth and a gentle glow. It was around four o'clock in the afternoon; these winter evenings felt unbearably long to Rita.

She had been reflecting upon the previous Christmas Eve when she drove wildly around the chaotic streets in Paris, singing carols. She pressed her hand on her enormous tummy, and in response, felt a small kick. The baby was due any day now. Her pregnancy had progressed exceptionally well, and the doctor anticipated a straight-forward birth. She had decorated the nursery in crisp white frills and a beautiful hand-crafted cot. Tiny toys and fluffy teddies waited patiently on shelves. All the room needed now was the baby.

Henri found her at the window watching the landscape change.

"I waddle like a duck and can't even drink champagne. It's Christmas Eve!" she complained.

"Our life is a little bit different this year, isn't it?" he replied softly.

She growled and shook her head when he suggested a game of cards, which she usually loved. They ate a quiet dinner together, although Rita pushed the food around her plate lazily. The roasted pheasant stuffed with chestnuts and served with a delicate red wine sauce was usually devoured, but tonight she barely ate. She nibbled on a bread roll, although she did manage to eat most of the chocolate and cinnamon mousse.

"I do hope our child doesn't have your fussy eating habits," Henri commented jovially.

"Well if *he* does take after me, at least we know *he'll* like champagne," Rita replied.

"Or *she* will," Henri said with a wink.

Rita frowned slightly, rubbing her stomach with gentle circular strokes. She wanted their baby to be a boy. If she was honest with herself, it was because Henri already had a daughter. It stung her to realise this was not his first child, yet she also knew the circumstances of Sophia's birth were completely different. Rita and Henri were married; Henri had not been married to his daughter's mother. Thinking about the whole situation frequently left Rita feeling simultaneously guilty, jealous, and confused.

After dinner, Henri took Rita's hand, and they walked across the hall to the living room.

"Do you mind if I have a brandy?" he asked.

She shook her head, and a wicked little grin teased her lips. "Do you mind if *I* have one?"

"Why not? It might help to relax you."

She had genuinely been joking about having the brandy, but actually, she liked the idea. It might curb the rising feeling of agitation she was feeling.

Henri poured a small amount of brandy into a warmed glass and handed it to her. She took a small sip, and to his absolute horror – it was a Remy Martin rare edition cognac – she instantly hurled the glass down onto the floor. Gathering her breath, she looked at him with wild eyes, unable to move.

He bolted towards her. "Rita? What is it?"

Although it should have been evident that a woman at the end of her pregnancy, gripping her stomach, was perhaps in labour, Rita couldn't catch her breath for long enough to tell her husband the news.

"Get the doctor, Henri," she hissed through clenched teeth.

"Is it time?"

In her head, she wanted to say *no, she was just about to waltz around the ballroom floor*, but sarcasm was poor camouflage for the sudden and excruciating pain consuming her. Henri flung the rest of the brandy down his throat, muttering apologies, and rushed off to call the doctor.

He returned a short while later, victorious. "The doctor will be here shortly."

Rita nodded. "How many babies did you say you wanted, Henri?"

"Ten," he replied then ducked to avoid the cushion she

fired at him.

Rita managed to hobble to their bedroom, holding onto Henri's arm. By then, she could barely walk and was panting heavily. "The baby is coming! I can feel it!" she cried. She crawled onto the bed and gripped the bedsheets until her knuckles turned white, lifting her knees towards her chest.

A knock at the door snapped Henri out of his frozen state of panic. The doctor waltzed in carrying a black leather bag, looking unimpressed. He had been enjoying a brandy himself at home, he confessed to Henri.

The doctor examined Rita and turned to Henri, looking surprised. "It appears this baby is very impatient."

Rita interrupted with a loud wail, and the doctor ushered Henri quickly out of the room.

Henri paced the corridor outside; the shouting and yelling almost drove him crazy with worry.

At last, there came the sound of a lusty newborn baby.

Henri pushed down the door handle and ran inside, ignoring the doctor's glare of disapproval. Rita was putting their baby to her breast for the first time. Tears streamed down her face, but she looked ecstatic.

"Henri, he's so perfect. I told you he was a boy!" she said.

He looked down at the small, pink face and thought his chest might explode with joy. He kissed Rita's head, smoothing back the hair stuck to her forehead.

"We'll have a girl next time, my darling," he said.

Rita rolled her eyes.

"Do you think we should call him Noel? It is *almost* Christmas after all. And it's French!"

Henri glanced at the clock. An hour ago they had been eating dinner. He closed his eyes, feeling tears swell in the corners.

"I think the name is perfect," he whispered.

In one astounding year, all their wishes had come true. Henri picked up Rita's hand and kissed it, feeling the blue diamond touch his moustache. She gently retracted her hand and burrowed it underneath Noel's blanket.

Henri was puzzled. It was almost as if she was *hiding* the ring. His brows knit together as he considered her reaction. He had been about to tell her the diamond felt like their lucky charm. Yet he now had the strangest sense that he really shouldn't say that to her right now. He quickly brushed the outlandish thought aside and reassured himself he had misjudged her. She wasn't hiding the ring – why would she?

Yet as he watched Rita gently reposition their baby son at her breast, the diamond caught his eye again. He couldn't shake the inexplicable, illogical sense that something just wasn't quite right.

Rita snuggled Noel towards her chest protectively, pulling the blanket over him and burying her left hand, and the diamond ring, safely underneath.

Her body throbbed with tiredness. The room was warm from the well-stocked fire, but the heat had drained instantly from her skin the moment Henri touched her ring. It was irrational, she knew – probably the result of overexertion and lack of sleep.

She watched her husband from the corner of her eye. Snatching her hand away from him had left him crestfallen and confused. This was not the behaviour of a loving wife to her husband and the father of her child. But she had reacted on instinct. An instinct that for one irrational moment had left her needing to protect the ring more than the baby.

The baby. Her son. Henri's son. That was what was important now. She reached out her right hand and squeezed Henri's fingers, giving him a reassuring smile. As he searched her eyes looking for clues to her earlier behaviour, she wedged her left hand further under the blanket. She had no answers to give him.

CHAPTER 26

ENGLAND, 1926

The next few years flew by for Henri and Rita. Their life was a perfect whirlwind of long summers in St-Tropez and Paris, and the rest of the year in England.

Noel was five years old and full of mischief and boundless energy. When he started school, the house became much quieter suddenly. A second baby had simply never happened, much to Henri's disappointment.

Rita hosted constant parties, and he would often find her indulging in an afternoon soirée of some description. Noel had made her infinitely more sociable, which surprised him. Some days he felt his wife was speeding up when all he wanted to do was slow down. Henri was sixty-four by then and the last few years had been the happiest of his life, but also the most exhausting.

He had just returned from a business trip to Paris, and the journey home had felt exceptionally long. He was still digesting the sobering news he had received in Paris when he walked in through the front door. He removed his hat and listened for the usual voices and noise.

Hearing nothing, he took refuge in his study. He sighed

as he sat at his desk, ruminating on the dilemma he was facing, churning different solutions over and over in his head.

He had no idea how he was going to tell Rita.

Even the sunshine had taken shelter behind dark, heavy clouds. Henri felt like a condemned man awaiting the wrath of a mighty storm. He jumped when he heard the front door slam shut, and her voice perforate the silence.

"Henri? Are you home?" Rita called.

She sounded happy. Henri shook his head sadly, knowing her bubbly mood was going to be short-lived. He cleared his throat. "I'm in my study," he shouted back. He heard her high heels clatter down the hallway. He stood up unsteadily, tightening his fingers under the edge of the desk.

"Henri!" Rita burst into the room, smiling. She didn't notice anything amiss as she planted a cherry-red kiss on his cheek. 'How was Paris?"

"Rita, darling, please could we talk?" Henri said soberly.

"Sounds serious. Do I need a brandy?" She laughed, dismissing the suggestion playfully with her hand.

Slowly, he nodded. Rita raised her eyebrows and sat upright, folding her hands neatly in her lap.

"It's Nicole, Sophia's mother," Henri said.

"I know very well who Nicole is," Rita snapped.

"She's dead." Henri blurted the words out before he lost the nerve. "The funeral is next week. I will be returning to Paris."

"Why?" Rita interrupted sharply.

Henri took a deep breath and exhaled a long sigh. He eased himself back in his chair, allowing a few moments for the rising heat of tension between them to cool.

"My daughter's mother has died. And I have been asked to attend the reading of the will," he continued mournfully.

Rita scoffed and leapt up off the chair. Henri saw that her hand shook as she poured herself a neat brandy. She drained the glass with one gulp and smashed it back down on the table.

"What has that got to do with *you*, Henri? Is she leaving you money?" She laughed sarcastically, rolling her eyes.

Henri felt a surge of anger and disappointment. He decided not to soften the blow. "She is leaving me her daughter. *Our* daughter."

Rita gasped. "No… No Henri. No!" She shook her head, backing out of the room.

"Sit down, Rita!" Henri's tone was unusually harsh as he pointed to the chair in front of him. Reluctantly, Rita sat down on the edge. Her eyes blazed at him, but he continued, unfazed. "I will suggest Sophia lives in England with us, if that is her wish. She will transfer school and live in our home as part of this family. It is non-negotiable."

Rita stood up, defeated and furious. She slammed her hands onto his desk and looked directly into his eyes. "If you had told me before we married that this would be a possibility, I would never have married you," she said.

Her caustic tone told him she meant it, as she swivelled on her heel and flounced out of the room. Moments later, he heard the front door slam and her car roar down the driveway. Something inside him quietly snapped. He sat in his chair and stared out of the window, remaining there deep in thought, long after the dust from Rita's Silver Ghost's spinning wheels had settled.

Rita avoided him for two days, and when she did pass him finally in the corridor, her eyes bore into his with unconcealed contempt. The night before he left for Paris, he tried to speak to her, but she threw a Baccarat crystal vase at him in a rage. It smashed as it collided with the wall, shattering into a million dazzling pieces.

When he closed the front door behind him the next morning, dressed in a dark suit, his heart had never felt heavier. The grey clouds looming overhead drizzled raindrops onto his hat, complimenting his mood. He had never felt older or sadder in his entire life; or as resentful towards anyone as he did his wife.

In contrast to England, the weather in Paris was notably sunny and warm. Henri reflected wryly that the chill in England, however, was not just due to the weather.

Walking down the Champs-Élysées, strangers smiled and greeted him simply to be friendly. When he sat down at his favourite café and ordered a double espresso, he felt immediately welcome. The street was lined with trees and tall buildings, making him pleasantly inconspicuous among the crowds of people. Just hearing the French accent and rapid conversations around him gave his spirits an imperceptible lift.

The funeral was taking place that afternoon at a small church nestled in the southern part of the city. He thought about Sophia and tried to recall the image of the fifteen-year-old girl from the handful of photographs her mother had sent over the years. He expected Sophia to be resentful towards him, but he knew he had to try and reach out to her if he could. She was staying with a neighbour and close friend of her mother's. That was the only information he had been given.

The will was being read the following afternoon. The solicitor had given him the address and time of the reading. Henri knew other men in his situation would not go, but Henri was not that kind of man. He had once cared for Nicole and felt dutybound to hear her final wishes. He fully expected Sophia would be orphaned now and he would not let that happen to her. Nicole had no family that he knew of.

Henri breathed in the buttery sweetness of warm croissants floating past his table. He lifted his arm to attract the attention of the waitress, unable to resist the temptation. As Henri bit into the delicate layers of crisp, fluffy pastry, he felt the warm comfort of home overwhelm him. Emotion caught in his throat, making it difficult to swallow.

The waitress reappeared looking concerned. "Monsieur, are you alright?"

Henri nodded, smiling weakly at her. Being in Paris felt painfully nostalgic, especially now. The sounds and smells surrounding him were comfortable and familiar. Returning to Paris always gave him a feeling of homecoming, but today he was filled with an acute sense of longing. Perhaps, he considered, it was because his wife had ostracised him. Or perhaps because he was about to see his daughter for the very first time that afternoon, at her mother's funeral.

Henri stood back from the small crowd of mourners gathered outside the church as the hearse arrived. He tipped his head respectfully towards the coffin, whispering a prayer under his breath. He raised his eyes to see a black limousine stop behind the hearse.

The door opened, and young girl stepped out. She was noticeably tall, and her hair was as blonde as her mother's had been, swaying like spun gold down her back. She wore a simple black dress and flat pumps on her feet. Her eyes were shaded by a delicate black veil, but she looked straight at him. Henri recognised his own face staring back. He wanted to step forward towards her but didn't quite dare. His heart ached as she walked alone behind the pallbearers, her eyes fixed on her mother's coffin.

Henri sat a few rows behind Sophia during the service. When she stood up to read a short poem, he thought he might burst with sadness and pride. Guilt surged through him as he watched her – how could he have cut her out of his life all these years? His eyes followed Sophia as she returned to her seat, sobbing. Her shoulders shook as she flopped her head against the woman next to her. The woman put an affectionate arm around her, hugging her close.

Henri couldn't stand it a moment longer. He stood up, apologising to the people who had to move their legs as he gently pushed his way towards her.

She looked up as he sat down beside her. She held his gaze for a few moments and then carefully laid her hand on top of his, curling her fingers into his palm. Henri offered her a lopsided smile, unashamed as tears coursed down his face.

✧ ✧ ✧

The solicitor's office was basic and not overly comfortable. Henri shifted in the thinly upholstered chair, noticing the desk was chipped and the polish peeling. He didn't like the look of the solicitor either; he seemed decisively shifty to Henri.

The only other person in the claustrophobic, threadbare office was the same woman Henri saw Sophia with at the funeral – the same woman who had put her arm around Sophia's shoulders. Her name was Madame Duval, and she had lived across the street from Nicole ever since Sophia was born.

The solicitor read the will solemnly.

Henri interrupted him, partly to get some reprieve from the monotony of his speech. "As Sophia's father, I intend to care for her now."

"Monsieur Brienne, with the greatest respect to you, the will cannot be disputed," the solicitor replied.

Madame Duval, Nicole's close friend and neighbour who had been named executor of the will, looked uncomfortable.

"She has no other living relative," Henri insisted.

"Monsieur Brienne, her mother wished for her to remain in France under Madame Duval's care."

Henri straightened his back, feeling the bones click. He turned to Madame Duval. "Please tell me, in your own words, what Nicole wanted."

The older lady, he guessed to be in her sixties, puffed up her chest. "Nicole was a good woman. She loved Sophia more than life itself." Madame Duval dabbed her eyes with a handkerchief, remembering her friend. "Nicole wanted Sophia to remain in France and be educated at the same school. Monsieur, she wanted her to live with me until then."

Henri nodded, believing the woman. Nicole had made provision without any further contribution from himself, using her savings and money from the house he had bought her to fund her wishes. Her integrity left him speechless. Everything Nicole had done and planned for was entirely for the wellbeing of their child.

Henri sat quietly, contemplating his options. He wanted to be a part of Sophia's life if he could. But he acknowledged that taking a traumatised teenager away from everything familiar to her, and bringing her to a new country, to a new life, and crucially to a stepmother who didn't want her, would be cruel.

He turned to Madame Duval and smiled warmly. "Thank you for your honesty. Would you mind if I made some suggestions about the arrangement?"

Madame Duval sat up straighter. "Of course, Monsieur."

The solicitor watched the exchange, his pencil poised. Everyone in Paris knew Henri Brienne. Maybe there was an opportunity for more business.

Henri guessed what the solicitor was thinking but ignored him and focused all his attention on Madame Duval. He liked her and understood why Nicole had entrusted their daughter to her. She was older than Nicole, which initially concerned him, but he could hardly criticise – they must have been similar ages. Henri promised to continue contributing towards Sophia's school fees and fund all her other living costs. What she inherited from her mother would be held in trust until she was older. The solicitor, seeing an opportunity, interjected.

"Monsieur, may we draw up an agreement to this effect? I'd be happy to arrange this."

Henri held up his hand firmly. "I have people who will do it. This unfortunate situation reminds us that we should all review our legal affairs periodically."

Henri briefly considered himself what he meant by this. In his heart, he knew he was also referring to Rita. He turned back to Madame Duval. "With your permission, I'd like to be part of Sophia's life. Maybe have dinner with her when I'm in Paris. Perhaps write letters to her. Would that be acceptable to you?"

Madame Duval beamed. "Monsieur, I am certain that would make Sophia very happy."

Henri took her hands into his own and beamed back at her.

The solicitor nodded, returning to the official paperwork. "There is just one final request in the will." All eyes back upon him, the solicitor adjusted his spectacles and continued reading. "A painting that was given to Nicole as a gift is to be returned to the person who gave it to her."

Henri closed his eyes, remembering the blonde woman he had once cared for deeply. Nicole had always said she would give the painting back to him. He had almost forgotten about it, although it was a sin to forget such a work of art. The romantic in Henri had been unable to resist buying it for her, as there was a startling resemblance between Nicole and the woman Renoir had painted. Nicole had been overwhelmed by the beautiful gift and had displayed it in her home ever since. The Renoir, purchased from a private gallery, was also an insurance policy for her and Sophia.

As Henri listened to Nicole's wishes being read, he genuinely marvelled at the lengths a mother would go to in order to protect her child. He was quite sure, by sharp comparison, he had never witnessed such maternal tenderness from Rita. Yet Nicole was right, this painting was already among the most sought after in the world, especially since Renoir's death in 1919. Nicole had had the canvas for almost twenty years, tucked away in a modest townhouse south of Paris. It was a risk to leave it with Madame Duval, which was why Nicole had made this particular request in her will.

The solicitor fetched the canvas from a large safe and handed it to Henri. Henri studied the Renoir and was struck by the delicate yet powerful way this exceptional artist captured emotion. He marvelled again at the striking resemblance of the portrait to Nicole. He knew instantly what he had to do.

"This belongs to Sophia," he said.

Madame Duval nodded with relief. "May I suggest, Monsieur, that you take the painting temporarily for safekeeping?" she said. "Sophia will be old enough to own it herself one day, and it will remind her of her mother."

"I agree. It will always be hers," Henri said.

And so, in that small, tired solicitor's office, the future fate of the painting was sealed.

❦ ❦ ❦

Madame Duval invited Henri back to her home later that afternoon for tea with herself and Sophia. Henri gratefully accepted. It would be an opportunity for father and daughter to meet again. He thanked her profusely and promised he would be there.

Seated in Madame Duval's living room several hours later, Henri sipped tea from a delicate china cup. He felt both nervous and excited. The front door opened and they heard Sophia arrive home. Henri's hand shook as he set his cup down.

"*Lou*?" Sophia called out.

Henri loved the sound of his daughter's French accent. Madame Duval smiled; Sophia had always called her by an abbreviation of her first name, Louise, she explained to Henri.

"In the lounge, my dear," Madame Duval called back.

They heard bags drop to the floor, and a few minutes later, the living room door opened. Sophia walked into the cosy, softly lit room, and caught sight of Henri. Her eyes told him she was pleased to see him.

"Hello," she said in flawless English.

Henri stood up. "Hello, Sophia. Thank you for agreeing to see me."

She gave a shy smile, and he noticed with delight that she bore a resemblance to him, just not her mother.

Madame Duval watched with interest, her arms crossed over her ample chest, her eagle eyes watching father and child.

Henri and Sophia eased into a comfortable conversation.

They talked about favourite songs, whether hot chocolate should be served with or without whipped cream, and paintings at the Louvre they loved.

Madame Duval replaced tea with sandwiches and later bowls of casserole, followed by coffee. It was only then they appeared to remember she was also in the room with them.

"Don't apologise," she said, holding up her hand while the other hand poured dark coffee into tiny cups. "It is wonderful to see you both talking so much."

Yes, they had missed out on many conversations over the years, Henri mused. He was determined to make up for lost time. He tried desperately not to think of Rita as he took Sophia's small hand and kissed it. This time, he was not going to let her go.

CHAPTER 27

Paris, 1935

Henri grinned as he watched Sophia run down the steps towards him, her nurse's cape and blonde hair flying behind her. She was late as usual. He glanced at his watch, rolling his eyes, but he didn't mind. He had been enjoying his second café au lait and reading the newspaper.

Several heads turned to admire Sophia as she weaved her way past people and tables, apologising profusely and earning smiles in return.

It was August 1935, and the sun was shining brilliantly across Paris. The city was teeming with people, although most Parisians took a vacation from July onwards.

Rita was already in St-Tropez with Noel, but as always Henri spent the first week of their summer break in Paris with his daughter. Sophia worked tirelessly as a nurse in the central hospital. Henri often remarked her shifts were gruelling, but she loved nursing. She was also dating one of the doctors. Henri frequently teased her that it was her boyfriend who kept her at the hospital beyond her usual shift, not the patients.

Spending time with Sophia constantly reminded him

how much energy young people possessed. Although, when he compared his two children, not all young people applied that energy quite so selflessly. Whereas Sophia had devoted her life to helping others, Noel seemed more of a gadabout. At fifteen, he indicated no ambition towards a particular career. His mother indulged him with fantasies of frolicking on the French Riviera once he left education. Henri hoped, by then, Noel would realise summer did eventually change into autumn, and the French Riviera would hold less appeal.

Not that anyone listened to Henri's opinion.

Henri had grown used to his wife and son pursuing their interests, regardless of him. Rita had distanced herself from her husband years ago. She had told him she would *never* welcome Sophia into their family, and Henri had informed her he would continue a relationship with his daughter no matter what she thought.

Rita's wrath had been wearing. She took any opportunity to mock, jibe, or be sarcastic. One day she pushed Henri too far, and he lifted his hand as though to strike her before abruptly pulling away. Rita punished him with silent, arctic hostility for the rest of the week.

But Rita was a very different person when she was in St-Tropez. Inebriated with sufficient French wine, it was possible to glimpse the carefree, funny, and charming woman he had fallen in love with. People, especially men, found her enchanting. She had invested considerable effort, time and money on maintaining her beauty as she matured. Even in a bathing suit, she could easily rival women half her age. Her skin was unlined and plump, her body lithe, and her hair as dark as it had been in her twenties. He missed the woman she had been back then.

Henri pushed Rita far from his mind as Sophia reached his table. She leaned down to kiss him.

"You look so well, Papa!" she said cheerily.

Papa. He loved hearing her call him that.

"I feel old," he complained, shrugging.

He had just turned seventy-three, and although he was quite spritely for his age, he had begun to feel the pangs of getting old. His hair was thinning, the skin under his chin was beginning to sag, and his hips seemed to creak. He had developed a growing list of ailments, including daily discomfort in his shoulders and arms.

They ordered coffee and a selection of pastries. Henri had just arrived in Paris, and they would meet later for dinner, after Sophia's shift at the hospital. Sophia ordered for them in flawless French, which Henri loved to hear. She spoke English equally as well, but like Henri, the French language was ingrained. She asked after Rita and Noel, as she always did. It touched him that after all these years of rejection by her stepmother, Sophia had the grace to be polite. It was a testament to her character, of which he was exceptionally proud. He told her as such, and she brushed the compliment away with a smile.

"And how are you, Papa?" she asked, her eyes searching his face.

It had only been two months since he had last been to Paris, but it felt longer. It always did. Sometimes he wondered if he should move back. Rita probably wouldn't even notice.

"I am fine, darling. Maybe a bit tired, but nothing to worry about."

Their coffee arrived along with warm croissants stuffed with ham and oozing cheese. They made general small talk as they sipped and nibbled, but Henri thought Sophia seemed distracted.

"Is something on your mind, Sophia? You've picked up that piece of croissant and put it back down several times."

She grinned and sat back in her seat, pushing the plate away.

"You know me too well, Papa."

"You knit your eyebrows in the same way I do when I have something on my mind," he said with amusement. "That's how I know."

"So now you tell me!" She laughed.

"I'm getting old. I may as well share a few secrets."

Sophia leaned over and took his hand. "Don't say you are old, Papa."

He knew she worried about losing him. Her mother dying at such a young age had left her with scars that would never heal.

"I'm sorry, that was insensitive of me," he said and gave her an apologetic smile. "So, what's on your mind?"

"I was going to talk to you about it over dinner tonight. Maybe we should wait..." her voice trailed off.

"No," he said firmly. "It will bother you all day. And me as well." He gently squeezed her hand reassuringly. "You can tell me anything."

Sophia signed and then nodded.

"I have been thinking about the painting of the woman

that looks like mama. You told me one day I could have it, but I feel so guilty asking," she said.

Henri turned her chin gently so that she faced him squarely.

"My darling girl, the painting is yours. I'm so sorry I haven't returned it to you. I promise the next time I see you in Paris I will have it with me. I know what it means to you."

Sophia pushed her chair back and reached forward to throw her arms around his neck. "Thank you, Papa!"

They spent the next hour lost in comfortable, animated conversation. The Parisian sunshine beamed down on them like a blessing.

When Sophia reluctantly got up to head back to the hospital, she held her father tightly, as she always did.

"I'll see you tonight," he said brightly.

"I love you, Papa. See you tonight."

Henri watched Sophia leave. She turned to wave just before disappearing. He shook his head and laughed as he saw her checking her watch, no doubt realising she was running late.

He decided to sit here a while longer. The sun felt warm, and he was enjoying the world revolving around him. Besides, he felt short of breath and had the rumblings of heartburn. It was unsurprising he was suffering from such discomfort, he chided himself, given the brunch they had just devoured.

Paris would always be his home. Henri *belonged* here. He had continued to stay at the house on the Champs-Élysées, although now the long halls were silent, and dust gathered on the furniture. Yet he felt happiest here, in the city he loved, with his daughter. It was nice to have those feelings of love reciprocated for a change.

Henri made a decision. He would return to Paris after St-Tropez, open the house up properly again and spend the majority of his time there. If Rita behaved petulantly about his decision, he would come back even sooner. He would hire servants, a chef, even a gardener. And as a priority, he would ship the Renoir back to Paris.

He felt motivated and excited, though his back ached. He'd been sitting down a long time and felt unbearably stiff. He stood up and stretched, deciding to go home and take a nap before dinner with Sophia tonight. He would tell her his plans then.

Back at the house, Henri turned the key in the lock, pushing his weight against the heavyset doors until they opened. The midday sun felt intolerable as he stumbled inside and tugged at the top button of his shirt. It had been a mistake to walk back. He mopped the sweat off his forehead with a handkerchief, steadying himself by holding onto the doorknob. A cool breeze of air greeted him from the marbled entrance hall – a welcome relief.

Closing the door behind him, Henri staggered into the hall, catching his breath. He felt his legs turn weightless beneath him as he tumbled towards the floor. The room began to spin, and his chest got progressively tighter. He opened an eye and saw the chandelier dangling above him. It really did look like angels' wings to him. Images darted through his mind of all the times he had looked up at this chandelier. The last time was Christmas Eve 1919 when Rita came down the stairs before dinner at the Ritz, a few months before they moved to

England. The same night he gave her the blue diamond.

He writhed in desperation as a crushing pain seized his chest, constricting it even tighter until his arms and legs abruptly flopped by his side. Henri's body lay motionless underneath the chandelier as fragments of tiny light bounced off the crystal and scattered across the floor. Thirty minutes earlier he had kissed his daughter goodbye. Neither of them had known it would be their final farewell.

CHAPTER 28

The weather in Paris refused to be bleak as the large group of mourners gathered for Henri's funeral. Those who knew Henri could well believe he had ordered the sunshine, set high in the flawless pale blue sky. The city he loved radiated an abundance of light as though to celebrate his life.

Friends and business associates who had travelled from England cursed the Parisian heat under their breaths, much preferring the more subdued English climate. Even though there were less than three hundred miles between Paris and London, the two cities may as well have been on opposite planets. Both British and French mourners, however, did have in common their respect and love for Henri Brienne and united on this, they filed into the church.

Senior politicians were in attendance as well as the Chief of Staff of the army, President of the Senate, businessmen from several countries, and many associates who came to pay their respects. Their cavalry included private bodyguards and police officers. Henri had few close colleagues, possibly his closest being his solicitor, Claude Bisset.

Claude sat ashen-faced next to Rita and Noel. A very challenging few days lay ahead of him. After the funeral would come the reading of Henri's will. He felt compelled to sit with Rita, but his eyes scoured the rows of faces for Sophia. Henri's daughter was a delightful girl, and Claude had grown very fond of her over the years.

Claude had been acutely aware that Rita had gone to great lengths not to publicise the funeral arrangements. He had sidestepped Rita's deliberate attempt to cut Sophia out of her father's funeral and informed her personally of where and when it would take place. Claude had never liked Rita. He disliked the woman even more now.

He glanced at Rita as she sat rigidly beside him. He watched her smooth her skirt and adjust her hat. She was a beautiful woman; there was no doubt about that. She wore sheer stockings and heels, a black blouse, and a small black veil to cover her face. Her lips were red, although a slightly softer shade than usual. Her eyes, however, were dry and devoid of emotion. He marvelled how she could shut herself off so easily. It was a well-practised skill, he was sure. It made him feel sorry for his friend, gone so suddenly, now laying in the coffin at the front of the church. It was French custom for the coffin to be open, but Rita had refused. It was not how things were done in England, she declared. Claude knew that Henri was only being buried in Paris because he had passed away here. If he had died in England, Claude could not imagine this sour-faced woman going to the trouble of reuniting him with his family plot in Paris.

As the mourners poured into the church, Claude glanced

around again. He nodded at faces he recognised. There was still no sign of Sophia. Settling back in his seat, Claude felt the chill emanate from Rita's arm as it brushed up against his. He wondered what had changed the carefree, happy woman he had met years ago. Henri had mentioned several times that having Sophia in his life had changed Rita, and Claude could understand that to an extent. But the situation with Sophia hadn't *changed* Rita; it had *corrupted* her.

He was anxious, wondering where Sophia was and what Rita would say if she saw her. Would Rita even know what Sophia looked like? Hopefully not, he thought. Claude looked at the coffin at the front of the church and decided his friend was in a safer place if she did.

Rita shifted in her seat, frowning. Her head throbbed, even though the church was quiet. Claude wouldn't stop wriggling next to her and appeared to want to acknowledge everyone he knew. She wanted to tell him it wasn't a social event but bit her bottom lip. They were in the front row; every row behind them was full. It was a highly visual testament to how many people loved and respected Henri. Regret gnawed at her – once, she too had been among Henri's admirers.

She had the unsettling feeling that his daughter would be here in the church somewhere. Sophia had been the unfortunate one who found him in the hallway of the Paris house. Rita closed her eyes and waved a fan in front of her face to quickly dry the lone tear that teetered on the edge of her lash. She visualised the entrance hall underneath the chandelier, recalling countless, wonderful memories of time spent with her husband in that house.

Before she left for England, she would go to the house in Paris. She wanted to see it one last time before she sold it. She had briefly considered keeping it, but she'd already had three agents provide a valuation for sale. The sum they suggested was staggering.

The choir stopped singing, nudging Rita's thoughts back to the service. She had bowed to French tradition, perhaps because she didn't have the energy to do otherwise, and the service was therefore lengthy. The endless, yet touching tributes appeared to go on for a considerable length of time.

She offered a faint smile to her son when he stood up, clutching a piece of crumpled paper in his hand. He read out a poem in flawless French, although Rita had no idea what he said. Despite his private education in England, he much preferred speaking French. A typical teenager, Noel would invariably find ways to provoke his mother. If she offered him toast for breakfast, he would ask for a croissant. During a heated argument, he would respond in French, because he knew she didn't understand. He had adopted many French customs, such as the French way to serve coffee, and he adored the smelliest of French cheeses. He had told her that one day, he would live in France.

Rita gently patted his hand when Noel sat back down beside her. Noel bent his head low and shrugged her affection aside, turning away. Rita gracefully folded her hands in her lap, leaving her son to handle his emotions in his own way. She was confident he would feel better when he was back beside the cobalt blue sea of St-Tropez, socialising with his friends in beachfront restaurants and relaxing in their villa.

As soon as the will was read the following afternoon, she would quickly conclude her business in Paris, and they would head south for St-Tropez.

Sophia crept into the church behind the late arrivals, nodded in by security. Claude had ensured her name was on the relevant guest list, unbeknown to Rita. She managed to weave her way slightly forward, enough to see her father's coffin.

A sob caught in her throat. She wanted to run to the front and touch the casket, just to feel near him again. The image of pushing open the doors and finding him on the marble floor would torment her forever. He had been dead for several hours by the time she found him. She had cradled him in her arms, only letting go when the ambulance crew gently peeled her away.

Sandwiched in-between black suits and dresses, Sophia listened to the voices from the front of the church. She couldn't take her eyes off the tall, lanky boy that stood up and read a poem she instantly recognised; she knew from photographs it was her half-brother, Noel. He didn't look like their father, which always surprised her. She watched him walk back to his seat. Next to him, she recognised Claude. The woman whose face was concealed by an elaborate black veil, she assumed was Rita.

She lowered her head when the service was over, as the chief mourners led the way out of the church behind the coffin. Claude gently touched her hand as he passed. She lifted her head and smiled weakly. He had told her she needed to be at his office promptly at 1:30 pm the day after the funeral. She had begged him not to have to go, but he told her there was no choice.

Sophia shrunk back against the crowd of people as Rita walked past. Yet it was intoxicating seeing Rita this close: the sound of her heels on the stone floor, the heady scent of her perfume, the way her hair bounced as she moved.

Sophia's palms and face felt hot suddenly. Tomorrow she would meet her stepmother face-to-face for the first time.

Claude's offices in central Paris were light and airy with a view across the Seine. The main reception desk was large and highly polished, with paperwork stacked neatly on top. Claude was waiting by the desk, talking to one of the other Senior Partners when Sophia arrived. Sophia walked towards him, looking like a young doe. The other man patted Claude on the back.

"Good luck," he said enthusiastically.

"I'd rather be fastening a firestick to a tiger's tail," replied Claude and sighed. His colleague stifled a smile and walked off down the corridor before Sophia heard them.

"Hello, Sophia." Claude kissed her cheeks, affectionately. He noticed she was shaking as he pulled away.

Rita had already arrived and was waiting in his office.

He had just dropped the bombshell that Sophia would be attending the reading. Rita's shrill response had been heard all the way down the corridor to the reception desk.

The receptionist peered over her glasses sympathetically at Sophia, who looked exceptionally pretty in a plain white linen dress, her hair tied back, and wearing only the tiniest hint of make-up.

Claude gave Sophia a few moments to gather herself before leading the way to his office. There was an unmistakeable tension in the air. Claude had left Rita pacing furiously when he told her Sophia had arrived. He tentatively opened the door to his office and saw that Rita was seated with her back to them. Sophia demurely sat down in the seat Claude had left out for her. Rita twisted her body away, refusing to acknowledge her.

Claude sat down at his desk opposite them. Deciding there would be no need for introductions or pointless pleasantries, he reached for his spectacles and read the will of Henri Brienne in full.

Afterwards, he pushed his spectacles further up his nose and tilted his head, allowing for the bifocals to bring the two women who sat in front of him into focus. Sophia was deathly pale. Rita looked like she was about to explode.

"I will contest it," she said icily.

Claude had been expecting her to say this.

"On what grounds, Rita?" Claude was calm. "Henri revised his will almost five years ago, lodging it through all the formal channels. He was of sound body and mind. He appointed executors and an impartial legal firm, *and* had the document witnessed by highly regarded professionals. It might even be embarrassing for you to contest it."

Rita's face turned crimson, her eyes blazed. "I am his *wife*. She..." Rita turned to Sophia, "is his *bastard*."

Sophia flinched, but Claude shrugged dismissively.

"Henri *obviously* did not see Sophia this way," he said.

Rita slammed her hands down on Claude's desk, her veins visibly pulsating. It was impossible not to notice the blue diamond iridescent on her finger. Rita swung round to face Sophia, jabbing a finger at her. "*She* will get nothing," she seethed.

Claude pounced. "You do not have that influence, Madame Brienne. The will is legal and binding. The executors, of which you are not one, have full power to carry out Henri's wishes." He stood up, signalling the meeting was over.

Rita took a sharp intake of breath. "Claude, you will regret this," she vowed.

Unimpressed, Claude looked her straight in the eye. "Given your behaviour, my dear, I suspect not as much as Henri did marrying you. Good day to you."

Open-mouthed, Rita pushed back her chair and stormed out of the room, angrily rubbing the tears off her cheeks.

Claude slumped in his seat. "I should not have said that – it was unnecessary."

Sophia reached over and took his hand reassuringly. "I can't imagine Papa with her."

Claude shook his head, wishing his old friend had chosen differently. He turned back to Sophia, who was still in shock. "You need to get some investment advice now. You are a very wealthy young woman."

She nodded quietly. Henri had left her the house in Paris, which had been Rita's tipping point, plus a substantial trust fund.

The figures were lodged officially on the paperwork and undisputed. Henri had left half of his overall wealth to his daughter – his wife and son shared the remainder.

Sophia left Claude's office and strolled back over the bridge with the Seine gently flowing beneath her. She was in shock. Her heart rate had not slowed down since the confrontation with Rita. She had never expected her father to leave her such a vast fortune. She hooked her arms over the edge of the cool concrete bridge and closed her eyes. She missed her father desperately. She could still hear his voice, smell his cologne, feel his soft stubble on her cheek when she kissed him goodbye.

Not far from here was her father's house. Her house now. She felt giddy with disbelief and, if she was honest, excitement. It was a beautiful building, and she would never sell it. She lifted her head and opened her eyes as it dawned on her that he must have known that. It was why he had left it to her.

But one thought weighed heavily on her mind. There had been no specific mention of the Renoir in her father's will. That was the sole reason she had gone to the reading – she had felt certain the painting was the only thing he would leave to her. It was a mystery why he hadn't done so. Perhaps he didn't want Rita to find out about the painting. Perhaps he had intended to return it long before he passed, but fate had caught him out.

There was no way Sophia could simply ask her stepmother for the Renoir or offer to buy it. The sentimental value would provoke Rita to damage or destroy it. Of that Sophia was certain. It needed to remain invisible among other paintings hanging unappreciated and unloved until enough time had passed for Rita to forget about its existence.

Sophia made a promise to herself. She didn't care if she had to pay for someone to steal it with their bare hands; the Renoir would one day return to her in Paris where it belonged.

PART SIX

CHAPTER 29

London, 1968

Charlie had promised Maggie a September wedding, and true to his word, two weeks after the blue diamond went on her finger to confirm their engagement, a cream Rolls Royce pulled up outside her home just after 2 pm to take her to the registry office. The driver got out and rolled a cigarette. He was early.

Maggie stood at her bedroom window, shouting for her mother to come quickly and see the car. Two long, white ribbons had been tied to the bonnet of the Spirit of Ecstasy and stretched back over the car like wings in full flight. The wheels shone like mirrors, and the paintwork gleamed.

Maggie's mother, Linda, rushed into the room. "Oh my, look at that car!" She peeked behind the net curtains, noticing a neighbour doing the same. Tutting, Linda dropped the netting.

In the bedroom that had once been her nursery, Maggie gently swayed her hips which were swathed in yards of white satin and lace. It had not been easy getting the dress to fit over her bump; the dressmakers had made final adjustments only the day before.

"What do you think, Mum?" Maggie asked.

Linda stood back to appraise her daughter and felt a wave of tiredness wash over her. She'd been on the go since seven o'clock that morning, making endless cups of tea, spritzing countless shots of hairspray, and adjusting the ribbons at the back of the dress several times. Her own hair was still in curlers.

"You look…" She paused, trying to find the right words. "You look like an angel."

Maggie squeezed her mother's hand, handing her a tissue.

"Stop, Mum. We'll both be crying in a minute."

A song by the Beatles came on the radio, lifting the mood. Maggie turned up the volume and the women sang along to the chorus together, feeling giddy with excitement.

"I'd better go and get these curlers out," Linda said, suddenly flustered, and scurried out of the room.

Maggie stood in front of the mirror, smoothing down her dress. She touched her necklace which was interlaced with pearls and tiny diamonds. She had recently bought it from a boutique jeweller's at Hatton Garden, parting with an entire bundle of rolled-up notes – it was to be her something *new*. Her hair had been swept up into a twist, pinned into position with hundreds of hairpins. The thin tiara on her head had been her mother's, which she'd borrowed. She checked that the delicate, lace handkerchief was neatly folded and tucked into her clutch bag. It had once belonged to her grandmother, Violet. Her mother guessed it must have been in the drawer for at least forty years. She smiled at the thought; something *old*.

Maggie lifted her hand, swivelling the blue diamond around until it sat perfectly central on her finger. She couldn't help wondering if any other woman had worn this diamond on their wedding day. It was a strange subject to enter her thoughts just hours before her wedding, yet she couldn't stop thinking about it. Charlie had told her the diamond had originated in South Africa. The exotic location made the ring seem even more mysterious. Who were these other women from whom this ring had been passed down?

Her brow knit in concentration as she watched the blue light of the diamond flicker and sparkle. Aware of a movement towards the back of the room, she turned her head. "Mum? Is that you?"

After a pause, her mother's voice echoed from the bedroom down the corridor. "I won't be long!" she chirped.

Strange, thought Maggie. She had been certain someone was in the room. She shrugged – her nerves were fraught; that would probably explain it.

Half an hour later, Maggie lifted her dress to walk down the stairs, treading carefully onto each step. Her mother had just slipped a sixpence into her shoe, which wasn't altogether comfortable.

Her father, Jim, waited for her at the bottom of the stairs.

"You look handsome, Dad," Maggie said as she dropped the layers of her dress to the floor. "Are you alright?" she asked, noticing he was unusually mute.

"I'm… I… Maggie, you are beautiful." He gently touched her arm, afraid to mess up any part of her ensemble. "I'm so proud of you."

She gasped, and tears immediately sprang to her eyes. Her father had *never* said those words to her before.

Jim held out his arm and helped her negotiate the narrow hallway and front door. Outside, their neighbours stood on the pavement to glimpse the bride – many of them remembered the day Maggie arrived home in her mother's arms.

The driver opened the door of the gleaming Rolls Royce. There was suddenly chatter, noise and squeals of excitement as little girls left their mothers' sides and rushed to see the pretty bride.

Maggie laughed as she backed into the seat, swinging her legs inside, and hauling in the heaps of fabric, making sure nothing got too creased. Jim got in beside her and squeezed her hand.

As the car slowly eased away from the curb, everyone called out their good wishes, shouting "Good luck, Maggie!" Maggie waved back in response. It was a moment she would never forget.

Charlie stood by the steps of the registry office in an immaculately pressed suit. A starched white handkerchief with his initials, CW, was tucked into his breast pocket. His hair had been combed until the quiff was perfect – not a single hair was out of place.

He saw the Rolls Royce and quickly threw his freshly lit cigarette down, extinguishing it with a sharp twist of his shiny leather shoe. He hurried inside and took up his position, shuffling nervously from foot to foot. The voices in the room became hushed whispers and were finally drowned out as their chosen song, 'Stand By Me' by Ben E. King started playing.

Charlie knew Maggie would walk through that door any second. It was unbearably warm in the registrar's office, even though the windows were open. He loosened the collar of his shirt, which had started to choke him, then took a deep calming breath.

Plain and rather unattractive blinds shielded the view from the windows. There wasn't as much as a breeze entering the room. The music continued to play. Charlie twitched nervously. How long was this song going to last? he wondered.

There was a pause as the song came to an end and the next one, 'Here Comes The Bride', began. There was a shift in energy as everyone sitting in the chairs stood up and turned to face the door. Charlie swivelled on his heel and faced the aisle. He lifted his head and waited until his eyes found hers. He was filled with pure joy as he watched Maggie take slow, elegant steps towards him, holding onto her father's arm. He absorbed every detail: her brilliant white dress encrusted with tiny pearls, the delicate lace veil flowing down her back, and her painted pink nails. She clutched a small bouquet, and when she finally reached his side, he could smell the sweetness of lily of the valley. He knew the scent well; it was her favourite. Lily of the valley was out of season, so the florist had offered white freesias as an alternative, but Charlie insisted on following Maggie's wishes and hadn't hesitated to pay a staggering sum for the delicate white scented bells.

The music faded just as Maggie eased her arm from her father's and took Charlie's hands. The registrar glanced around the room, waiting for the shuffles and whispers to silence, and then turned to the bride and groom with a beaming smile.

The ceremony was conducted pleasantly yet formally, reinforcing the binding laws of marriage and commitment. Everyone was silent as the registrar spoke, and Charlie and Maggie exchanged their vows.

Charlie held the blue diamond in his hand as he lowered the wedding band carefully onto Maggie's finger. It reminded him briefly of the night he had stolen the diamond ring. He replaced the engagement ring on her finger and their eyes fell upon the two rings side-by-side, representing love and togetherness.

"May I present Mr and Mrs White," the registrar announced proudly to the room. People cheered and called out their congratulations as Charlie leaned forward and kissed his new bride tenderly.

"I love you, Maggie White," he said.

Maggie's eyelashes fluttered rapidly, dispersing tears.

Charlie offered his arm, and they walked down the aisle and outside into the lovely September sunshine. Confetti danced in the air around them as the photographer worked tirelessly taking pictures of the happy couple. Afterwards, the Rolls Royce took them to an exclusive restaurant in Kensington, although several guests may have choked on the perfectly pink fillet of beef had they known the cost of the meal. Champagne flowed, laughter filled the private room, and when everyone left just before midnight, Charlie and Maggie were driven home.

Their home was a pretty white townhouse, which they

had only moved into the week before. Maggie hadn't spent a single night there yet, but already there were dozens of bags and boxes piled up high in every room, waiting for her to unpack. New furniture sat awkwardly in unopened boxes, many of them delivered straight from the department stores. There hadn't been any time to get properly moved in and settled before the wedding.

Outside the house, Charlie looked at the half-dozen steps leading to the front door. "I think I've drunk too much champagne to carry you over the threshold," he said, pulling a face.

Maggie laughed and swiped him with her bouquet. She knew she should have followed tradition and thrown the flowers to the guests outside the registry office, but it was only a small gathering, and besides, she couldn't bear to let her flowers go.

"I think you mean I'm too heavy," she said.

Charlie simply replied with the smile that had won her heart the first time they met. He helped her inside and let her scream and fuss over the several dozen roses he had organised, and then he slipped outside for a smoke.

Charlie had a job coming up in the next few days, which wasn't ideal timing, but Bobby didn't trust anyone else. It would pay well, but the caveat was if he got caught, he would go to prison for a very long time. In his line of work, the balance of risk and reward was always on a razor edge, especially a few days after getting married and with a baby due any day.

Maggie was so preoccupied with opening boxes and settling into their new home that she didn't complain too much when Charlie said he had to go away.

"At least you will be out from under my feet, Charlie White."

Truthfully, she was disappointed. But she wasn't going to start nagging less than a week into their marriage. Maggie understood as few women did that Charlie had to work. Money didn't fall from the sky after all.

"At least you won't have to cook for me," Charlie teased.

She pretended to agree then they both laughed. Maggie had not cooked a single meal since they moved in. Her mother arrived every day with pies, casseroles, and Tupperware brimming with trifles, or cakes.

"Mum, people will think I'm just fat, not pregnant if you don't stop," Maggie had said, glancing out at the street before shutting the door firmly behind her mother.

Linda began to stock the fridge with a variety of meals, telling her daughter how to re-heat each one as she loaded it onto the shelf. "Do you want me to stop?" she asked, turning round to face Maggie.

"Never." Maggie declared with feeling.

Mother and daughter knew there was more truth than jest in what Maggie said. Both women worked tirelessly in the house, unpacking and rearranging. Maggie fussed and fretted about the cot and baby clothes. There was so much left to organise. The chaos kept her busy, and from thinking about what her husband might be doing.

CHAPTER 30

In theory, the job was simple. Charlie had to drive a van to Scotland and drive it back the following day. The back of the van was stacked with what appeared to be large cans of paint, sealed as if they were brand-new and never opened. Inside the cans were stashed bags of tightly wrapped bundles of cash. Charlie would exchange the cans of paint for similar cans of paint containing packages of cocaine. The street value was phenomenal, as was the risk.

He looked over the van he was using, appraising it as a suitable cover. It had false number plates, fictitious company details plastered down both sides, and looked suitably battered and bruised. Inside, it even smelt of tools and paint – a proper decorator's van. Charlie reluctantly removed his leather jacket and pulled on a pair of dusty overalls. But he refused to mess up his sleek hair. Surely even painters and decorators kept a comb in their overall pockets, he reasoned. He found a cap on the driver seat; Bobby knew him well. His hair was the only thing he was precious about, but he'd wear the damned cap.

The paint cans were already loaded, and the tyres inflated

with extra air. Charlie never, ever asked how much cash he was carrying. Bobby would have told him, but Charlie always held his hand up to stop him. He jokingly said it might soften his nerve if he knew.

"I'd better not tell you what you're bringing back then, or how much," Bobby had said drily.

"I know what I'm bringing back. But I don't want to know how much until I get back with it. Or you can visit me when I'm banged up and tell me," Charlie replied.

Although they had laughed, there was an undercurrent of tension in their exchange. Charlie knew this was a big job, and there would be no defence if he got caught.

He climbed into the van, laid the map flat on the seat beside him, rammed the engine into first gear, and flicked on the radio. Bobby Blower shook his head and grinned as Charlie took off with 'Jailhouse Rock' blaring out of the open windows.

Charlie's meticulous planning estimated a ten-hour drive, with a stop in Manchester. He wouldn't dare leave the van and would sleep bolt upright in the driver's seat, reclining it as far back as he could and tipping the cap over his eyes. If he got stopped by police, he had a plan A and a plan B, depending on what happened. He adopted the behaviour of a legitimate workman, playing the part like a true actor. He whistled to music, banged his hands on the steering wheel in time to his favourite tunes and flicked countless cigarette butts out the window.

He forced himself to take regular breaks and a short nap on the journey. He couldn't take the risk of falling asleep at the wheel and drawing attention to himself. Waking up from a brief doze, he rubbed a small amount of cocaine on his gums to keep alert and washed it down with coffee sweetened with two sugars. He had brought a flask and homemade sandwiches that were neatly wrapped in greaseproof paper, just like regular workmen. In the footwell, a collection of wrappers and leftovers had already accumulated. Usually, he hated mess, but Charlie was enjoying the novelty of playing a part. The corner of his mouth twitched whenever he saw a police car, but he didn't even look at them; he just carried on singing and driving.

It had taken Bobby years to negotiate and organise this deal. The purity of the cocaine was around ninety per cent, which was almost unheard of, and the volume being traded was one of the highest ever attempted. A trawler carried it from The Netherlands, but before then a complex ghost network had moved it around. This run was a trial. If successful, more frequent and even larger volumes would follow. It was like exposing a vein to see how easily the blood would flow.

Bobby had let Charlie go alone. A second man would have made the job lighter, but Bobby knew not to question Charlie about his decision to go solo. If he was happy to lug the heavy paint pots by himself and take the fallout from any disaster, Bobby would trust him.

By the time Charlie pulled into Peterhead in the small hours of the morning, he was physically and mentally wired. The address was a block of garages near a row of houses. If anyone stopped him, his alibi was well-rehearsed. He was packing his van for an early start on a job, which was technically correct after all. Charlie had to work fast, knowing every second could make a difference. The trawler had arrived into Peterhead the night before, and the garage would now have been stocked with paint cans full of cocaine. He observed a light above the garage door was on; this signalled the job was ready for him.

Using the key Bobby had given him, Charlie quietly opened the garage door. He was on full alert for anything unexpected. He stood back from the open doorway and waited a few moments. No one rushed out. Pushing the garage door up to its full height, Charlie walked inside, poised to attack or defend at any given moment. His van headlights shone fingers of light into the garage, but they barely penetrated the darkness inside.

Charlie saw the paint cans piled high, sealed tightly. Bobby had told him the deal was good, but Charlie preferred to check. If he was going to get caught, it would be for the real thing. Using his knife, he burrowed through the seal, ripping the lid wide open. Inside were neatly stacked blocks of tightly wrapped white powder. He bore into a random one with his knife, extracting a generous scoop. Even in the faint light, the powder was not the consistency he expected. But when he inhaled some up his nostril, he knew for sure. It probably wasn't even cocaine. Bobby had been set-up.

How Charlie behaved now was critical. He had to play along. There was a good chance someone was watching from a distance. He lifted the cans from his van and carried them into the garage. But instead of exchanging them for the ones filled with drugs, he carried the same ones back out again. It was an onerous task, but crucial. It looked as though the cash had been switched with the cocaine and the deal completed. If the police were behind the set-up, he was done for either way. It would be marginally simpler if he only got caught with the cash, however. He'd sit through the interrogation, shrugging off their questions, playing psychological games with the officers in front of him. They would let him go eventually. He was fairly confident about that. The only high-risk element of this job had been carrying back the cocaine. But now, that risk had been eliminated.

He finished off-loading and re-loading the cans then quietly drove off with Bobby's cash still in the back of the van. Stopping down a quiet residential street, Charlie threw the cap off and wriggled out of the overall. He was Charlie White now, not some poxy decorator. He was doing what he loved, and what he did best.

Making sure the van was locked, and there was no one loitering around suspiciously, Charlie crept back to the garages. He had a hunch that whoever was behind the set-up would appear before long. If the police were involved, Charlie would take a very different route back to London or change his plan entirely. He crouched down low beside a line of trees next to the garages and waited.

For almost two hours, Charlie sat there, occasionally lighting a cigarette to pass the time. His legs ached, and his mouth felt parched, but his gut feeling told him to be patient a little while longer.

Finally, a car pulled up. Charlie watched two men get out. One of them pulled a long jumper down over his bulging stomach, sliding his fingers underneath to twist his belt around until he was more comfortable. He ran his fingers through slicked ginger hair then wiped his hands down the legs of his jeans. Charlie squinted to see better in the dark. The man didn't look like a copper. Neither did his companion, who opened a can of beer and slurped it thirstily, wiping splashes of foam from his beard with the back of his hand.

Charlie crept forward, trying to listen. The men's Scottish accent was thick and they spoke fast. He couldn't decipher anything they said, and certainly nothing of interest. It didn't make sense why these two oiks were handling a job this big.

Charlie cursed silently to himself. He could have, *should* have, driven straight back to London. He'd just got married, and his wife was due to give birth any day. A few weeks earlier he'd been sat in prison. Yet Charlie was riled. He'd been about to leave a serious amount of cash in an abandoned garage and take an unknown substance, which wasn't cocaine, back to Bobby. Charlie had already decided he needed to take back more than just the cash. He'd tucked a bag of the fake cocaine in the glove compartment of the van. He was also going to take these two men.

He watched them lift the garage door and step inside. He knew he had a split second opportunity to surprise them. He pulled his knife out of his pocket, leapt to his feet, and sprinted towards the garage. He rolled under the man-sized gap of the partially opened garage door. Pulling himself quickly up onto his feet, a heavy blow caught his cheek, and he tasted blood. Then adrenaline took over. He picked up a paint can and swung it at one of the men. It smashed into his belly, sending him reeling. The second man lunged towards Charlie, but

Charlie was faster and more nimble. He ducked, and sprung the pocketknife open. He pushed it deep into the man's leg several times until he buckled. Charlie hit, punched, and kicked his assailants until bones cracked and blood squirted. Both men lay still, clutching their injuries.

Charlie shook his head; he had expected more of a fight. Again, it irked him why these two imbeciles had been sent to pick up the cash. The job was top-end. Huge. He had assumed elite criminals would be handing the entire operation. Bobby would have to work that one out, he decided.

Lighting a cigarette, he quickly tied the men up and stuffed their mouths with shreds of material he'd ripped from their shirts. He figured they'd be quiet until he came back with the van and they'd probably stay silent for most of the long drive back to London.

Charlie tipped cocaine from a small bag tucked in his leather jacket onto the lid of one of the paint cans. He cut two neat lines and shot one straight up each nostril: one for the extreme tiredness he felt and the other for luck. He'd be driving home with two Scotsmen tied up alongside several hundred thousand pounds rolled up in paint cans. He'd need all the luck he could get.

CHAPTER 31

Maggie eased herself into the bathtub. The warm water felt heavenly as the muscles in her back began to unknot. Her back had been aching all day. She was staying with her mum while Charlie was away. She felt too shattered to look after herself as well as a new house.

She had spent the last few days at her own home, unpacking suitcases and boxes. Furniture had been fixed into place, bedlinen ironed and smoothed onto beds, and the kitchen filled with pots and pans. Even the nursery had been finished. It had been a mammoth task, but finally, the place looked and felt like a real home. But with Charlie away she missed having company and felt slightly anxious on her own. Living back with her mother at least meant Linda didn't have to bring food all the way across town to her.

It struck Maggie as ironic that she had been desperate to be married and have her own home, yet here she was in her family's bathtub as always. Not quite the start to married life she'd dreamed about. But perhaps it was just her hormones making her morose, she decided.

She could smell fresh bread baking, and if her nose was correct, there was roast chicken too. The bath water had cooled, and her skin had turned wrinkly. Heaving herself up, she suddenly felt a bulging pressure in her abdomen followed by a strange pop.

Reaching for a towel, she quickly dried herself, but it was clear by then her waters had broken.

"Mum? Can you come here?" Maggie called, trying to keep her voice even.

"What is it?" replied Linda from downstairs in the kitchen. "I'm just peeling the potatoes, love. Can it wait?"

Maggie felt her tummy tighten like an elastic band and then release. "No!" she yelled, panic rising.

Maggie heard her mother's rapid footsteps on the stairs.

Linda knocked on the bathroom door. "Maggie, love, are you alright?"

"I think it's time."

There was a pause as Linda composed herself.

"Open the door, Maggie."

The bathroom door opened, and Linda pushed her way inside. Maggie was already on the floor, clutching her stomach.

"Jim?" Linda shouted down the stairs, her voice shrill. "You'd better run to the phone box and call the midwife. The number's on the hall table."

They heard something drop on the floor, followed by silence, then footsteps out in the hall. A few moments later, there was the sound of the front door closing. Maggie and her mother exchanged a look. He'd be heading for The Stag's Head afterwards. The baby would probably arrive long before he returned home.

Linda helped Maggie to her bedroom and onto the bed. She sank back against the pillows, bracing herself. There was no way to avoid the pain of childbirth, she knew that, but at the same time, she just wanted to run away. As the practicalities of what was about to happen set-in, she began to focus. When the pain came in overwhelming surges, she squeezed the pillow her mother gave her and gritted her teeth. The agony was unrelenting, with only fleeting moments when the tightening, pulling and pushing subsided just long enough for her to take a deep breath. The midwife was visibly impressed when she arrived. The room was ready, Maggie was panting, and Linda had a pot of tea brewing. It looked extremely civilised.

The atmosphere grew gradually more charged over the next few hours. Maggie's pain rose to an intense pitch, and after several cups of tea, the midwife finally whispered to Linda. "The baby is big."

Maggie released a hideous wail as the midwife and Linda stopped and stared at her. She looked almost demonic.

"I can't do this!" Maggie hissed through clenched teeth.

Linda sat down next to her daughter, wishing she could help more but knowing there was little she could do. Encouragement at this late stage was the equivalent of applying a plaster to a deep flesh wound. She was almost afraid to say or do anything now that Maggie was hysterical.

"Right." The midwife drew back her shoulders and seemed to have formulated a plan of action. "Let's move you onto your front, up on all fours."

"What?!" said Linda, shocked.

"It's a new position that some mothers find works very well," the midwife replied brusquely. And besides," she continued as she helped Maggie manoeuvre, "we are running out of options."

Linda knew running out of options meant calling in the doctor, which could result in a forceps delivery, involving irreversible physical and mental scarring. "Alright, let's move her," agreed Linda.

Another hour passed and still, no baby arrived. The midwife coaxed Maggie kindly but firmly, and things finally started happening. The baby's head became tantalisingly visible then disappeared back inside again. Maggie seemed to be running out of energy – her face sagged with exhaustion, her hair matted to her head with sweat.

"I can't do this anymore," Maggie sobbed. "Just let me sleep," she begged.

"Right, let's get some food in you," said the midwife. "Linda, can you fetch some biscuits? Linda? Did you hear me?" she repeated, exasperated.

Linda shook her head.

"Do you have any biscuits, Linda?" The midwife spoke slowly and calmly.

Linda looked shocked at the idea of biscuits at such a critical time, but she did as she was instructed and rushed downstairs. A few minutes later, she returned with honey and oat biscuits, baked only that morning.

The midwife nodded her approval. She put her arms around Maggie to support her weight and motioned to Linda to help at the other side. "Maggie, I want you to turn over for a moment."

They heaved Maggie over and sat her up. The midwife handed her the small plate of biscuits. "Eat these. Just one will be fine."

Maggie didn't have the energy to do anything but obey. She ate the biscuit followed by some water.

The midwife looked pleased. "That, my dear, will give you the energy you need to push this baby out." She turned to Linda. "We'd better have one too, don't you think?"

Linda nodded, and for a surreal moment, all three women silently munched the biscuits. The midwife swept a few stray crumbs from her skirt and turned to Maggie, a look of determination on her face. Maggie nodded back, knowing that the midwife was telling her it was time. Maggie was ready. She looked ahead, focused on what she had to do.

The midwife repeated words Maggie would never want to hear again once this was over, "Push and pant, push and pant."

It was all she heard and all she did. The pain intensified, but Maggie kept going. Finally, on the wave of a forceful contraction, the baby whooshed out and lay motionless on the bed. Maggie began screaming as the midwife turned the baby upside down. Seconds passed that felt like hours. Then they heard a loud and gusty cry. The midwife quickly wiped away tears of relief and joy before wrapping the baby up in a clean, warm towel.

She leaned over Maggie, whose cheeks were wet with a mix of tears and sweat. "May I present your daughter? She's made quite an entrance, wouldn't you say?"

Maggie touched her baby's silky black hair for the first time, in awe of the angry little face staring back at her. Linda couldn't resist holding out her arms to take her first grandchild, feeling her heart melt. The little girl looked at her grandmother with wide eyes, flexing her tiny fingers. Maggie was surprised at the instant connection Linda had with the baby, talking to her as though they were the only two people in the whole world. Maggie had never expected to feel such overwhelming love for the baby herself and was doubly shocked to see her mother talk with such unbridled tenderness.

"What are you going to call her?" the midwife asked.

Maggie had thought about this a lot. If she had a girl, she wanted to call her something that was associated with the name Maggie, or Margaret. She had considered the name Peggy – it was a sweet name, but it didn't suit the little girl in her arms. Rita, another derivative, also felt wrong somehow. Marjorie was a pretty name, but Linda was adamant on that one – the landlady at the Stag's Head was named Marjorie, and Linda often accused Jim of having a soft spot for her, so that was out.

"What about Daisy?" Linda suggested.

Maggie had read in a baby name book that Daisy was a French nickname for Margaret, and she was instantly drawn to the name. Neither Linda nor Maggie could think of anyone else they knew who was called Daisy. It was a unique name for a unique baby, they decided.

"Will Charlie like it?" Linda asked.

Maggie laughed. "He won't have much choice. We agreed he could name a boy, and I could name a girl. I always knew I was having a girl."

"How did you know?" the midwife asked, bemused.

"Just a feeling," Maggie said, contented.

Grandmother, mother and daughter enjoyed a few more precious moments of silent contemplation. Then Linda suddenly jumped up and rushed from the room. Maggie heard her rummaging around in her bedroom, pulling out drawers and banging open and shut her wardrobe door. She returned a few minutes later with a small box.

"This was given to you by your grandmother, Violet, at your Christening. You'll see why when you look at it. Quick, open it." She handed the box to Maggie, beaming at her excitedly.

Maggie opened the box and pulled out a small necklace with a tiny pearl in the centre of it. Confused, she looked back at her mother.

"It's lovely, Mum. But why is a pearl necklace so significant at a Christening? I don't understand."

"Your name, Maggie, means Margaret. Yes?" Linda said.

Maggie nodded wearily.

"Well, the name Margaret means 'pearl'. That's why your grandmother got this necklace for you. And if Margaret means pearl, then *Daisy* also means pearl! So this is for her."

Maggie touched Daisy's soft cheek, marvelling at how perfect she was. Her diamond ring shone bluer than ever against the baby's milky skin. She felt quite overwhelmed at the thought that one day it would belong to her daughter. An unusual smell wafted under her nose and pulled her out of her reverie. Knitting her brow, she turned to her mother. "Mum, what's that smell?"

Linda looked at the baby, but Maggie shook her head.

"No, it's a strange smell. Like one of those incense sticks. Can't you smell it?"

"No, I can't," replied Linda, shrugging.

Maggie tilted her head and breathed in deeply. It was a pleasant smell – sweet but woody. She had never smelt anything quite like it before so had no frame of reference. But somehow it triggered something in her memory. The smell intensified, filling all her senses. It became so strong that it was as though there must be something burning right next to her. Linda and the midwife exchanged bewildered looks. They could smell nothing. With a shake of her head, and putting it down to a fresh batch of hormones, Maggie gave up trying to fathom out what it was or where it was coming from. She was too physically and emotionally drained to think about it.

Linda retrieved her granddaughter from Maggie's arms and began rocking her, gently humming a song.

Maggie listened carefully. "I've never heard you hum before, Mum."

"Me neither, I just felt like it." She gave a relaxed laugh and snuggled the baby closer before commencing to hum again.

Maggie frowned, her mind now drifting back to that strange scent in the room. Somewhere at the back of her mind she vaguely remembered reading that some cultures burnt a special blend of herbs and plants when a child was born, to cleanse the air and protect the spirit of the baby. She seemed to think drumbeats, or perhaps humming, was part of the ceremony too.

She sniffed the air again, but the scent had faded. She

glanced at the small pearl necklace left on the bedside table and smiled, remembering her grandmother, Violet.

Maggie loved knowing her name was linked to her daughter's, and that it had a shared meaning: pearl. She wondered if she might have another daughter one day – if so, she would continue the tradition. If not, perhaps Daisy would.

Maggie used her elbows to lift herself up slightly and get more comfortable in bed. As she did so, her ring caught on a stray loop of the woollen blanket and twisted, gently pinching the skin of her swollen fingers. The South African blue diamond shone steadfastly as always. Maggie touched it with the finger of her other hand, feeling the smooth surface and the platinum claws holding the jewel firmly in place. She felt her eyelids get heavy and begin to droop as she nestled against the soft pillows.

Her mind was foggy as she dozed and drifted into a dream. She could see a handful of dried plants, or herbs, burning. She tried to reach them, but the smoke masked her view, making her feel as though she was wading through clouds. Anxious, Maggie walked faster, trying to push the fog away with her hands. It swirled around her, creating ringlets of pale grey smoke. She could hear drumbeats getting louder and louder. Suddenly, they stopped. A young woman with long dark hair and blue eyes emerged from the smoke. The woman smiled, offering a small hand for Maggie to take. Maggie shook her head. The woman smiled again then sat down. She was clutching a teacup. She swirled it around and appeared to be peering inside. Maggie felt herself walking backwards, hearing a baby cry. *Her* baby.

Her eyelids fluttered open to reveal her bedroom. She felt heavy with exhaustion. Her mind began to drift once more, thinking of her new baby, Pearl. No, *not* Pearl – Daisy.

She felt someone tugging her arm gently.

"Maggie, love? I've put a cup of tea on the side for you," Linda said.

A cup of tea. Maggie could still see the woman holding the teacup in her dream. A woman she felt she should have known somehow. But the memory was just out of reach.

"Thanks Mum," Maggie said, watching her mother cradling baby Daisy. "Mum? Is it normal after giving birth to feel a bit… strange?"

Her mother laughed. "Completely normal. Welcome to motherhood!"

Maggie half-heartedly joined in the laughter. No, 'strange' wasn't the right word for what she was feeling right now. The smell, the humming, the drumbeat… the dream… they had all felt very… There wasn't a word to explain it after all.

CHAPTER 32

The day after Daisy was born, Maggie moved back to her own house. The baby was feeding and sleeping well, and Charlie was due home any day. There had been no way to reach him and tell him about the baby.

When she opened her front door, it felt unfamiliar and uncomfortably quiet. Her mum bustled behind her, lugging bags and dragging the pram inside. Maggie held Daisy to her chest, swathed in a crocheted blanket her mum had made.

"I'll put the kettle on," said Linda, disappearing towards the kitchen at the back of the house.

'Thanks, Mum," replied Maggie. "I'll be there in a minute."

Maggie heard a kerfuffle in the kitchen, something about teaspoons being in the wrong drawer, and smiled. Her mother had been a godsend. She had offered to stay until Charlie came home, but Maggie knew sooner or later she'd have to cope on her own.

"Cottage pie alright for your tea tonight, love? I'll stick it in the oven to warm through," called Linda from the kitchen.

Maggie grinned. "Lovely. What's for pudding?"

The reply from Linda was immediate. "Treacle sponge."

Having her mother to fuss over her had taken the sting out of Charlie not being there when Daisy was born. He had missed those unrepeatable, precious moments immediately after the birth. Even now, coming 'home', the house felt empty.

"Your tea's on the table, love." Her mother's voice interrupted her sullenness. "And a piece of fruit cake. You need to eat to keep up your strength."

Maggie kissed the tip of Daisy's nose. "Your nana is going to make me fat," she teased.

But looking around the hallway, there were still several boxes to unpack; she'd need all the energy she could get. She felt surprisingly alert, despite everyone telling her to stay in bed. Her mother fussed, but what she wanted right now was some space to adjust to her new role in life. She was also still quite unsettled by the images that had troubled her sleep immediately after giving birth. She wasn't frightened as such. If anything, the experience had been calming. She felt as though someone was watching out for her or, more worryingly, trying to warn her somehow.

Every time she made a cup of tea, the image of the woman with blue eyes peering into the teacup flashed through her mind. She had been smiling and gently reaching out to touch her. Maggie still had no idea what the sweet, woody smell had been – she couldn't place the scent at all. Or the drumbeats. She wondered if she'd suffered some kind of temporary insanity or hallucination straight after Daisy was born. But asking anyone about that would make her sound completely daft. There was just no way to express how *real* the whole thing felt, despite its dreamlike quality.

The experience spurred Maggie on to get back to normal as quickly as possible, whatever 'normal' was. She'd only been married a couple of weeks, was living in a brand-new house and had a newborn baby. It was no wonder she was beginning to question her own sanity, she told herself, as she drank the cup of tea her mother made and tried not to fixate on the bottom of the cup.

Charlie was still away, but she had a hunch he would be back today.

"I'll only be a couple of days, Maggie," he'd said before he left.

"You'd better not be longer than that, Charlie White," she'd warned, wagging her finger.

"I promise," he'd said firmly.

She'd been sure he had been crossing his fingers, but she didn't press him. His business was *his* business. She knew it was dangerous – rolled-up bundles of cash didn't magic themselves out of thin air, and diamond rings didn't miraculously appear.

Maggie looked down at her engagement ring. Her mother had just left and she was busying herself folding baby clothes and putting them neatly in the drawers in the nursery. The waft of homemade cottage pie baking downstairs felt comforting. Daisy was fast asleep, contented after a long feed. With a few minutes to herself, Maggie set down a baby vest and studied her ring more closely. Where had it come from *exactly*? She'd never questioned it properly before. Life had been a whirlwind of wedding preparations and home-making since Charlie gave it to her. Then again, Maggie also knew sometimes it was better not to ask these things.

The blue light of the diamond seemed to draw her into a

trance and she had the same, strange feeling she'd had when Daisy was born. "I must be going mad," she said to herself.

A loud knock at the door made her jump. The knock turned into a rapid succession of bangs. Maggie leapt up and raced downstairs. She was going to give whoever was at the door a piece of her mind. She might even throttle them if they woke the baby.

Charlie was fully aware as he stood on their doorstep that he didn't look pretty. He'd not taken a key with him, on purpose. If he'd got caught, he would have ended up emptying his pockets in a police station. If a gang had outnumbered him and got hold of his house key, well, there was no telling what level of punishment would have resulted.

He smoothed his hair back, knowing it was a mess. He hadn't slept for days. The deep cut on his head, inflicted by the first man in the garage, had swollen and was still seeping blood. He dabbed it with a handkerchief whenever he felt it trickling down his face. He had dark, heavy lines under bloodshot eyes. His clothes were dirty, several days of perspiration causing them to cling to him like a filthy second skin. Even his shoes were flecked with grime.

He'd driven straight back to London from Scotland, only stopping for fuel and coffee. The men in the back of the van had stirred several times but were bound so tightly that any movement was excruciating for them and they soon gave up struggling. Charlie kept the windows down, allowing a breeze to alleviate the stench that inevitably occurred when two scared, fully-grown men were gagged and thrown into the back of a van for hours on end.

When Charlie made it back to the workshop, Bobby was waiting for him. He steered the van in through the gates. He was struggling to focus and narrowly missed scraping the side of the vehicle. He slammed the gears into neutral, yanked the break on, and turned off the engine. He was beyond tired. It took all his will power to get out of the van and make it over to Bobby.

The cold air revived him slightly and Charlie began to tell Bobby what had happened, producing the bag of 'cocaine' he had sampled. This operation had taken military precision to get right; now the fragile trust between the partners had been sabotaged.

It was the first time Charlie could recall Bobby losing his cool. He watched with mild horror as Bobby's hands began to shake violently, his body twisting as he clasped his head and moaned as though in physical pain.

"Those *bastards!*" Bobby spat. He kicked a bottle lying on the ground, causing it to hurtle against a wall and smash. "*Bastards*," he repeated. The van moved slightly, catching his attention. "What the hell is going on in there?" he said, turning to Charlie.

"Two of those bastards you were talking about," replied Charlie nonchalantly. "And all of the cash. I didn't swap the cans."

Bobby stared at him. "You didn't *actually* swap the cans? The cash is *still* in there?"

Charlie nodded. "And two Scotsmen. They showed up a couple of hours after I was meant to have switched the cans. I thought you'd appreciate a souvenir."

Charlie opened the back of the van. The tightly bound men wriggled slightly, squinting against the bright light.

Bobby peered in, shaking his head. "Thanks for the souvenirs. Much appreciated." He patted Charlie on the back, grinning. "Go home, lad. Get some rest. Take these." He reached inside and pulled out half a dozen cans. "Decorate your new house," he said and winked. "I'll get a driver to take you home now."

Charlie fell asleep on the back seat as the radio quietly played, the paint cans by his feet. It felt like just a few seconds later when the driver gently nudged his shoulder to let him know they'd reached their destination. He pulled himself up off the seat, shaking himself awake. Every part of his body thumped, ached or throbbed. Pushing open the car door with his foot, he dragged himself out onto the pavement. Reaching back into the car, he picked up the paint cans, hanging three over one arm and three over the other. The cans seemed to get heavier with each step he took towards the house. He set them on the step and put all of his remaining energy into banging the front door as loudly as he could.

No answer. He banged again.

When Maggie finally swung open the door, she looked furious. He noticed something different about her as her eyes drilled into his, then softened into a smile. The smile quickly faded as she pulled the door wide open and dragged him inside.

"Charlie, what has happened to you?"

"Hold on," he replied.

He opened the door again and grabbed the paint cans, holding them up to Maggie like a gift.

Maggie raised her eyebrows. "Are we decorating?"

Charlie opened his mouth to answer then froze. From upstairs Daisy began to cry. He dropped the cans and reached for Maggie, looking at her midriff.

"Maggie White, why didn't you tell me?!"

"*When* could I have told you? *How* could I have told you?" she said, laughing.

Charlie kicked his shoes off and ran up the stairs following the infant cries. Maggie watched from the doorway as he crept into their bedroom and peered over the edge of the crib.

"Oh, Maggie, look!" he whispered. He wanted to touch the baby but didn't quite dare.

Maggie walked over to him and placed a gentle hand on his back. "This is your daughter, Daisy."

"She's beautiful," he replied, staring at the little face.

"You get in the bath, Charlie White," said Maggie, appraising her husband. "Then you can cuddle your daughter."

He nodded and peeled off his clothes. Maggie ran the bath, pouring several caps of antiseptic into the running water. It turned the water white, which frothed slightly as the bath filled. As Charlie eased himself into the hot water, he began to relax.

Maggie leaned over him and examined his head wound. "That cut needs stitches, Charlie," she observed.

"Have we got any plasters?" he asked.

Maggie nodded, watching droplets of blood drip into the water and disperse. She reached into the cabinet and found something suitable. As she busied herself tending to his injury, she brought up the subject of the paint cans sitting in the hallway. "The house has just been painted, Charlie. What's going on?"

He was too tired to lie. "There is money in each one. A *lot* of money."

Maggie sat down on the edge of the bath.

"How much?"

Charlie shrugged. "Honestly? I don't know. Thousands. Tens of thousands, maybe."

Maggie felt suddenly faint. She wasn't sure if it was the steam from the bath or the notion of tens of thousands of pounds just sitting in her hallway that caused her to feel so woozy. She opened the bathroom window to let in some fresh air.

"Oh, Maggie! It's freezing. Shut that window!" Charlie whined.

"Don't complain, Charlie. I need fresh air to think."

"About what?"

"About *what*?" she repeated. Then she realised – this was normal for Charlie White. He would get home, empty his jacket or something else loaded with cash, and think nothing of it. "Don't worry," she said, composing herself. "I'll think of something to do with it."

Charlie rolled his eyes. He did not doubt that. Not for one moment.

CHAPTER 33

London, 1973

Maggie watched the van reverse into the warehouse, her hands placed firmly on her hips as the vehicle moved slowly backwards. If the driver misjudged by a few inches and the van's brand-new white paint was stripped off the side, she'd be having very strong words with him.

Maggie let out a sigh of relief as the manoeuvre was completed successfully. The driver was a young lad who had just been given the job. He looked petrified as he jumped down from the driver's seat and tipped his cap to acknowledge the boss. It wasn't Charlie White they all feared – Maggie paid their wages. And, as one or two of her employees had discovered, her tongue could be more fearsome than Charlie's menacing stare.

Maggie peered into the back of the van.

"Are all the deliveries done, Jack?" she asked before the lad scarpered to take his tea break.

"Yes, Mrs White. I'll put the paperwork in your office, as usual."

Maggie nodded. Every single piece of paperwork was

accounted for and rigorously checked. If ever she couldn't locate a delivery note or an invoice, for example, or one of the girls in the office misplaced the item, Maggie investigated its whereabouts relentlessly. If any stock went missing, she found out why. Charlie often teased her that she should have worked for an interrogation agency, but whatever she did, it was effective.

Maggie turned on her heel and walked out of the warehouse. She looked up, as she often did, and smiled. Above the doors and nailed into the brickwork was the company name: White Electrical.

The sign would be coming down soon though – she was moving the business to much larger premises the following month. She already had a stack of job applications on her desk to go through, even though she had not actively posted vacancies. As tough as she was to work for, she paid well and was fair. She also paid a staff bonus out of the profits, which was virtually unheard of. Maggie had a staunch view that people working together, not individuals, created success. Therefore, why reward just one person? Her theory worked extremely well for both her staff and her balance sheet. Her business was surfing on an upward curve that appeared to have no end in sight.

Maggie often referred to the start-up inspiration as 'the paint can idea'. Apart from Charlie, no one knew why she kept a used paint can on a shelf in her office. It always made her smile and reminded her where it all began. And, importantly, why.

When Charlie came home the day after Daisy was born, a

deep cut on his head and comatose, Maggie had watched him holding their daughter. The image frightened her – she saw a man who lived his life on the razor-sharp edge of a knife. In his arms, was her precious, newborn baby. The strange, eerie feelings she had been getting since Daisy's birth began to make some sense. Perhaps they *weren't* hormones. Maggie began to realise that her husband wasn't just a dangerous man who lived a perilous life; he could go away for a couple of days and *not* come home. Ever. How long would the rolls of cash she had stuffed into shoes, stacked behind tins in the larder, or sunk into the paint cans, last then?

Maggie had helped Charlie to bed that night, folding the bedsheets over his exhausted body. She'd kissed his forehead – he'd already fallen asleep by then. After checking on Daisy, who was sleeping soundly in her cot beside their bed, Maggie had crept out of the bedroom and gone back downstairs.

She had emptied every single paint can, watching as the rolls of cash spilled onto the kitchen table. She made herself a cup of tea and stared at the money for a long time. Draining the last of the tea, she glanced in the bottom of the cup. Smiling, she remembered the strange dream: the woman with blue eyes staring at her and peering inside a teacup.

"Shame, I've used a tea bag," she joked to herself.

Maggie put the teacup down and glanced around the room. She'd brought some new crockery that needed to be unpacked and put away. The dishes from dinner hadn't been cleared and remained stacked beside the sink. The fridge made a sudden clunking noise, reminding her to get it fixed. Or better still, get a new one.

Sat alone in her kitchen, surrounded by money and an old fridge making sporadic groans, Maggie tapped a fingernail on the edge of a paint can. In that moment, her idea was born.

Over the next few months, Maggie purchased hundreds of fridges and many other household electrical items. She used some of the money from the paint cans to buy a few items of wholesale stock, which she sold within days. Two months later, she rented her first warehouse and hired a van and a few lads to deliver bulky items. The demand for electrical household items was unprecedented, and Maggie created the perfect brand. She was the epitome of a young mother running a household, and everyone wanted to look as glamorous as Maggie did standing next to their fridge or holding an electric whisk.

Daisy spent most of her first year bouncing on her mother's hip, or with her nana and grandpa. Jim and Linda doted on her, and eventually decorated Maggie's old bedroom for their granddaughter.

"She needs somewhere to nap when she's here," insisted Linda.

"Of course, Mum. Thank you." Maggie leaned over and kissed her mum's cheek. She had felt closer to her mum since Daisy's arrival. It was though they worked as a tag team sharing bottles, blankets, and baby toys.

Daisy thrived living between her parents and grandparents over the next five years. It gave Maggie time to grow the business, which she loved. She was steadily building a safety net around them all, even Charlie. By then Maggie had fully realised that what ensnared her husband to the criminal underworld was not money. He had other, more sinister commitments.

Charlie veered into an empty parking space outside the warehouse, stepping hard on the brake. His brand-new 3.0 litre V6 Ford Capri growled then yawned as Charlie turned the key and jumped out. A few lads wandered out of the warehouse to admire the glossy red car, making sure they stood well back. Charlie ran his hand over the bonnet, flicking off a leaf, and carefully checked the car up and down. He made sure he looked at all the lads loitering nearby – both they and he would know he'd seen them if anything happened to his precious car.

In her office, he found Maggie checking paperwork. She glanced up as he came in. "Am I forgiven?" he asked grinning.

Maggie put down her pencil and papers. "That cost us a large commercial fridge, Charlie White. I've just seen the van come back from delivering it."

"She deserved it."

Maggie shook her head, smiling. "I'm never going to ask you to pick Daisy up from school again."

"Okay." He laughed, and Maggie threw a hard ball of elastic bands at him.

A girl from school had been teasing Daisy for weeks but had managed to inflict her nastiness without a single adult witness. Charlie decided it was up to him to do something about it. He waited until the last parent had filed out of the school gates one morning. He walked casually into the cloakroom and caught the girl hanging her coat on her peg, teasing Daisy and kicking her. Charlie had gripped the girl's jumper at her neckline and pulled her backwards, using his vice-like grasp to keep her feet slightly elevated off the floor. He dropped her before the teacher arrived, although not before he had whispered into the girl's ear to leave his daughter alone.

Maggie had received a phone call a short while later from a traumatised headmaster. Charlie had told him, and anyone else who wanted to hear, that he would be very *unhappy* if his daughter was bullied again.

Maggie had donated the new school fridge as a peace offering. She gently suggested to the headmaster that it would be sensible to leave it there and not involve the police. It wasn't the slur on her business that concerned her or what the playground gossips said. She knew that when Charlie made a threat, it wouldn't be an idle one.

After five years of marriage, Maggie had soaked enough of Charlie's blood-stained shirts to understand his business involved violence. She'd only seen him physically hurt the night he returned home with the paint cans – a thin silvery scar now ran down the side of his face as a constant reminder. On the surface, she was nonchalant about what he did, brushing it aside with humour. But deep down, she knew what *fuelled* him.

She often found crumbs of the silky white powder scattered on the windowsill in the bathroom. She quickly swept it up and flushed it down the toilet. He'd been more careful about tidying up for a while, but she always found tiny specs. It was unusual for Charlie to be slapdash, but he seemed not to care as much anymore. Once or twice, Maggie had handed him a tissue and told him to blow his nose.

Occasionally, she wondered if he dallied with other women. But there had only been one time when she had detected a slight hint of perfume on his shirt as she shoved it into the washing machine. It could have been her imagination or the new fabric softener, she rationalised.

Charlie still made her heart leap. He only had to smile, and something inside her melted. It didn't matter what shady activities he was involved in – she still loved him.

Maggie turned her attention back to her husband. If he was bored, she had plenty of jobs he could do. She began to list the tasks in order of priority, but he cut her off mid-sentence, spinning round on his chair before leaping to his feet.

"No, I'm too busy, Maggie. Got people to see." He winked. "I just wanted to say I've got tickets for Christmas Eve – a little jazz club."

"That's two months away!" Maggie exclaimed, pointing at the calendar on the wall.

"That should give you just about enough time to find a dress, eh?" He gave her one of his dazzling smiles and waved goodbye.

She shook her head, grinning.

A few minutes later, she heard the roar of his car engine. He was too aggressive with that accelerator pedal, she thought, rolling her eyes and tutting. She glanced out the window and saw Charlie's red car thunder out of the car park. She'd noticed the glassy shine casing his eyes earlier and was pretty sure he'd recently snorted cocaine. Maggie turned back to her work, wondering what it would take before he finally addressed his problem.

CHAPTER 34

The Christmas tree was draped in zigzags of thick, glittery tinsel and sparkled with blue, green and red lights. Daisy had also hooked large baubles in random places, typically on the very ends of the bottom branches. Charlie had lifted her to place the angel on the very top. The overall look was haphazard, including the tilted angel. But at five years old, Daisy would be sure to notice if anyone moved anything or 'fixed' the tree even slightly. She appeared to have developed Charlie's knack for such awareness of detail.

When Maggie walked into the living room on Christmas Eve, she found Daisy playing dominoes with her parents. Daisy wriggled free from underneath her grandpa's arm and ran to her mother.

"Careful, Daisy!" warned Linda.

"She's alright, Mum," said Maggie, smiling affectionately at her daughter.

Daisy appraised her mother's long red cocktail dress. "Your dress is very pretty, Mummy."

"Thank you. You look pretty too, Daisy."

Daisy giggled as Maggie pulled her carefully onto her lap. Maggie could smell her perfume on her daughter's hair. Daisy had wandered into Maggie's bedroom while she was getting ready earlier. The little girl was fascinated with all the glass jars and pretty bottles on the dressing table. She had helped herself to a generous squirt of her mother's favourite perfume, Chanel No.5, saying she wanted to be able to smell it on her nightdress all night long.

Maggie turned as Charlie came into the room. His pristine black suit, complete with a white shirt and bow tie, suited him to perfection. Out of habit, Maggie sought out his eyes – it was her way of 'reading' him. But he made sure he avoided her gaze. It didn't matter; she could tell from his bounciness something was amiss. This appeared to be the normal state of affairs these days.

"Are we ready?" he asked, bubbling with excitement.

"I think so," Maggie replied.

She picked up the small beaded handbag she had left on the side and swooped down to deliver a final kiss on Daisy's forehead, leaving a bright red lipstick stain there, on purpose. "See you in the morning. Not too early!"

Daisy grinned and watched her mother slip the full-length mink coat over her dress. Maggie and Charlie strolled outside together, looking like movie stars.

Maggie turned and saw Daisy looking out of the window, waving to them. She blew her daughter a kiss and mouthed "I love you" just before stepping into the waiting car.

"Charlie, look it's snowing!"

Charlie reached for her gloved hand outside the jazz club just as the first snowflakes began to fall. It was bitterly cold, but the stunning display of lights framing the front of the club made it worth standing outside in the cold for a few extra minutes. This club was highly exclusive and by invitation only. Heavy-set bouncers stood at the door, but Charlie and Maggie needed no introduction. Charlie kissed Maggie, just as a photographer pointed his camera at them and the flash exploded.

They joined the train of other mink coats and bow ties walking inside, feeling the warmth instantly thaw their cold cheeks. The jazz band was playing upbeat carols in the background, creating a lively, festive vibe.

Maggie leaned over to Charlie, who had just returned from the gents, and handed him a hanky. She pointed discretely to the fine white powder clinging to the hairs at the edge of his nostrils. He thanked her, apologising with his eyes. She shook her head. Once Christmas was over, she was going to have a serious conversation with Charlie about this. At some point, Daisy would become aware, and she couldn't bear the thought of exposing her daughter to any part of the seedy drug world.

Maggie was so distracted with her thoughts, she didn't see the tall, blonde girl walking towards them. She felt Charlie's arm stiffen by her side.

"Hello," said the blonde, looking directly at Charlie.

"Hello," he replied blankly. "This is Maggie, my wife."

Maggie was certain she saw the blonde woman flinch. There was something familiar about her face. Maggie tilted her head, trying to place her.

The sequin-studded black dress she wore was cut too low, emphasising small breasts pushed up deliberately high. Her face may have been naturally pretty, but she wore far too much make-up.

Maggie knew her face from *somewhere*. At last, she remembered. "Susan? That's right, isn't it?"

The blonde girl looked shocked, as did Charlie.

"Yes," the girl replied gingerly.

"Bobby's daughter?"

They'd been introduced at one or other of Bobby's Christmas parties in the past. It had been a few years since the last party and this woman had been a teenager then – she suddenly looked very grown-up.

Maggie had noted the way she looked at Charlie. When Susan nodded to confirm she was Bobby's daughter, Maggie decided to put her firmly in her place. "My, you look very grown-up. I like your pretty hair and make-up." Maggie was careful to temper her patronising comments with just the right amount of pleasantness. Susan smiled awkwardly and walked away, stopping a waiter to help herself to a flute of champagne.

Maggie looked at Charlie to gauge his reaction, but he was already talking to someone else, dismissive of the uncomfortable exchange. She wasn't sure why the girl had looked at Charlie that way, but she seemed to have disappeared into the crowd, and Maggie decided to forget about her for now.

It was a magical evening of dancing, champagne and laughter. Just after midnight, Maggie collapsed into a chair, exhausted but happy. She saw Charlie leave the dancefloor and head towards the main foyer, probably to visit the gents. It was perhaps time they went home anyway, she thought. It was getting late. She picked up her bag and followed him but got distracted by a couple of friends who were also about to head home and wanted a farewell chat. After a flurry of goodbyes and promises to catch up in the New Year, she began to wonder where Charlie had got to. She fiddled with the ticket for her coat as she joined the queue for the cloakroom, glancing around anxiously. Surely he should be back by now?

Suddenly a fist of anger gripped her. Was he taking more of that cocaine in the toilets? He did it all the time, and it infuriated her. Frowning, she took deliberate steps towards the gent's restroom, knowing full well it was unheard of for a woman to do such a thing.

Once inside, she glanced around. The place looked empty. She momentarily thought how bad it would appear if someone came in and saw her, but she shrugged off any fear of embarrassment. Over the past few weeks, she had grown aware just how much cocaine Charlie was snorting, and enough was enough. This time she was going to flush whatever he had down the toilet and read him the riot act.

Lifting her dress, she squatted and peered under the cubicle doors. It didn't take long to find Charlie's distinctive black shoes, standing motionless. She walked into the cubicle next to him and shut the door. There was still no noise from his side. She waited a few moments, feeling the adrenaline rise like acid in her throat, then she deliberately flushed the toilet. Using the noise to disguise the sound of her heels clambering onto the toilet lid, she balanced carefully. She wasn't sure whether to laugh or scream; surely this was insane behaviour?

She peered over the cubicle. Her eyes locked on Charlie as he gazed up at her in shock. She opened her mouth to speak, but words failed her as her heels slipped and she immediately fell backwards. She steadied herself, wincing in agony. She heard him call out her name as she grappled with the door. The clasp pinched her skin as she fumbled with the lock. Yanking the door open, Maggie hurried out of the gents. Her long dress swishing around her feet made it difficult to move quickly, and her ankle started to throb.

She pushed her way past people who were leaving the club, burrowing through the queue. They raised their voices but she didn't stop or apologise. She needed to get outside and find a cab.

The sharpness of the cold air nipped at her skin but heat was radiating from her core; sweat gathered on her brow and froze in situ. The mink coat felt like a concrete slab on her back. She threw her hands up and waved frantically, trying to catch the attention of a cab. She felt her eyelashes stick together as salty tears coursed down her cheeks. Clumps of fluffy snowflakes fell steadily from the ominous sky, obscuring her view. She stepped forward, limping. She couldn't bear to put any weight on her right foot.

She saw a cab approaching and threw her hand up again.

Maggie didn't hear the screech of wheels as the car lost control on the freshly laid snow or the blast as glass shattered from the windscreen. Her head began spinning, then her entire body seemed to float through the air.

All Maggie could see was Charlie's face and his black trousers pushed down to his knees. The blonde, Susan, reclined back against the toilet cistern. Her eyes had taken in every painful detail in that split second: her dress heaved-up, her legs wide open, naked breasts exposed. The images replayed over and over in her head like a horrific kaleidoscope.

There was an abrupt thud and Maggie could no longer see, hear or feel anything.

The ambulance fought through the stationary traffic with full sirens blaring. They could see the commotion ahead but couldn't reach it. One of the paramedics jumped out of the ambulance and sprinted towards the accident. He arrived at the scene and found a hysterical man rocking a woman in his arms. Her small frame flopped like a limp doll as he held her.

As the paramedic went to touch her, the man raised his hand, and the paramedic stepped back.

"I can't help if you don't let me see her, sir."

Charlie was blinded by emotional pain and torment, unable to let her go. Finally, a voice he knew, jolted him back to reality. It was Bobby Blower.

"Charlie, let them help Maggie."

Maggie. The woman he loved in a way he could never love anyone else. In his mind, he saw her the day she visited him in prison, her eyes dancing and her stomach swollen with their baby. Then on their wedding day, with lily of the valley woven into her bouquet. Then tonight as they twirled around the dancefloor, her eyes midnight blue and radiant. And now, her eyelids closed and motionless. He watched as the paramedic gently turned her onto her back and shone a light in her eyes, then reached for her wrist. A trickle of bright red blood seeped from her head and dispersed into the brilliant white snow beneath her.

The paramedic pulled back slightly, defeated. There was no point peeling the mink from her body to perform CPR – she had died either upon impact or soon after.

Charlie lifted Maggie back into his arms, ignoring the onlookers who had gathered around him. In that precise moment, nothing but Maggie existed. He touched her face with shaking fingertips, then rested his cheek against hers. He smelt Chanel No.5 in her hair, and her lips were still bright with fresh lipstick. He felt the warmth of her skin against his, almost as though she were simply sleeping. He felt his heart being torn from his body and his soul shatter.

"I'm so sorry, Maggie… I'm so sorry," he whispered into her hair, desperately wishing she could hear him. He took her hand into his own and squeezed it tightly until the diamond ring she loved dug deep into his palm. It seemed wrong that the gem should still be sparkling so beautifully.

The paramedics were waiting to take her. With the same instinct that had made him pick it up that night in the mansion, he gently slipped the ring off her finger and clutched it tightly in his hand.

Sobbing, he let them lift her from his arms. The people gathering nearby watched in horror; most were crying too. Several of them had known Maggie. It was a sharp reminder that fate could steal mortality at any point.

As the ambulance drove off with Maggie's body, Charlie

came undone. His eyes filled with anger, his fists clenched, and his body shook uncontrollably. He felt a strong pair of hands grip his shoulders. He turned and saw Bobby Blower. The two men locked eyes as they had done many times before – but this time was different. Charlie was a dangerous man, fuelled with the lethal combination of incandescent rage, a broken heart and nothing to lose. His target would be Susan.

"Come with me, son. We need to get you out of here," Bobby said.

Charlie knew he didn't have a choice. He could kill Bobby with his bare hands if he had to. They walked down the steps towards the bowels of the club, which Charlie often privately thought of as the Devil's lair. Now he followed the Devil himself, not knowing or caring which way this would go.

CHAPTER 35

Bobby nodded at Charlie, silently directing him to take a seat on the vacant chair in his office. Charlie shook his head. The simple gesture of defiance marked a shift of power between the two men.

Bobby was the first to break the icy stand-off. "Charlie, I'm so sorry about… about Maggie."

"*Are* you?" Charlie spat the words at his employer and Bobby fell silent. Charlie began pacing, threading his hands through his hair, pulling it as though trying to yank the words straight from his head. "You *told me* to do *it*!"

Bobby glanced over Charlie's shoulder – for once, there was no bodyguard at the door. The irony was almost laughable; in almost forty decades of crime, he'd never been without a heavyset bouncer guarding his door. Now here he was, face-to-face with one of the hardest killers he had ever come across, with no back-up.

"Charlie, no, I… I just wanted you to look after Susan."

Charlie laughed bitterly. "You said you wanted us to get married one day." He paced the length of the desk between them. "Yes, that's what you said. Tell me, what would you have done to make that happen?"

Bobby shook his head, holding his hands up defensively. "You aren't thinking straight, Charlie."

"I think I am. *I think* you wanted Maggie out of the way."

"No!" Bobby shouted.

"*Yes!*" Charlie boomed. "Your daughter followed me into those toilets. My head was spinning. I thought someone had…" Charlie stopped. He shook his head in disgust as he began to join his theory together. "I thought someone had spiked my drink. I couldn't even see properly. I felt sick – that's why I'd gone into the cubicle. Susan followed me and she started to touch…"

Charlie stopped pacing and closed his eyes, remembering. "Then Maggie looked over and saw us. Susan was trying to…" Charlie noticed Bobby's face was stony white.

"Charlie, I don't need to hear…" said Bobby assertively. Then his tone changed and softened. "Susan loves you, Charlie."

Charlie froze. He pulled the pocketknife from his jacket and flicked it open. Twisting it around, he slammed the sharp tip straight into Bobby's desk. The wood splintered, leaving a deep gouge.

Charlie spoke the three forbidden words. "I want *out*."

Even though he had just been threatened with a knife, a knife belonging to a ruthless killer, Bobby shook his head. "You can't ever leave – that's the deal. You know too much."

"Then you will have to kill me." Charlie leaned across the desk and looked Bobby squarely in the eye. "But I will kill your daughter first."

Bobby knew he could have thrown the threat back at

him – threatened Charlie's daughter, Daisy. But he didn't need to voice the warning. Charlie knew how things worked in their world.

"What do you want, Charlie?" said Bobby, sighing. He sat down and crossed his legs, business-like. But this wasn't a negotiation.

Charlie took a steadying breath. "I want your guarantee that I'm out. And that my daughter and wife's family are left alone."

"I can't control what others do, Charlie. And people will be worried about what you know about their business."

Charlie shook his head. "You *can* control it, Bobby. I'm going to slip away for a while, so no one has to be worried. But if *anything* happens…"

Bobby held his hands up and nodded – he didn't need to be told again. Charlie leaned forward and held out his hand. Reluctantly, Bobby accepted the handshake.

The deal was done.

◈ ◈ ◈

Charlie asked the cab driver to stop several streets away from his house. It was four o'clock in the morning and still dark, but most people had their Christmas lights on. It was, after all, officially Christmas Day.

And the worst day of Charlie's life.

The snowflakes that had powdered the ground the evening before had now melted into a thin layer of slush. The streetlights glowed a dull orange and beckoned the way home

– Charlie knew there were precisely five more lampposts between where he stood and his front door.

As he approached, he saw the police car leaving. He held back, waiting until they had gone. His heart sank knowing his in-laws had just been told the news about Maggie. He wanted to run away, to avoid the truth, but he knew he couldn't. They were good people and deserved more. What they didn't deserve to hear was the *actual* truth.

Charlie slowly climbed up the steps towards the front door, remembering coming home on their wedding night. Maggie had been holding her bouquet of lily of the valley in her hands, laughing. She'd teased him about being too heavy for him to carry her over the threshold.

He stopped and stared at the front door. Less than ten hours earlier he had watched her lift her mink coat and sidestep towards him, revealing delicately heeled shoes. Her red dress had swished around her ankles and fitted snugly around her narrow waist. He remembered her hair had been curled and tied with a satin ribbon. Charlie surprised himself – considering his head had been swimming in cocaine, he remembered everything.

He remembered that Bobby hadn't baulked when Charlie accused him of being involved in Maggie's demise.

Charlie clenched the railing beside the first step, feeling the world begin to spin. Stale alcohol gurgled in his stomach, rising as a bitter, acid taste in his mouth. He spun around and sat on the step, steadying himself. He shivered and rubbed his shoulders in a futile effort to bring some feeling to his frozen body. He should go inside, but he needed to think. He wanted to do anything other than see Linda and Jim's faces, or witness his little girl sleeping on Christmas morning, oblivious to the knowledge that her mother was dead.

Charlie couldn't stop the tears. It was an unfamiliar sensation as the warm, salty water trickled from his eyes and splashed onto his jacket. He dropped his head into his hands and began to sway gently.

He couldn't go inside. Charlie White was feared by some of the toughest, most ruthless men in London, but right now he wasn't capable of facing his five-year-old daughter. He patted down his clothes, thinking about what he had on him. A bunch of keys – Charlie glanced down the street at his Ford Capri. On the keyring was also a small, silver key. It opened a garage tucked away in south London where he had several changes of clothes, weapons, and enough cash to disappear for a few years – maybe to Cornwall. Charlie ferreted in his pockets and pulled out Maggie's ring. Those were the only two items in his possession as he slid behind the wheel of his car and pulled away from the kerb: a bunch of keys and the South African blue diamond.

CHAPTER 36

Charlie's head was in such a dark place, he almost fled London without a word to anyone. It was only when he pushed the last bag into the back of his car and slammed the boot down, he knew he had to face his father-in-law. He was the only one Charlie could trust.

Charlie tailed Jim discreetly from his house to the Stag's Head. Just as Jim reached the door of the pub, Charlie called, "Jim! Wait!"

Jim turned on him, his eyes blazing. "What the *hell* are you doing here? And where the *hell* have you been?"

Charlie recognised the anger, sadness, and pain in Jim's eyes. He saw the same emotions in the mirror himself. But he saw Jim's anger deflate at the sight of the raw, bloody gash next to his son-in-law's eyebrow. It was a stark reminder of the world Charlie operated within: a sinister world fraught with danger and corruption.

Charlie needed to leave London quickly. What he had done would stir up the criminal underworld like a tornado. Charlie needed to sidestep the core of the whirling storm, avoid its path of destruction.

"Not here," replied Charlie, looking over his shoulder. "Can you meet me tomorrow?"

"Why not now?" asked Jim.

"I'll explain tomorrow."

They met at a café they both knew just after the breakfast rush at 10 o'clock. A burly waitress plonked two cups of tea down on the red and white checked cloth, apologising cheerily as the hot milky tea sloshed over the edge of the cups.

"Sugar's in the bowl, dears." She pointed to a chipped ceramic bowl with dregs of crystallised sugar stuck to the bottom, then wandered off.

Charlie tutted and reached over to lift the sugar bowl from the adjacent table. He heaped two mountains of fresh sugar into his tea and carefully stirred it. He slid the sugar bowl across to Jim without looking at him.

Charlie had tried to mask the cut running alongside his eyebrow but it was too fresh to conceal, and still weeping. A plaster made it look worse – the blood soaked into the fabric and drew attention to the wound. He hoped the air would speed up the healing process. He'd been able to hide the other bruises and cuts underneath his clothing. His right shoulder was the worst affected and still throbbed in agony from where his attacker's knife had sliced straight through his leather jacket and pierced his skin.

Bobby Blower had not honoured his handshake with Charlie. When Charlie had pulled away from the kerb in the early hours of Christmas morning, he'd noticed a car following him. He had weaved through the empty streets for almost an hour, calculating his options. In the end, he had driven south as planned, reluctant to reveal the whereabouts of his garage but knowing he wouldn't be able to defend himself without going there.

The car was seconds behind him as he yanked on the brake of his Ford Capri and jumped out. He would run the rest of the way to buy a few extra minutes before they realised what direction he'd taken after abandoning his car. He flipped open the garage and ducked underneath the door. Inside, he pulled off his dinner jacket and replaced it with his leather one which was hanging on a peg. Being meticulous about his belongings had paid off: a brand-new gun was ready and loaded, and his collection of knives were lined up like a row of soldiers. There was a safe concealed behind some workbench drawers; he'd recover what was in there later.

Charlie knew they were approaching. He could sense if not yet hear them. He would recognise each one as soon as he saw their faces. Unlike Charlie, they had wives or girlfriends to hurry home to, someone to spend Christmas with. Charlie knew Bobby hadn't sent them to offer a warning – it was to finish him.

Deep down, Charlie had always known there was a risk their deal could backfire. A gentleman's handshake usually meant a seal of honour. But these were no gentlemen.

Charlie saw an outline of a man crouched at the edge of the garage door. He flung a knife sideways and heard a thud followed by a loud yelp. He moved quickly forwards and hunkered down behind the brickwork adjacent to the doors.

The underside of a hand holding a gun nudged forward just above his head. Charlie took out a blade and swiped it across the exposed wrist. Before the arm spewing blood could retract, Charlie grabbed the man's arm and pulled him forward. He thrust the gun to his ear and squeezed the trigger.

Charlie waited silently for Bobby's next killer to emerge. Not one, but three men burst into the garage, waving knives and brandishing guns. Charlie ducked to the ground, shooting at their legs. It was then he felt the knife pierce the flesh on his shoulder, and an excruciating pain incapacitated his arm. Fury, pain, and grief fuelled a fresh surge of energy, and he launched a ruthless attack. Charlie didn't register any feelings; he just focused on his bloody onslaught until all the men fell completely silent. He dragged their bodies inside and pulled down the garage doors.

Only then, covered in blood and in agony, did Charlie collapse to his knees and cry. Warm tears and cold blood dripped from his face onto his hands and onto the grey concrete floor – merging with the blood of the dead men. Bobby had sent four hitmen to kill him, and he had destroyed them all.

That left just one man to deal with. This thought pulled him out of his self-pity and gave him sudden purpose.

But first, he had to deal with his wound. Charlie knew first aid; he'd had to learn over the years how to repair the damage his line of work inevitably inflicted on his body. Often, as with this injury, he needed a doctor. But they asked questions, and he had just murdered four men.

Charlie applied pressure and pulled out the knife that

was wedged into his shoulder – there was no gentle way to do this. He pushed a thick dressing onto the cut until the bleeding began to clot. Luckily, his leather jacket had taken the brunt of the attack, and only the sharp tip of the knife had penetrated his skin. Charlie bathed his shoulder with antiseptic and tightly bandaged the area. It throbbed but it was manageable.

He pulled on his leather jacket; he'd get the slit fixed at some point. It took him half an hour to empty the garage and drag the men into a heap. When he had finished, he quietly pulled down the doors behind him. He would never come back here again.

The inky dark sky was beginning to lighten. Charlie got in his car and flicked on the lights, illuminating the road ahead. A cut above his eye made him squint, and he felt slightly dizzy. Composing himself, Charlie opened the glove compartment and placed his gun carefully inside. It was time to go and hunt down his former employer. Bobby Blower would not be carving the Christmas turkey this year. Or any other.

Charlie studied his father-in-law carefully, as Jim dropped half a spoon of sugar in his cup and stirred.

"Thanks for meeting me, Jim."

"Where have you been? Since… Maggie…"

Both men looked down into their teacups in silence at the mention of her name.

"I had no choice. I'm sorry, Jim, I can't explain," said

Charlie, after a long pause.

"What about Daisy?" hissed Jim.

Charlie closed his eyes. It was because of Daisy he had stayed away. It was also why he had to leave – it was the *only* way to keep her safe.

"Jim… I have to leave. After Maggie… I had some business to sort out, and…"

Jim put his hand up.

"Don't tell me," he said firmly.

Charlie nodded. He could never tell him everything that had happened. He would have to carry those secrets like punishing weights for this rest of his life.

"I need to leave straight away. Will you and Linda… look after Daisy?"

Jim looked shocked. "Of course we will. She's our granddaughter… and *all we have left*."

Charlie felt a fresh stab of guilt. He knew he couldn't explain all the reasons why he couldn't stay. It was too dangerous, even though Bobby was no longer a direct threat.

"I'm sorry," Charlie said hoarsely.

He knew Maggie had taken care of their finances and Daisy would be provided for. He also knew he had no choice but to vanish – for now.

"Where will you go?" asked Jim.

"I'm not sure yet," Charlie lied. "Jim, I have Maggie's ring."

"Keep it," Jim replied adamantly.

"Maggie wanted Daisy to have it one day."

The mention of Maggie again forced Jim to look away. He brushed tears from the corners of his eyes and glared back at his son-in-law.

"No. Once you leave, stay away forever."

Charlie shook his head.

"I can't do that, Jim."

Jim stood up suddenly, pushing back his chair. Charlie met his eyes squarely.

"We are better off without you. *Daisy* will be better off," Jim said, his voice slightly raised.

A few people turned. Charlie had expected Jim to be upset. He couldn't blame him.

Charlie stood up slowly. His voice was quiet but uncompromising. "One day, I *will* give Daisy her mother's ring. I *promised* Maggie."

It was true. On Christmas Eve as Charlie slipped the ring off Maggie's finger, he had gently pulled her hair aside and whispered into her ear. He had been certain her eyelids had momentarily fluttered, and that she had understood.

Charlie did not move until Jim broke the silence.

"Ok, Charlie," Jim said with a heavy sigh. "I know I can't stop you. I just hope I'm dead before you come back."

"Oh, I won't be gone that long, Jim."

"Answer me something," Jim said. The conversation was surprisingly refreshing – neither of them had to pretend anymore. "Did you have anything to do with… with what happened to my… daughter?"

"No," replied Charlie vehemently. "It was an accident… I… I saw it happen."

Jim flinched and steadied his arms on the table. Charlie could see him trembling.

"Was it… did it…?" Jim struggled to find the words.

Charlie did the only kind thing he could think of.

"Jim, they told me it was instant."

The older man nodded and took several deep breaths. "A photographer dropped off a photograph of the two of you," he said, now crying openly. "He said he'd read about the accident in the paper. She looked so happy…" He swallowed slowly then reluctantly said, "You both did. We'll keep the photo for Daisy. You know, for when she's a bit older."

Charlie remembered a flashbulb going off when they arrived at the club. They had twirled around on the step outside, their heads touching. Maybe one day he would get to see that photograph.

Charlie studied his father-in-law. Jim was a good man. Charlie leaned forward and gently touched his hand. "Thank you, Jim."

The older man replied with a thin smile, his anger dispersed but not forgotten. Charlie watched him leave the café and shuffle down the street, his head bent low.

"More tea?"

The waitress reappeared, pointing at the cup. Charlie forced a smile. Even in this small Westend café, the British bulldog spirit of unrelenting courage and 'getting on with it' echoed from bygone eras. He was going to miss London.

"Yes, please. And a full English."

"Fried bread or toast?" she asked, scribbling on her pad.

"Fried."

After breakfast, he would drive south. He had no idea where he would end up or even stay that night. Maybe in a hotel or possibly even curled up on the backseat of his car. It didn't matter.

He reached inside his pocket and pulled out a recent photo of Maggie and Daisy. It had been taken around Daisy's birthday in September, a few months earlier. Mother and daughter looked eerily similar, although Daisy had her father's dark eyes.

"Your wife and girl?" commented the waitress, putting his breakfast plate down in front of him.

Charlie nodded. He wondered what the cheery waitress would say if he told her his wife was dead and he'd recently killed five men.

Charlie tipped the bottle of ketchup upside down and thumped the bottom until thick, red sauce gulped out of the neck onto his plate. He dunked his fried bread into a runny egg and looked out of the window. Mothers walked past juggling pushchairs and bags of shopping from the market, old people shuffled along with walking sticks, black cabs beeped their horns at other drivers hurtling past, and the drizzly grey skies overhead embraced them all. London was his home, and one day he *would* come back.

He picked the ring up and dangled it on the tip of his finger. He remembered the night he gave it to her; she had been radiant with excitement. Perhaps he was drunk-tired or just overwhelmed, but as he stared at the diamond, he felt a cold shiver across his shoulders, giving him the surreal sense Maggie was close by.

Brushing the thought away, Charlie tucked the ring and photograph back in his pocket. After leaving some notes on the table and catching the waitress's eye, he walked outside to where he'd parked his car.

Adjusting the radio channel, he recognised the tune and stopped twizzling the knob. Their wedding song 'Stand By Me' by Ben E. King, was playing.

"Strange…" he smiled, turning up the volume.

He lit a cigarette and wound down the window, glancing out occasionally as he drove away from the heart of the city. He kept driving south, thinking of Maggie. He would not break the promise he made to her. One day, he would make sure the diamond in his pocket was put directly onto their daughter's finger.

But he knew that wouldn't be for a very long time.

PART SEVEN

CHAPTER 37

LONDON, 1989

The mid-afternoon sun shone brilliantly, flooding the pale blue sky. The couple walking through the park towards the cemetery squinted against the bright rays. The warmth was welcome on their skin; their fingers and toes were numb with cold. Crisp white frost was painted thickly on the ground, and puddles of dense ice cracked beneath their heavy boots. Bright white branches of weeping willow trees hung low like long silvery hair. Occasionally, a robin darted between the branches, its red breast flashing brilliantly in the sunlight.

They took turns throwing a ball for the puppy at their heels, their breath creating swirls of mist. The puppy bolted in-between them, his tongue and tail wagging, his paws filthy.

"Winston!"

"You sound like your grandfather," said Daisy, laughing.

George rolled his eyes and repeated the puppy's name, this time emphasising the soft, distinct twang inherited from his father's native tongue.

The puppy looked confused and cocked his head, waiting to hear his name in the familiar sweet voice Daisy always used.

Daisy threw his ball and Winston instinctively fled after it. She watched the jet-black Labrador disappear into a hedge, then spring out moments later with the ball in his mouth. Just up ahead was the familiar gate leading into the cemetery.

"No more balls, for now, Winston," said Daisy softy.

"Are you sure you still want to go?" asked George.

Daisy looked shocked. "I go every Christmas Eve."

George nodded and rubbed her back reassuringly. He had been coming with her for the past three years, but Daisy had not missed visiting her mother's grave on Christmas Eve since she was six years old. Her grandparents used to take her when she was younger, but as they got older, they preferred to come in the warmer months. This year marked sixteen years since her mother had died.

Daisy put her hand on the cemetery gate and pulled it slightly ajar, cringing as the ancient hinges squeaked. Winston tried to wriggle through, forcing his nose through the gap, but George scooped him up.

"We'll head home then," George said. "Are you sure you don't want any company? We can tie Winston here."

He pointed at the railing, but Daisy shook her head.

"No, he'll only howl." She smiled, ruffling Winston's ear.

"See you back at home?" said George, planting a kiss on her forehead.

Daisy nodded, thinking how strange that sounded – *home*. She still thought of the narrow, terraced house she had grown up in as home. Not the four-storey house she had recently purchased outright about half an hour away from her grandparent's in a leafy neighbourhood close to

Hyde Park. It was an attractive house, rendered cream at the bottom with brickwork up to the top. The second floor had an ornate balcony overlooking a community park, and there was a surprisingly spacious garden at the back of the house. The house had been fully refurbished before they moved in. It had been decorated in soft shades of pale cream and fitted with light caramel-coloured carpets.

For weeks they had sat on or stepped over boxes and suitcases. George was either there for days at a time, getting under her feet, or not there at all. Up until the previous year, he had been training as a hospital doctor. The wage didn't reward the long hours, and he was always studying. Even now, the only change since qualifying was his wage. Their spare room was stacked with medical books and journals which George read frequently and flatly refused to part with. In the end, they built bookshelves that almost reached the ceiling and put a desk and a small sofa in there. They had four other bedrooms, including their own on the top floor with panoramic views of the garden and the tips of the city skyline.

Daisy quickly discovered that living with someone required substantial personal adjustment. She wasn't used to seeing George's clothes strewn across the bathroom floor, a trail of shoes in the hallway or half-nibbled slices of toast left randomly on plates in odd places.

"You aren't a student anymore," she would chastise, throwing clothes into a pile and grumbling as she squirted washing-up liquid into the kitchen sink.

"I'm sorry… I will tidy up, I promise," he always replied, offering her his winning smile.

His beeper was always going off, especially first thing in the morning. He would shove a piece of toast between his teeth while he grabbed his jacket and shoes, dropping the toast onto a plate as he tied his shoelaces before rushing out of the door, leaving the toast forgotten.

When George finally got home after an extended shift, he was so exhausted he peeled his clothes off and left them where they landed. Daisy learnt to be tolerant – providing he put his shoes away when he walked in. Her grandmother had instilled this particular discipline in her, and it had stuck. Daisy would stand at the door with her hands on her hips whenever George came home, and he would shake off his shoes and drop them into the shoe box.

The arrival of Winston disrupted everything even further. Just as Daisy had unpacked every box and meticulously arranged every item in drawers, wardrobes, and cupboards, George arrived home with a small, black-haired bundle wrapped in a blanket. The puppy wriggled out of George's arms and scampered up the hallway towards Daisy.

"George, what have you done?" she asked, aghast.

"He'll be company for you when I'm working such long hours at the hospital."

Daisy eyed him suspiciously. "And?"

George shrugged then laughed. "And he will be messier than I am. In theory, you won't notice my mess as much."

Daisy frowned, watching the puppy dart up and down the hallway and then skid to a halt. It looked up at her imploringly.

"I suppose we have to keep him," she said.

"Come on – he's cute! Admit it," George replied.

It was true; Daisy was struggling not to smile.

That had been two months ago, and Daisy had more or less got used to muddy paw prints on the white tiled kitchen floor, black hair clinging to the sofa, and the odd household item being chewed. She certainly didn't fret over George's clothes or abandoned bits of toast any longer.

By Christmas, they had settled into a comfortable routine. The week before Christmas Eve, George had heaved their Christmas tree through the front door and up a flight of stairs to their lounge. They decorated it together, thinking how far they had come in a remarkably short amount of time.

♦ ♦ ♦

Daisy watched George and Winston walk away before she shut the gate behind her. The temperature felt as though it had dropped. She pushed her hands deep into her pockets and burrowed her face into her scarf.

Her thoughts drifted to her mother, as they always did the moment the gate closed and she was inside the cemetery. The squeaky hinges, which had made the same noise since she was a child, signalled to Daisy that this was her time to think and grieve. Except this year she would also crouch by her mother's graveside and thank her for the most extraordinary gift.

When Daisy had turned twenty-one a few months earlier in September, the full extent of the trust fund her mother had left was passed over to Daisy.

It had been a shock to everyone.

Her grandparents had barely touched the full funds

available to them via the trust fund. They had raised Daisy in the home they had raised her mother in, anchored by precious memories.

It turned out Maggie had thought of everything. She'd even made her dad, Jim, a director of her company, White Electrical. In an unprecedented move, he picked up the reins and ran the business for ten years after she died. Maggie had created the workings of a highly successful business engine that motored on even without her. Jim had only sold the business when he realised it was growing faster than he could handle, and it needed more dynamic leadership. The company had sold for an exceptionally large sum and still continued to do a thriving trade under the household brand name Maggie had inspired.

The new management board had organised an impressive anniversary party a few years earlier in 1984, when the company had been officially trading for fifteen years. Daisy had been invited, along with her grandparents. The small warehouse her mother had initially rented in 1969 had exponentially flourished into a business justifying a glass frontage suite of executive offices in central London, with five large depots dotted throughout the country. What touched Daisy the most was seeing a portrait of her mother in the London office. A gold-plated plaque underneath the photograph presented Maggie as the original founder. The Chief Executive Officer, Mr Clarke, had personally commissioned the picture to be displayed in the main foyer.

Daisy had tried to glimpse the elusive Mr Clarke at the anniversary gathering, but her grandpa told her he was a 'silent partner'.

"He's put the money in but doesn't want the headache of running the company," her grandpa had explained. "Apparently he met your mum once."

Daisy remembered feeling a flush of excitement at that news. "When?" she asked.

"I'm not sure. It's just a rumour I heard. Knowing your mother, she probably sold his wife a washing machine," Jim said, laughing.

"Is he married?"

Her grandpa shrugged. "I don't know. No one knows much about him."

"It's a shame he wasn't at the party."

They had both agreed that it would have been nice to thank him personally. It was a thoughtful sentiment to keep Maggie's memory at the heart of the business, where it began.

Daisy passed the familiar wooden bench, which she knew was dedicated to someone who used to tend the cemetery. She often sat there, when the weather was warmer. She glanced at the seat as she passed, and shivered; frost glistened on the panels of damp wood. The branch of an English yew tree covered the bench like an umbrella. In summer, it was a lovely place to sit. Today, it looked cold and gloomy – even though the sun was shining.

Daisy was reminded of the photograph of her parents on the mantelpiece at home. The sun had been shining beautifully on their wedding day too. The photo had been snapped just as they left the registry office, their heads lowered as the deluge of confetti was thrown up into the air around them. Daisy cherished the photo; it set the bar for how love should look and feel.

Her father Charlie had always been a mystery to Daisy. She had only vague memories of him – snippets of moments caught in time. Her grandparents had told her they didn't know where he was, but there was always the possibility that he might come back one day. Over the years, they glossed over the details of who Charlie was – and who he had been. As Daisy grew up, she gathered information from a confusing tangle of stories – often compiled from whispers of conversation heard from behind closed doors. That's how she'd learnt Charlie had been in prison, that he mixed with dangerous people, and that he was better out of their lives.

Her eyes didn't deceive her, though. She *knew* her mother had loved him. She could tell by the way she looked at him in the photograph, and the way he smiled back. But either way, the handsome man in the photographs was gone.

Photographs of George's family were placed on the opposite side of the mantelpiece: one of his father and grandfather, a smaller photograph of his parents on their wedding day, and a very old, sepia photograph in a small frame of his great-grandfather. George looked distinctly like the line of men he had descended from, just as Daisy resembled Charlie and Maggie.

The photographs on the mantelpiece were precious to both George and Daisy. George's father had died after a short battle with cancer a few years before he met Daisy. George had been at medical school at the time, and almost flunked his degree, but his grandfather had insisted he honour his father and finish. Daisy could imagine his grandfather doing that – at eighty-three, he was spritely and liked to make his point by waving his walking stick. "You don't ever expect to bury your child," he had told Daisy wearily.

"I'm so sorry, Grandpa," she had replied.

He had quickly changed the subject to try to lighten the mood. "When are you going to have my great-grandchildren?" he said, a familiar twinkle in his eye.

There was a gap in the middle of the row of family photographs on the mantelpiece. Daisy thought about what George's grandpa said and wondered if one day, pictures of their children might be placed there. But it was pointless to even think that now. They weren't married or even engaged. She remembered the striking diamond engagement ring her mother had always worn. As a child, she used to twizzle it round her mother's finger and watch the blue light sparkle. Daisy often wondered where the ring was now. Her grandparents had always been tight-lipped about it; either they didn't know, or were refusing to say.

The familiar pathway veered around to the left, past uneven rows of headstones. Even though the sunshine poured down from the sky, branches from overhead trees stemmed the warmth. Most of the grass was tipped with frost, creating an eerie blanket of white. The cemetery was not at its most welcoming at this time of year. The trees creaked when the wind was unsettled, and their swaying branches created unnerving shadows. Her preferred time to visit was in mid-spring when wild snowdrops, crocuses and bluebells sprang from the ground and appeared everywhere, creating a colourful fusion of bright, crisp colour. It was, however, depressing to visit a couple of weeks after the heads had flopped and the vibrant coloured flowers had shrivelled to brown carcasses. When it rained, it was even worse.

She felt close to her mother here. But at the same time, she was also conscious of how time had created an unmistakable distance, clouding her memories. She often couldn't decipher between what was a genuine reminiscence and what was just wishful imagination. Daisy had felt incredibly proud when she had stared up at the portrait of her mother in the offices of White Electrical. Her mother represented the empowerment of women in a man's world, of success, and courage. Her pride was tempered by a sting of sadness. Maggie had been stolen from this life just when she was on the crest of her success and when Daisy was only a child. Thinking of the injustice of this inevitably led Daisy to give in to feelings of anger. *Why* had she been in such a hurry to leave the club that fateful Christmas Eve? Why had she *not* been with her father? And where was *he* now?

The same questions plagued her regularly, but were always at the forefront of her mind when she came here on Christmas Eve. She glanced down at the small wreath she had brought with her: seasonal holly interlaced with mistletoe, tied cinnamon sticks, and dried orange. She knew it would go soggy in a few days' time, but she loved the combination, and it smelt lovely. Not that it would matter here, she thought sadly.

Maggie's grave was up ahead, in front of a long hedgerow, behind which was a bank of old, weeping willow trees. When her grandparents had brought her here as a child, Daisy used to race ahead and dangle daisy chains over the edge of the headstone or gently place flowers into the vase, enjoying those few moments alone to 'talk' to her mother. In all these years, visiting the grave had never got easier.

She stopped suddenly a few feet from the grave.

An old lady tending to a grave nearby called over, "Are you alright, dear? You look like you've seen a ghost!" The old lady laughed lightly at her joke, but her amusement quickly changed to concern. "Are you ill?"

Daisy shook her head. "No, I'm fine. It's just… I'm sorry, excuse me."

On Maggie's grave, a dozen perfect red roses lay against the grass, tied with white ribbon. The petals were free of frost, meaning someone had left them recently. There was a card tucked in-between the roses.

No one had ever left flowers before, and especially not on Christmas Eve.

Daisy crouched down and picked up the card, feeling her heart thump painfully. She pulled off her gloves, no longer feeling the chill. She dared herself to look. The card said simply: 'Forever, C'.

"My dad, that's my dad! He was here!"

She looked around nervously, but apart from the old lady shuffling towards her, the graveyard was empty.

"He was very charming," said the old lady.

Daisy's eyes flew open. "You saw him?"

"Yes. He left a short while ago," she squinted and pointed at Daisy's face. "You have his eyes."

Daisy felt frantic. Should she run and try to catch up with him? Should she call out and hope he was still close enough to hear?

The crunch of footsteps on frozen grass caused her to look round. She couldn't move. It wasn't a daydream or a hallucination. Her dad, Charlie White, was walking slowly towards her.

Charlie looked pale as he took small steps forwards, unable to take his eyes off her. Daisy looked so similar to Maggie – it was like seeing his wife when she was young. This was the closest he had been to his daughter in a very long time. He had always been in the shadows, watching from a distance.

The old lady slowly walked away, sensing something significant was happening and her presence would be intrusive. Charlie was aware of the old lady's movements, but he wasn't sure Daisy had even blinked. He couldn't rush this. He had to wait for her to make the first move.

Daisy hesitantly stepped forward. Charlie couldn't recall how many times he had imagined this moment, but he could tell how apprehensive she felt. He inched towards her, offering his hand. He was close enough to see fresh tears glistening in her eyes. Daisy tentatively reached for his outstretched hand until their skin touched and their fingers intertwined then locked.

"Hello, Daisy," he said breathlessly.

She began to gently sob, overwhelmed and overjoyed to

see him. Charlie tenderly pulled her towards him and into his arms. He held her as tightly as he dared as her body slowly eased into the embrace. He felt her silky hair on his cheek and the sweet smell of her perfume – he had waited a very long time to hold her in his arms, and it had been the hardest jail sentence he had ever served.

"I can't believe you're here," she said, touching his cheek.

He couldn't find the words to tell her everything he wanted to say. So much had happened. How could he tell her he had never been that far away? Or that he had watched her come here so many times on Christmas Eve? Or that *everything* he had done since he left had been to protect her? That he had vanished – presumed dead – for a *good* reason? How could he explain the timing had to be perfect for him to return? Or even that he had told her grandpa, Jim, that one day he would come back for her. Or the promise he made to her mother seconds before she died. Even when the medics told him Maggie had died on impact, he would always be convinced he saw her eyelids flutter when he whispered to her – when he *promised* her he would make sure Daisy got her ring.

Charlie kissed her hair, feeling his hand quiver as he tucked her head underneath his chin. He was astounded at how relaxed she seemed with him – he had half expected her to reject him after all this time.

"I'm sorry I left, Daisy. I'll try to explain it to you in the best way I can and hope you'll understand."

She peeled her face away from his chest and looked into his eyes. Even Charlie could see how similar they were to his own.

"I'd like that, Dad."

Dad. That single word was enough to melt his heart. He smoothed her tear-stained hair away from her face. The lump in his throat melted and he pulled her into his arms again.

Glancing over Daisy's head, he saw Maggie's grave behind her. He mouthed "I love you" into the air, thinking of the girl he would always love.

For sixteen years he had held onto Maggie's blue diamond ring – usually tucked safely in his jacket pocket. After a while, he had come to think of it as his lucky charm.

CHAPTER 38

Daisy stood at the bus stop, deciding which route to take. She wanted to rush home and tell George about meeting her dad, but she knew she *really* should go and tell her nana and grandpa first.

She raised her hand decisively and got on the bus to her grandparent's house. It was not going to be an easy conversation, but it was a necessary one. Daisy knew they regarded her father's name as blasphemy, although she was never quite sure why.

The bus dropped her off a few steps from her grandparents' house. Until recently, this terraced house had been the epicentre of her life. She had felt safe and guarded against the rest of the world here. She craned her neck to look at 'her' bedroom window above the front door. That room stored a host of memories: tales of her mother's wedding day; the day Daisy had been born; and the years she spent there, growing up.

This house would *always* feel like home. She couldn't imagine not being able to push her key through the lock and walking into the hallway, as she did now.

"Nana? Granddad?" Daisy called.

She kicked off her shoes and placed them neatly in the cupboard. The hallway was dark but there was a light coming from the half-open door to the kitchen at the end of the hall.

"Daisy? Is that you?" Linda shouted.

"Yes, Nana."

Linda appeared in the doorway, rubbing flour off her hands with her apron. "You must have known I'd just made the jam tarts." Linda went back into the kitchen and returned holding a tray piled with warm tarts. Daisy was drawn to the golden pastry and glossy jam and tried to grab one. Linda grinned and held out the tray, luring Daisy into the kitchen.

Jim was seated at the table and looked up from his newspaper. "Didn't we raise you to chew slowly?" he said, pointing at the crumbs tumbling from the edges of Daisy's mouth.

"You *can't* chew these slowly, Grandpa. They taste too good."

Daisy joined her grandfather at the table. She sat in 'her' chair, watching patiently as her nana poured fresh tea, before sneaking another tart off the tray. It was a tradition in their house to bake jam tarts on Christmas Eve, a tradition that pre-dated Daisy. Maggie had never liked mince pies.

Usually, on Christmas Eve they all sat down and had a pot of tea and plate of jam tarts. But this year she'd told her grandparents not to expect her. She would be spending the day with George. The events at the cemetery had changed her plans. She would just have to wait to tell George about meeting her father. Her grandparents deserved to hear the news first.

"I went to see Mum today," Daisy began and waited for a response.

Both her grandparents looked down at their teacups. It still hurt them to hear about Maggie.

"Did George go with you?" asked Linda.

Daisy nodded. They had a soft spot for George, even though they couldn't understand the modern concept of dating. In their day, George and Daisy would have been married by now.

Daisy glanced through the kitchen hatch into the living room. She could just about see the photograph of her parents on their wedding day in the glass cabinet, and the one that was taken of them the night her mother died.

"There is plenty of space for another wedding photo," her nana would often tease her. George was a doctor, after all. He was 'a catch' as far as they were concerned – they were the perfect match for each other. Just like Maggie and Charlie.

Even her grandparents had admitted that Maggie and Charlie made a beautiful couple. Daisy recalled how they always spoke Charlie's name in a whisper, as though if they said it out loud, they might wake the spirits that kept the monster from returning. Except, unbeknown to them, as Linda stirred a spoonful of sugar into Daisy's tea, the 'monster' was already back.

Linda sat down heavily, staring at the tarts. "Would you like another one?" she offered.

Daisy shook her head. "There is something I need to tell you both."

She closed her eyes and took a deep breath. "I saw my dad

today. He's back."

There was a vacuum of silence. Jim rolled up his newspaper and blasted the table, muttering a swearword under his breath. Shocked, Daisy stared at him. Her nana was crying.

"Linda, pour me a brandy will you. You might need one yourself," Jim said, his voice shaking.

Linda nodded. She poured generous measures into three glasses.

"How was he, Daisy?" Jim croaked.

Daisy's face lit up. "Oh, Grandpa, it was *amazing* to see him. I can't believe it, after all these years."

Jim nodded. "He said he would come back one day."

"*What*?" Daisy squealed.

"I'm sorry, Daisy. We didn't want to give you false hope. We hoped he *wouldn't* come back," Jim replied.

Daisy looked horrified. "Why not? He's my dad!"

"He abandoned you! After… after Maggie… after your…" Jim couldn't get the words out.

"But why, Grandpa? *Why*?"

Jim dropped his tone to barely a whisper. "It was safer for you to stay with us. Charlie was involved with some bad people, Daisy."

It was the first time she had heard that said openly. Daisy knew very little about the notorious Charlie White. The truth about who he was, the crimes he had committed or the hearts and bones he had broken – it had all been hidden from her.

"Why has he come back now?" asked Linda, breaking her silence.

Jim let out a tired, heavy sigh, knowing he was going to have to talk to Daisy about the ring. Charlie would tell her anyway.

"Maggie's ring. He said he would one day give you your mum's ring."

Daisy looked perplexed. "He didn't mention that today."

"He will. He promised Maggie."

Daisy felt guilty at the sight of her grandpa's desperately sad face. She reached out and touched his hand.

"I don't want to upset you or Nana. But I would like to get to know my dad… Charlie…"

Jim patted her hand and nodded. "I know you do. We just don't want you to get hurt."

"I won't, Grandpa. Besides," she moved the chair to sit beside him and nestled her head on his shoulder, "I'll always have you to protect me."

Jim took a big breath and forced a bright smile.

"What does George say about it?" asked Linda.

"I came straight here, Nana. He doesn't know yet."

"Oh," replied Linda. "You'd better get home then."

"I am home, Nana." Daisy grinned, pinching another jam tart.

Daisy kissed her grandparents goodbye, promising to return for Christmas lunch the following day with George. She turned down the street she had grown up in, and took in her surroundings. The grey concrete pavement had chipped and cracked over the years, but they were the same slabs her mother had walked on. Weather and vandals had left the lamppost on the corner battered and peeling, but it stood firm nonetheless. The street looked exactly the same as it did when she was a child, as though the years had stood still. Except, this afternoon her entire world had spun on its axis.

She wondered how George would react to the news. What would be the emotional impact of Daisy reuniting with her father when *his* father was *never* coming back? She knew she'd have to choose her words with care, even though she couldn't conceal the fact that Charlie White had reappeared.

The bus was crammed with people doing their last-minute Christmas shopping, and Daisy was pleased to clamber over bags and feet and get off the bus at her stop. Their house was only a short walk away.

The familiar buzz of London traffic hummed in the background, although her street was quiet and brimming with festive cheer. Large bay windows boasted brightly lit Christmas trees, and beautiful wreaths hung from doors. This was considered an exclusive street. The houses here were mainly Victorian, tucked away from the mayhem of mainstream London. Daisy loved it here. Like her parents and grandparents, London was in her soul.

Sometimes George talked about visiting the country where his great-grandfather was born, although his grandfather said the village probably didn't even exist anymore. Daisy pushed the thought away – now was not the time to be thinking about faraway places.

She turned the last corner. The house was set back slightly

from the main road and not yet visible. A long row of cars lined the curb, blocking her view, although she could hear Winston barking. George was probably getting something from his car – they were lucky enough to have a private driveway. She heard raised voices. Pausing, Daisy strained to hear what was being said. It was a woman's voice and it was clear that whoever she was, she was upset.

Instinctively, Daisy knew something was very wrong. She inched forward towards the house. Their driveway was lined either side with dense shrubbery and she had to raise herself up on tiptoe to see over the top. George was crouched down, trying to calm the woman, who appeared to be hysterical.

Daisy felt panic grip her throat and steal her breath. George was trying to dampen the woman's shrill shouts with soft, gentle words. The woman was crouching down like a wounded animal on the wet floor, shaking her head and sobbing.

Daisy couldn't watch or listen a moment longer. Striding into her driveway, her dark eyes blazing, she confronted them. George turned pale. The woman stopped crying and looked up at Daisy with contempt.

"Is *this* her?" she asked, pointing a painted finger at Daisy.

Daisy spun around to face George. "What's going on?' she demanded.

The woman struggled to her feet, laughing. "Yes, what *is* going on, George?"

It was obvious the woman was drunk. Daisy appraised her briefly; if she had been sober and clean, she might have been pretty.

George mumbled something incomprehensible. He

stumbled towards Daisy then backed off, not knowing which way to turn.

"Can we go inside, please?" he pleaded.

The mysterious woman went to follow, but Daisy put her hand in front of her. "Not you!"

"You would prefer for me to scream and shout out here on your doorstep?" goaded the woman.

"No, I want you to *go away*," Daisy spat.

The woman lunged at Daisy, who saw the drunken arm swinging long before it came close. Daisy grabbed it and dug her nails deep into the woman's thin coat. The woman tried to hit her again, but this time Daisy clenched her spare fist and aimed it straight under her chin.

Blood trickled from the edge of the woman's mouth, which she wiped away in horror as she backed slowly out of the driveway. Daisy did not take her eyes off the woman until she had vanished from view.

Daisy walked inside and George followed, his head bent low. Winston bounced ahead of them both, seemingly oblivious to the tension between his masters. As soon as the door closed, Daisy turned to George.

"What the *hell* is going on?"

It was inconceivable how a few hours ago, they had been walking Winston to the cemetery, and now so much had changed. Daisy felt dizzy and sick as she waited for George to answer.

He slumped on the bottom stair and sunk his head in his hands. Winston sat between them, now wary, his eyes darting left and right, like judge and jury.

"She's a patient. *Was* a patient," he said quietly. "She was admitted a few times, always with an injury because she was drunk or high. She's led a sad life, and I felt sorry for her. One time I put my arm around her and told her she'd be alright. Next thing I know, she's kissing me. I pushed her away instantly, but she's been blackmailing me ever since."

Daisy absorbed the story, wondering how much more she could take in today. "How long ago was this?" she asked.

George dropped his eyes.

"Six months ago."

She should have shouted and screamed at him, but she was just too exhausted. "How has she been blackmailing you?"

"She said she would tell the hospital board I raped her. Daisy, I'd be struck off. Then she said she would tell you. I didn't believe her until she turned up today."

Daisy looked at him carefully – she believed him. She *knew* George, and he wouldn't have an affair. But it was still a lot to take in.

"What does she want?"

"She wants *me*. I have told her to go away, that I love you, but she keeps threatening me."

Daisy flicked on the light switches, transforming the lounge into a haven of tiny, sparkling lights. The fire had burnt low. She threw on a new log, concentrating on the pop and sizzle of the damp wood. She withdrew from the fire and closed the curtains, sealing off the world outside. She realised how naïve she had been; this had been going on for six months and she'd been blind to it.

"George, I need some space. It's been a very long day."

"I don't want you to be on your own."

"I *need* to be on my own."

George nodded. Daisy felt her heart swell and break as she watched him put his coat on. Winston barked enthusiastically, assuming this meant he would be taken for a walk.

"I'm sorry, Daisy. I will sort this out," George said gently.

"I saw my dad today," Daisy blurted out.

"What? Where? He's *here*?" George exclaimed, looking around.

"No, not right *here*," she tutted. "But he's back. I'll tell you about it later."

"Tell me now… please."

"No. I need some space."

She longed to reach out and hold him, but she felt too angry.

Daisy watched from the bay window as George got in his car and reversed out of the driveway. Thankfully, the drunken woman had gone, but she thought she saw the shadow of someone next to the railings of the community park opposite her house. Wisps of cigarette smoke drifted beyond the tall deciduous trees and drifted into the early evening sky. It was probably a dog walker, she figured.

George drove off and Daisy closed the curtains, glad to shut out the world. She slumped in front of the fire and watched the flames dance in the small fireplace. She missed George already. Everything he'd just said – every detail about that woman – went around in her head like a washing machine on full spin, until she felt dizzy and physically sick.

Deep down, Daisy trusted him. George had a big heart and would gravitate towards helping anyone. He eventually wanted to specialise in heart surgery, which was ironic, as he seemed entirely capable of breaking hers. Annoyance bubbled inside her. He had been trained to deal with potentially insane patients, surely. Or perhaps there was more to this, and she was simply making excuses for him.

She poured herself a large glass of vodka and orange – more vodka than orange. She drank until her shock and sadness began to slowly ebb. Pouring a second drink, she accidently knocked over the vodka bottle. She stared at the bottle for a moment and then sat down, leaving it to leak its contents onto the floor. Winston raced over to investigate. He sniffed the spilt liquid and quickly retreated, grimacing at the potent odours from the neat vodka soaking into the carpet.

It was difficult to absorb everything that had happened. Perhaps, she considered, she was going to wake up and find that the day had not been real. She rested her head on the arm of the sofa. Her head began to spin and she felt her body slide slowly off the seat and sink towards the floor. Her stomach began to tense and ache. She had to get to the bathroom.

Winston fidgeted around her feet and started whimpering. Even though she was inebriated, Daisy knew this meant he needed to go outside. She clambered up onto her feet and stumbled towards the back of the house, through the kitchen. Her vision was blurred, and she had to use the back of a chair to steady herself as she groped her way along the kitchen worktop to locate the back door. She pulled the door open and the sudden cold air hit her like an arctic blast. Winston bounded outside and barely made it to his favourite apple tree before lifting his leg and almost falling over in his haste to relieve himself.

Daisy dragged herself outside, rubbing her arms. She felt her stomach lurch. She grabbed the edge of a nearby plant pot and was violently sick. Pushing back her hair, Daisy lifted her head and tried to focus. Everything was either spinning, blurry or both – but she felt better.

She walked slowly inside and flicked on the kettle. A cup of tea might help. She also wedged two slices of bread into the toaster. She'd take two paracetamol, she decided. There was some in the bathroom cupboard.

Daisy padded slowly upstairs and woozily pushed open the bathroom door, waving her arm to find the light cord. Squinting as the light suddenly clicked on, Daisy moaned in pain. She opened the bathroom cabinet and focused on finding the paracetamol. Brushing aside several neatly stacked boxes of plasters and bandages, she found what she was looking for. As she pulled the box out, half a dozen tampons tumbled out of their packet towards her. She tried to catch them in her hands then swore loudly, letting them drop to the floor.

She looked at them, scattered around her. Once she'd taken the paracetamol, she'd pick them up. She turned on the tap and bent down to slurp the running water. She held the paracetamol in her hand and popped them in her mouth, swallowing them quickly. Wiping her mouth with her sleeve, Daisy let her body sink to the floor. She pulled a towel around her arms, feeling shivery. She noticed one of the tampons next to her knee and picked it up. How long had it been since she had used one of these? Probably before she moved in with

George – just under three months ago.

"No... no!" she shouted.

She got unsteadily to her feet. She had been so busy with the house move she'd not even registered the dates.

Her mind became suddenly clear. Over a year ago she'd had a pregnancy scare and had bought a pack of two pregnancy tests. It had been a false alarm but that meant the spare test would still be here, in the back of a drawer, or in a cupboard, *somewhere*.

She swept out the contents of the bathroom cupboard onto the floor. Nothing. She continued her frantic search in their bedroom and then the kitchen. No sign of the test. Then she remembered; she had tucked it neatly away with surplus toiletries stored in a box underneath her bed.

Pulling the box out, she ferreted through tubs of spare face creams, bottles of shampoo, and tubes of toothpaste until she found the pregnancy test. Her hand trembled as she ripped the cellophane off the box and pulled the test out and looked at it, mulling over the possible options and consequences. If she didn't do the test, she could pretend the possibility of a pregnancy wasn't real. If she did the test and it was positive, she couldn't undo or erase her awareness. Or she could do the test and it could be negative. She felt a surprising stab of disappointment at that last thought. They hadn't planned a pregnancy but hadn't been especially careful either.

Either way, she had to know.

She completed the test and sat on the edge of the bath, staring at the two windows. The first line appeared. She felt her heart fluttered nervously, even though the first line simply meant the test was working. Her eyes followed the liquid being absorbed along the window – it was the appearance or absence of the second line that mattered.

Two distinct pink lines stared back at her.

Daisy gasped loudly, feeling both panic and elation. A *baby*.

She decided not to tell George. He needed to sort out the situation with that woman first, and Daisy needed time to ensure it had been resolved.

She frowned. Wasn't she just doing what George had done? Trying to buy time until the situation was sorted out? Wouldn't she be equally guilty of keeping a secret too?

Daisy looked down at the pregnancy stick again. This Christmas couldn't possibly get any more dramatic – it was almost surreal.

She walked slowly downstairs and snuggled up on the sofa in front of the embers which still glowed in the fireplace. The Christmas tree twinkled, creating colourful shadows on the walls. Daisy pulled a blanket over herself and tucked it under her chin, curling her legs under her weary body.

It was gone midnight when George got home. He bent down and kissed Daisy's forehead, smiling.

It was then he saw the pregnancy test on the floor beside her.

CHAPTER 39

George gently nudged Daisy until she stirred. He could smell the alcohol on her, and his heart sank.

"Daisy, please, wake up."

His tone was soft but assertive. Daisy groaned and twisted away from him, pulling the blanket over her head.

"I'm asleep," she replied groggily.

"I know you're pregnant," he whispered.

Daisy flipped over and steadied herself on her elbow.

"How?"

George held the pregnancy stick up and the empty vodka bottle. Daisy lowered her eyes.

"I didn't know before I got drunk."

Relieved, George nodded. He listened as Daisy told him what happened after he left.

"I believe you, George, but I was so hurt and confused," she said, wiping away fresh tears. "My dad turning up was such a big deal. I was so excited to tell you."

"I'm sorry," he said. "It must have been an incredible moment seeing him."

Daisy smiled. "It *was* incredible. He looks the same as he does in the photos."

She looked across at the pictures of Charlie on their mantelpiece. His hair was now peppered with grey and his skin was more lined, but the years had not changed Charlie much at all.

George sat down next to Daisy. "I can't believe you're pregnant, Daisy. How do you feel?"

"Sick." She laughed half-heartedly.

"That might be the vodka. How do you *feel* about being pregnant?"

"I don't know yet. Happy, I think."

George took her hand and smiled. "I'm *thrilled*. I've wanted this for a long time," he confessed.

"You have?"

Her eyes opened wide in surprise. George nodded.

"I'm getting old," he teased.

"Hardly," replied Daisy. Then she felt the dark shadow between them return. "What about that woman, George?"

"I've spoken to the hospital and the police. This isn't the first time she's blackmailed a doctor. The police have been to her house to give her a formal warning," he said, feeling brave enough to pull her into his arms. "Daisy, I was trying to protect you by not telling you what was going on. I was wrong – I'm sorry."

Daisy snuggled into his chest – signalling he was forgiven. "Happy Christmas, George… what a year!"

George held her away from him slightly and looked into her eyes, grinning. "It isn't over yet!"

Daisy laughed. It was true. She let George's arms wrap tightly around her. In a remarkable turnaround of events, her dad was back after sixteen years, and she was having a baby. She wondered what could possibly happen next to eclipse that.

George and Daisy stepped out of the Bentley, awed by the sense of pomp as crowds of people gathered outside the brightly lit venue. Charlie had sent the car to pick them up.

"It's a Bentley Turbo R!" George had exclaimed when it pulled up outside their house earlier that evening.

"Stop drooling and put the curtains back," Daisy had replied, laughing.

"Do you think it's his car? Your dad's?"

Daisy shrugged. "I have no idea."

She spritzed her hair with hairspray one last time and reached for her bag.

"Where are we even going?" asked George.

"Dad said it was a surprise," replied Daisy. She pulled a tissue out of her bag and blotted her lipstick.

"I hope it isn't too posh for a lowly doctor," he teased. "I'm used to drinking tea out of plastic cups and eating whatever sandwiches have been rejected by the patients."

Daisy rolled her eyes. George frequently complained about the hospital food. He didn't, however, protest when he saw the car up close. George had a passion for cars, especially classic ones. He spent the entire journey to the venue inspecting the tan leather seats, the cream carpet, and the walnut dashboard.

"Can you sit still?" said Daisy, exasperated.

"I'm not sure I can," he teased.

Daisy shook her head and glanced outside, watching the New Year's Eve revellers filing into pubs, restaurants, and clubs. The atmosphere was energetic and full of hope.

Daisy placed her hand on her stomach. She was certain when she stood sideways in the mirror that there was a noticeable bump, but George told her it was too early. They guessed she was almost three months pregnant.

She wore a shimmering black cocktail dress, and her hair was pinned up high. Even though she knew she looked the same, over the past week she had felt totally different. Just knowing she was pregnant had changed everything.

Daisy felt George's arm guide her through the crowd of people and towards the door. The Bentley gracefully pulled away from the curb and disappeared down a side street adjacent to the building. She looked up at the archway of tiny, sparkling lights interlaced into the dense foliage, which was draped across the double glass doors, beckoning the way inside.

Two heavyset bouncers dressed in immaculate suits flanked the entrance. They peered down at George and Daisy and pulled the solid doors open, smiling at them both.

George and Daisy raised their eyebrows. "Thank you!" they chimed together, then laughed.

Inside, the lobby was stunning. Elaborate blooms of white lilies, pale pink roses, and silvery leaves were displayed everywhere, with candles in little glass holders placed intermittently between them. The ambiance was romantic and sophisticated. Luxurious mahogany wood furniture and twinkling chandeliers completed the picture.

"It's like a fairy tale," commented Daisy, gazing around.

"I bet the prices are enough to make us both run at midnight," teased George. Daisy laughed, waving her hand to silence him.

They walked into the bar, where a band was playing live jazz. The music was soft and melodic; it had already attracted a crowd. The seats all seemed to be taken by glitzily dressed people.

Daisy glanced around. She found Charlie resting an arm casually on the bar, watching them arrive. She smiled as their eyes met and tugged George's arm to drag him over to her father.

Charlie looked suave, undeniably handsome, and as formidable as the bouncers on the door – perhaps even more so, she thought. His eyes followed her until she reached him and tucked herself into his arms. She inhaled the woody, earthy scent of his aftershave mingled with fresh, crisp undertones. He had always worn the same scent, or something very similar, she recalled.

"You look beautiful," said Charlie, clearing his throat.

"Thanks, Dad."

That word was as strange on her lips as it was for his ears. Although it was still very early days, they both felt comfortable with the newfound closeness.

Even George had grown used to Charlie's dark eyes interrogating his own, like an unspoken inquisition.

Daisy watched as George leaned forward and offered his hand. Charlie accepted with a warm smile.

"This place is incredible," remarked Daisy, looking around, wide-eyed.

"It only opened two years ago," Charlie said. He appeared to be an encyclopedia of knowledge about the building: from the first brick that was laid in the eighteenth century, to the team of designers who had worked tirelessly to create a fusion of bygone glamour and modern luxury.

A waiter appeared and directed them towards a table in a private area of the lounge. Two sofas in Louis XV style were positioned opposite each other, with a low table between them. Adjacent was an elaborate mantelpiece, crammed with freshly cut flowers and candles gently burning on tall candlesticks. The scene looked lavish and romantic.

Daisy sat down, wriggling into the luxuriously upholstered seat. "Dad, how did you manage to get this for us?"

The waiter smiled, handing them flutes of bubbling champagne and placing delicate china plates boasting handmade canapes on the table. He explained the name of each one in a soft French accent. Daisy and George stared in awe. Charlie sat back, amused by their reaction.

"Enjoy your canapes, Mr Clarke," the waiter said and nodded respectfully at Charlie, then at Daisy and George.

"Why did he call you Mr Clarke?" asked Daisy, confused.

Charlie lit a cigarette and took a deep drag, then rested it in the crystal ashtray on the table. He looked steadily at his daughter and she met his gaze, instinctively knowing she needed to brace herself for what he was about to say.

♦ ♦ ♦

Charlie had mentally prepared for this moment for sixteen years. It had started the moment he left the café in London after meeting Jim before he drove south in his Ford Capri.

He had never known *how* he would get to this moment, only that he *would*. Now that moment was here, he could hardly find the words, even though he had rehearsed them hundreds of times.

Even now, he couldn't tell her the entire truth. He had spent long hours trying to decide what would be necessary and what would be damaging to share with her. Looking at her tonight and seeing Maggie reflected back at him, he forgot what he had decided. She was beautiful and innocent – and she deserved to stay that way.

Charlie had asked his staff to make sure no one interrupted him. Even if someone important walked through the doors, he was not to be disturbed. If a catastrophe erupted behind the scenes, he didn't want to know. The staff had been instructed that when Daisy and George arrived, only the head waiter, Pierre, was to tend to them.

A few curious members of staff couldn't resist peeking. Charlie guessed they'd be whispering questions to each other. Who was this woman in the stunning black cocktail dress? And the gorgeous man by her side? If they were smart, they could easily work it out. It was impossible not to see the resemblance between Daisy and her mother. Everyone who worked there had seen the picture of Maggie hanging in his office and knew who she was. Or rather, who she had been. The portrait had been painted by the same artist as the one in the lobby of White Electrical offices.

Charlie focused on Daisy's question. He had known at some point he would have to explain why he no longer called himself Charlie White.

"I changed my surname when I left London sixteen years ago," he began in a sober voice. "It was better for people to think I had vanished."

"*Vanished*?" interjected Daisy.

Charlie nodded. "Yes, Daisy. I knew some dangerous people."

"Were *you* one of those dangerous people? Grandpa always said you were…" Her voice trailed off and her cheeks blushed crimson.

"Yes," replied Charlie, honestly.

George squirmed in his seat and took a large gulp of champagne. Charlie didn't blame him.

"Where did you go?" whispered Daisy. Charlie laughed and turned around, looking for Pierre. He ordered another double brandy.

"I don't suppose anyone cares anymore, Daisy." He smiled and continued. "But they would have done at the time. I went to Cornwall. A quiet little place called Polperro. I liked it there." He looked up and thanked Pierre who had placed a glass of brandy in front of him. Charlie swirled the warm liquor around in the balloon glass, casting his mind back. "I still have a house there."

"When did you come back to London?" asked Daisy.

Charlie frowned. This was not an easy question to answer. Should he tell her he'd been back more often than he wanted to admit? That he used to watch her walking through the school gates, or sometimes playing in the park? Or that he'd seen her play truant once from secondary school? How would she react if he told her he knew the film she saw at the cinema on her first date with George?

"I've been back and forth," he said honestly, hoping she didn't press him for the details. "But that's why I used a different name. It was safer."

Daisy nodded, trying to absorb the information.

Suddenly, she gasped. She stood up, sending her untouched champagne flute tumbling. George leapt forward and caught it.

"*Mr Clarke!*" she shrieked. "You *own* mum's company!"

Charlie was unable to resist a smile; she was a bright girl. "I do," he replied simply.

"Why?" Daisy exclaimed.

"I remember the first electrical item your mum sold," began Charlie, remembering the cash Maggie had used from the 'paint can job'. He still had the thin silvery scar from that misdemeanour. "I kept a close watch on the company's performance. When Jim was ready to sell, I was ready to buy." Charlie dropped his eyes, unable to camouflage the raw emotions. "I couldn't let her go."

Daisy reached out for his hand. Charlie watched her curl her fingers around his, squeezing tightly. He wished Maggie could be here to see this. Daisy looked so much like her; it unnerved him. It was only when he looked into her eyes that instead of midnight blue, he saw his own dark brown gaze reflected back.

"I miss her," Daisy said in a tiny voice.

Charlie nodded, feeling the warm tears fall unashamedly down his face. He had missed Maggie every day since she'd been gone. Everything he had done since then had been leading to this moment with Daisy, right now.

"Your mum was very lovely and very special, Daisy," Charlie said tenderly. George turned away, but not before Charlie noted that he was crying too. "I named this place after her. This is where we got engaged."

Daisy's hand flew to her mouth. "*Here*?"

Charlie nodded. The club had come up for sale a couple of years after Bobby Blower died, and Charlie had managed to secure the purchase. He'd done nothing with it for a long time until renovation works started around two years ago. By then, he'd made his fortune. Charlie Clarke owned a truck company in Cornwall that had expanded nationally, as well as several clubs and restaurants in London, including 'Maggie's'.

The first thing he did when he arrived in Polperro was breathe in the clean, salty air. From that moment on, he had never touched cocaine again. He had instead invested all his energy and cash into clawing his way back to where he belonged – in London, with Daisy.

"You *own* this place?" asked Daisy, shaking her head in disbelief.

"Yes. You probably didn't see the sign when you came in. I asked them to hurry you through. I wanted to tell you myself. But I bought it with the full intention of naming it after her."

"Maggie's," said Daisy wistfully.

"When we got engaged, she was pregnant with you," Charlie said softly.

"I know. Nana told me."

"And now *you* are pregnant."

Charlie and George exchanged a look. Charlie reached into his pocket, feeling the diamond ring against the silky lining. For sixteen years he had kept it safe, like a guardian, and now the timing was perfect. Charlie had the same inexplicable feeling he'd had that night in the mansion, the very first time he saw the ring next to the gloves on the mantelpiece. It was like a drumbeat in the distance, ringing in his ears and thumping in his chest.

George looked at him and nodded. George fell onto one knee and turned to face Daisy. She gasped.

Charlie reclined back in his seat and looked away, recalling the moment Maggie had visited him in prison, and they had agreed on a September wedding. He swallowed the lump of emotion sticking in his throat and closed his eyes.

"Daisy, will you marry me?" asked George solemnly.

Charlie smiled. He heard Daisy squeal with delight and opened his eyes to see her throw her arms around George's neck.

It was time.

Charlie took the South African blue diamond ring out of his pocket for the last time. It had been twenty-one years since he had taken it from the mantelpiece in the mansion. Since then, Maggie had worn it for five years and he'd carried it with him for sixteen more. Every business deal he'd done, every time he'd watched Daisy growing up from a distance, he'd had the ring on him. When George had visited him after Christmas and asked for Daisy's hand, Charlie had offered him the ring. He had been especially touched George had honoured the time-old tradition of asking the bride's father.

George took the ring from Charlie and gently slipped it onto Daisy's finger. All three of them stared at the ring, lost in thought.

"Mum's ring…" whispered Daisy.

In the background, a group of diners popped champagne corks and laughed.

Charlie handed her another gift, beautifully wrapped. For a man once so intensely submerged in the underworld of corruption and lacking emotional bandwidth, his attention to detail for his daughter was exquisite. She unwrapped the layers and gave a sharp intake of breath at finding a small bottle of her mother's distinctive perfume. She squirted the familiar scent around herself, laughing and crying, and threw her arms around Charlie.

"Thank you."

It was all she could say and all he wanted to hear. He hoped wherever she was, Maggie knew his promise to her had been fulfilled.

"The diamond came from South Africa," Charlie said, with a sense of déjà vu. George's head shot up, interested. "It would have been mined there, although no one really knows what happened to it after that."

Daisy and George fell silent, listening intently. Charlie would never tell them he had stolen it, so the ring would forever be shrouded in mystery. The story he told them was similar to the one he had recited to Maggie years before.

Daisy stared at the ring in awe. "It's stunning," she said and Charlie nodded. "I'll never take it off my finger," she said solemnly.

Charlie froze at hearing the *exact* words Maggie had said

when he gave the ring to her.

He watched Daisy and George admiring the ring and excitedly making plans. He could hardly believe that the baby he'd held in his arms was now almost a mother herself. Fate was constantly reinventing itself, he decided.

His thoughts turned once more to the ring. He thought about all the times the ring had been there during his lifetime with Maggie: when they got engaged, their wedding day, Daisy's birth, when Maggie died, and for all these years he'd lived without her.

Charlie wondered how many *other* people had also lived with the ring, and what had happened to them. Maggie had always believed in having a 'sixth sense' about the significant things in life, and he wondered how much influence his sixth sense had had on the decisions he'd made over the years. There had been that original picture of the *Titanic*, for instance. He'd paid an extortionate sum of money for it at an auction the previous year. The picture now hung in his office, and he would often simply stare at it. At the time, he couldn't fathom why he had felt to drawn to it – art was not his thing – but something inside him drove him to ensure that picture became his. Much like the way he was drawn to pick up that diamond ring, he mused.

He sighed in frustration at himself, wishing he'd paid more attention to the information Bobby had given about the ring all those years ago. It was entirely conceivable to Charlie that this ring had a backdrop of history he could only guess at. The mansion he had stolen the ring from had been impressive. He wondered briefly about the woman who lived there: Rita Brienne. He remembered her name from the newspaper. Charlie idly wondered if she had also sworn never to take the ring off her finger. But yet she had… for here it was, on Daisy's finger.

They moved into the restaurant and ate a sumptuous meal. Afterwards, Pierre reappeared with the drinks menu. "Will everyone partake in an after-dinner cocktail?" he asked politely.

"Not for me," said Daisy with a smile. "Could I have some tea, please?"

"Just two cocktails, thank you, Pierre," said Charlie. "And tea."

"Of course, sir."

A short while later, Pierre placed two chilled glasses on the table. The drinks looked intriguing: layers of dark, coffee liqueur and vodka, ice, and fresh cream floating perfectly on top.

"What's that?" asked George.

"A White Russian, sir," replied Pierre.

"Interesting," said Charlie. He'd never heard of this particular cocktail before, but it jogged something deep in his memory. The diamond had allegedly travelled from Imperial Russia after the 1917 revolution. Would a white Russian, or white émigré, have carried the diamond out of Russia? Charlie considered the idea then shrugged; he'd never be able to confirm the theory.

He focused on Pierre carefully pouring Daisy's tea through a strainer into a delicate china teacup. The waiter was a perfectionist; every drop of the pale tea swirled into the cup without a stray drip. He carefully removed the strainer and placed it on the holder.

Daisy peered inside the cup.

"Can't you tell people's fortunes from tea leaves?' she teased.

"It's called tasseography," replied George. "You know, when witches used to tell fortunes and provide herbal medicines? I remember reading about it."

"Do you believe in all that?" asked Daisy, laughing.

"Actually, I do," replied George. "There were women who used plants and herbs as medicine with phenomenal results. They saved many lives."

Daisy sipped her tea, noticing one or two slithers of tealeaf floating on the surface. "What about the tea leaves?"

"Apparently, the witches were incredibly accurate at reading the tea leaves," continued George. "They could see far into the future."

Charlie listened with interest but preferred not to comment. Maggie probably would have enjoyed their conversation, he thought. She used to be fascinated by the idea of this kind of thing.

In the background, the jazz band began to play. The saxophone and clarinet players had taken a break, leaving just the cellist and double-bass player entertaining everyone with a soft and haunting melody.

"It's a beautiful song," said Daisy dreamily.

"I think it's cello and violin playing," said George.

Charlie smiled. It had been a wonderful evening. He couldn't really explain how or why, but it *felt* as though the magic had been engineered. The ring caught his eye again.

It belonged to Daisy now. He had fulfilled his promise to Maggie. Yet a restless feeling began to creep around the edges of his contentment. A feeling deep in his gut – one that all the champagne, cocktails, love and laughter just couldn't silence.

CHAPTER 40

Daisy and George settled on a late spring wedding. Thousands of bright yellow daffodils had sprouted in the small churchyard. Flecks of vibrant red had begun to appear as early tulips started to open, and the scent of fragrant hyacinths clung to the warm air. Fruiting trees were bursting with a profusion of pink blossom, and their delicate petals floated in the gentlest of breezes like confetti.

In the hedgerows and treetops, a chorus of birds created a symphony of chirps, heightened by devoted nesting. They ducked and dived between branches, observing the wedding party with beady eyes.

The church bells were ringing as Daisy and George emerged from the church doors and walked out into the soft spring sunshine. The photographer kept them busy clicking his camera up close and using the stunning backdrop to take photographs that would remind them all of this precious day and their beloved family and friends.

Daisy couldn't stop the tears when the photographer asked her to stand with her grandparents. She squeezed her grandpa's hand tight.

"Don't cry on your wedding day, silly," he said sternly.

"You're crying too, Grandpa," she said with a sad smile.

Her grandparents had told her by then that Jim had prostate cancer. The prognosis wasn't encouraging, and Daisy knew they were on borrowed time. The medication was stalling the inevitable, but it made this moment with her grandparents now infinitely priceless.

Daisy noticed her dad watching from a distance. He nodded to her. She suspected he was struggling with his own emotions. Daisy had discovered her dad was a profoundly philosophical and emotional person when you peeled back the hardened layers.

"Charlie, come for a picture," called Jim, waving his arm. Even her grandparents had softened their resolve towards Charlie. They might never truly forgive him, but they realised they were punishing him for how much their daughter had loved him. That was no crime, they realised. Daisy had listened to all their stories, shared with more honesty than they would have dared before, and she began to understand.

She could see how time had slowly tempered the sharp edges of their pain and replaced it with acceptance. Her grandparents would *never* stop grieving for Maggie. The past meant heartache for them and they would always agonise over her stolen future. Yet they knew they couldn't change what had happened – none of them could.

Charlie walked over to them, and the photographer took several photographs. Daisy smiled brightly with damp eyes, knowing in years to come, she would always remember this moment.

George took her hand, and they made their way towards the waiting car which was adorned with white ribbons. The layers of Daisy's delicate satin dress swayed as she walked, and her veil tousled gently in the breeze. She turned as they reached the Rolls Royce, sharing a secret smile with her dad. Charlie had managed to hire the Silver Ghost for George, who had worshipped this particular classic car since he was a child.

Daisy settled on the backseat, smoothing her dress. George climbed in beside her, grinning.

"We did it!" he said, leaning over to kiss her. "Isn't this car unbelievable?"

"It is," agreed Daisy. "Are you ready for the reception?"

"How do you think everyone will react?" he asked nervously.

Daisy took his hand in her own, admiring the thin band of diamonds underneath the spectacular blue solitaire. "Let's find out!"

◆ ◆ ◆

The entrance to 'Maggie's' was lavishly decorated with a stunning floral archway. The solid glass doors were open wide to welcome the guests, who accepted flutes of champagne as they wandered inside. Musicians played in the lobby, accompanying a female singer dressed in shimmering silver.

Charlie acknowledged the singer with a smile when he walked in. She lowered her eyes and smiled shyly back, then lifted her head fully to hold a high note.

Guests stopped to listen as they drifted past. It wasn't only the woman's voice they were mesmerised by; she was a natural beauty. Her glossy, honey-coloured hair fell down her back in soft, natural curls. She wore only a touch of make-up, naturally accentuating sharp cheekbones and full lips. Charlie knew she usually preferred to tie her hair in a knotted headband and wear threadbare jeans, not formal gowns. He especially enjoyed watching her when she was oblivious to his presence. Recently, they had been spending a lot of time together.

He was beginning to think he might be falling in love with her.

They had met that New Year's Eve when Daisy and George had got engaged. She had been the lead singer of the jazz band.

The shroud had lifted from Charlie's heart when he handed Maggie's ring over to Daisy that night. In all the years after Maggie died, he could never commit to anyone. There had been lots of encounters with women, but the ties were always cut short.

When he met Jennifer, he felt a dormant light reignite.

"You sing like an angel," he had said to her the first time they met. She had laughed, shaking her halo of blonde hair.

Maybe after all these years, he was now free of the chains that had bound him. He couldn't change the cocky kid who had served time behind bars, or the madman in him who had killed in cold blood, or the criminal who had stolen a priceless Renoir along with an irreplaceable blue diamond. Or the husband who had watched his wife run into the jaws of an oncoming car, knowing he could not reach her in time. Or the father too spineless to say goodbye to his five-year-old child.

Charlie wondered whether he had now paid his debt. And maybe Jennifer was indeed an angel, sent to him as a sign.

He thanked the barman, who had placed a large brandy on the bar in front of him. It had been a perfect day so far. All he had to do now was get through his speech.

He swigged back the neat drink and merged into the swarm of people filtering into the bar area. As Daisy and George arrived, the energy in the room lifted, as did the music. Charlie would always remember the noise being a happy fusion of chatter, jazz, laughter, and Jennifer's overwhelmingly sweet voice reaching above it all.

The next few hours coasted by smoothly. There had been drinks in the garden at the back of the restaurant, followed by a sumptuous à la carte meal, topped off by coffee.

Charlie waited for everyone to settle before taking his daughter's hand. "I'm not someone who will ever make a long speech," he said, trying not to show his nerves. He glimpsed Jennifer out of the corner of his eye. Their eyes met, and she returned a bright smile. Feeling confident, he continued. "I want to say how proud I am of my daughter, and how proud her mother would be. You look exactly like her." He paused, tears welling in his eyes. He took a deep breath. "Maggie was a beautiful, spirited woman." Charlie looked pointedly at Linda and Jim. "I'm sorry she is not here today."

Turning back to Daisy, he swallowed the lump in his throat and continued. "I've watched with interest to see how you would cope with the big wide world. A dad can't ask for more than to see his daughter happy."

Charlie sought out Jim's face. Jim nodded, dabbing his eyes. In the end, happiness was all that mattered.

Charlie raised his glass as George stood up and shook hands with his new father-in-law.

George put his glass down as the room fell silent. His fingers shook as he picked up his rehearsed speech which he'd scribbled on several pieces of paper. After a jittery beginning, he eased into a more comfortable pace. Daisy caught his eye and smiled encouragingly; she knew what was coming next.

"We will soon be welcoming what my grandfather refers to as 'the next generation' into the world," George said.

George's grandfather was sat next to George. The older man's ears pricked up. With a grin, he raised his glass.

George continued. "My wife and I decided that our wedding day would be the perfect time to share something with you that surprised us both a great deal."

Everyone fell silent, curious to hear more. George and Daisy had agreed that they wouldn't tell anyone beforehand. George let the silence continue for a few moments longer, prolonging the suspense. He turned to his grandfather, knowing the news would mean the most to him. "We're going to have twins!"

The entire room erupted into squeals of delight and laughter, although several women clasped their hands over their mouths in sympathy. People rushed to Daisy and George to hug, shake hands and kiss them. Linda started fretting over the number of booties she had to knit, and Jim scratched his head, wondering where twins had come from in the family.

George focused on his grandfather. Something had changed in the older man. It was as though a light switch had flicked on as he got to his feet, gulping back his third whiskey. Clasping his walking stick, he slowly pulled his unstable frame up onto one of the chairs until he was standing above them all. He banged his walking stick loudly on the floor, commanding attention. George tried to help him down, but the eighty-three-year-old man waved his stick adamantly.

"I've just risked life and limb getting up here, boy. Besides, I have something of my own to say."

The room fell immediately silent again.

George's grandfather looked around the room, squinting at the wedding guests.

"For those of you who don't know who I am, my name is Kai. I'm the groom's grandfather," he said proudly. "I was christened with this name, which is Afrikaans for 'sea.'" He looked around the room and winked. "I think I was conceived on the long journey from South Africa to England."

The room erupted into low laughter. Kai straightened his jacket and tie and everyone fell silent again.

"I'm not drunk if that's what you're all thinking. Well, I've had a couple, but that's not the point. I want to share a story with you."

George and Daisy had heard this story a few times since New Year's Eve. It would be too awkward to try and remove

George's grandfather from the chair, so they gritted their teeth and let him continue.

"My father was not a man of many words," Kai began.

George bowed his head. His great-grandfather had once been their family figurehead, and in their culture, that commanded respect.

"But when my father did speak, we all listened. He didn't ramble on like some of us." Kai winked at Daisy, and she giggled; it was impossible not to.

The entire room was transfixed, waiting for him to continue. "I'll tell you his story, as I understand it, so you can realise why it is so important for me to stand on this chair today." He grinned, waving his walking stick as though he were a great conductor.

His natural skin was darker than George's, but not as dark as his father's had been. Marrying white women had diluted their genetic traits, but their heritage was undeniably still visible. Kai's features were more distinctive, and it was easier to tell he had inherited stronger genes from his father's South African ancestors. He had picked up the native dialect from his father and absentmindedly emphasised it now, even though his father had been a young man when he fled his home with a British nurse who shortly after became pregnant with Kai.

"As romantic as that tale was," Kai said, having relayed his family's history to the audience, "my father left his heart in South Africa. He never recovered from leaving his sister behind, or not knowing what happened to her. He was a *tormented* man." He shook his head, remembering the broken man who had never healed. "They had a connection few human beings ever share. I saw it in his eyes whenever he spoke about her. Without her in his life, he was truly lost."

He turned to George and Daisy.

"She was his *twin*," Kai, more determined than ever, turned back to the room. "People come into our lives, and people leave. Often we are not privileged to understand why, except I will tell you this: my father told me the last time he saw his sister, he put something in the palm of her hand. It was a blue diamond he stole from the mines when he was a negro slave at Kimberly, South Africa. He never saw his sister or the diamond ever again." Kai was now crying, as were many others in the room.

"I've never told anyone what I'm about to tell you now. George's great-great-grandmother was a sangoma in my father's village. She told my father and his sister they would bring prosperity to their bloodline. When he stole that diamond, it was in desperation to save himself and his sister." Kai stopped briefly to compose himself, remembering what he had tied on his wrist. He wriggled it off and held it up high for everyone to see. "My father and his sister were given a special bracelet by the sangoma. They would wear this to remember the prophecy passed down by the ancestors – that the bloodline of *those* twins would prosper. It has *five* pearls on the bracelet, which my father was told would prove the prophecy was real. *Five pearls*," he repeated. "He was told the number five was significant…"

Kai turned to Daisy. "The ring on this girl's finger is a blue diamond from South Africa. I'll accept *that* coincidence. I'll also take the news of these twins as another sign."

Raising his glass high, he looked up as though addressing the heavens.

"This is to celebrate the newlyweds and *their* twins. Secondly, to give thanks for the life of my father and *his* twin. I pray they are at last together. And finally, George's great-great-grandmother." He waved again. "I believe your prophecy has been fulfilled. Our bloodline has prospered. My belief is that diamond," he looked down at Daisy's finger, "was the very same one my father, Davu, took for his sister."

And with that, Kai finally stepped down, helped by George and Daisy.

For a long moment, no one spoke. Then waitresses slowly began to disperse among the guests, offering drinks. Chatter resumed, and music began to play in the background gently.

As everyone started to mingle again and talk about the incredible story, Charlie looked as though he had just seen a ghost.

As Charlie listened to Kai, he had an overwhelming sense he had been part of a masterminded plot. It suddenly made sense why he had felt compelled to take the diamond; it was intended for Maggie, and then Daisy. It sounded almost illogical, unbelievable maybe, but Charlie had no doubt. He remembered how he felt that night in the mansion, and then holding onto the diamond all these years since Maggie died. Strange, subtle, subliminal feelings and happenings which now somehow made complete sense.

He strained his memory back over the years, trying to locate any evidence to support the haywire thoughts now buzzing through his head. Bobby Blower could have sent any other man to steal the picture, but he waited until Charlie was out of prison. Why? Or why had the woman who commissioned the artwork theft chosen that particular time to take it? How had the coincidences perfectly aligned?

He remembered reading in the newspaper that Rita Brienne had not taken the diamond off her finger for over forty years. Dementia had caused her to leave the ring behind when she went to France. Was that also engineered?

Charlie closed his eyes. He could still see the blue diamond resting on the white glove in the mansion, where he had taken it without thinking of the consequences. He struggled to remember exactly what details had been relayed about the diamond's history. Charlie realised that if there were fragments of truth to the cobbled-together story, there must be gaps too. How did the diamond leave South Africa? What happened to Davu's sister? What happened to the diamond when it was in Russia? Who cut the diamond from a rough jewel? How did it escape the depths of the ocean, if it did indeed sail on the *Titanic*?

"Dad, are you alright?"

Daisy's voice interrupted his deep thoughts. George was by her side, with Kai, who was getting ready to leave.

Charlie looked directly at Kai. He had just been thinking about what the Polish jeweller had said about the ring.

"It is *five* carats," Charlie said, pointing at Daisy's hand. "I remember the jeweller telling me when I had it re-sized for Maggie."

"*Five*," repeated the older man. Daisy noticed the bracelet of blue and white beads was back on his wrist.

"Five pearls, look." She stroked the beads, realising the white ones were, in fact, tiny pearls. She instinctively touched her neck, where Maggie's christening pearl hung from another necklace. She had borrowed it, as was tradition. "Nana told me my name means Margaret, and so does Mum's. And Margaret means *pearl*."

Kai leaned on his stick as George quickly reached forward to steady his wobbly arm. "My father's twin sister," he said in a shaking voice, "she was called Pearl."

They all gazed down at Daisy's hand, resting on her stomach. The South African blue diamond glinted brightly.

"That's a lovely name…" she said, but she felt the warmth drain from her body; a chill chased along her spine. She tasted warm, salty tears as they gathered in the corner of her mouth and then splashed onto her dress. All she could think about was the mysterious twin called Pearl. What had she been like? What had happened to her? Was the diamond on her finger *the same one* her brother claimed to have stolen?

There were too many coincidences, gushing into her mind, flooding it with confusion. There were no clear answers. Yet the truth felt tantalizingly close.

Daisy closed her eyes, feeling slightly dizzy. She felt George's hand touch her elbow to offer support.

"I'm fine…" she said softly.

In her mind's eye, Daisy caught a fleeting glimpse of her mother. She held her breath, afraid to move. Maggie turned to face Daisy, offering her a loving smile. Daisy drew in her breath sharply, and her hand involuntarily reached out to touch her. But the image faded as quickly as it had materialised.

Her eyelashes fluttered slowly open and she noticed George's grandfather Kai was staring at her, his eyes glistening.

"You see, girl, now you believe?" he said.

Daisy cocked her head and gave a hesitant laugh. She longed to ask him if he knew how pertinent his question was. She touched the surface of the blue diamond, feeling a flutter in her stomach. She wondered which twin was nudging her to answer his or her great-grandfather.

Daisy considered her response. Was it conceivable a sangoma's prophecy had somehow come full circle, concluding with her own unborn twins? Was it fathomable the dazzling South African blue diamond on her finger had served as a talisman?

Daisy reached for George with her left hand. His fingers wrapped around hers, squeezing gently. She turned to Kai and smiled brightly, ready to answer his question.

"I believe everything," she said earnestly.

None of them took any notice of the young waitress hovering nearby. Her long dark hair fell down her back, tied neatly in a ponytail. The moment her shift ended she would wriggle the tight band free and let her hair flow freely. Occasionally she braided it, as her grandmother had taught her.

She stole a sideway glance at the bride, desperate to glimpse the ring on her finger. She kept her hands busy collecting glasses, but she wasn't paying full attention to her duties. Her mother, Anna, often chided her for being easily distracted.

But *this time* it was different. She had stood at the back of the room during the speeches. Her brilliant blue eyes, identical to her late grandmother's, had stared at Kai in disbelief.

She had heard the story of Pearl and the blue diamond before. Her grandmother had recited the tale many times; it formed the fifty-year love story between her and her husband.

"Sylvia?"

She jumped at the sound of her name – the same as her beloved grandmother's. Her manager ushered her towards the main dining room where the evening festivities were being prepared. She followed dutifully, glancing a final time over her shoulder at the bride and the people gathered around her.

Smiling, she carried on.

Printed in Great Britain
by Amazon